Prologue: Florida 2001

When Danielle was young, she took her beauty for granted. Now she was well into middle age. After agonizing over detail of the old photos that she had buried in boxes in the back of the closet, she guiltily acknowledged that maybe that had been her fatal mistake. Although she had to admit the smiling girl in the pictures, dressed simply in an embroidered shirt, jeans, and sandals, looked confident and happy. Her long black hair framed a face that could have belonged to her ancestors, Rebecca, Leah, Rachel, or Sarah. Even to Danielle's jaundiced eye, her body that had once been padded with baby fat looked sexy and nubile. Maybe, just maybe, if she had deigned to use her youth and lush body for fame or fortune, all the tragedy could have been avoided. But she was stubborn and had had her ideals. Now she was too old, so there was no longer any choice in that department. The evidence stared at her every time she looked in the mirror and saw the deepening lines etched at the corners of her eyes. Only now did she understand why they were called crow's- feet. Looking at her blotchy skin and the extra inches stubbornly attached to her waist, she was glad her eyesight wasn't as keen as it used to be. Though ironically, it seemed her memories had become clearer.

Danielle sighed as she wiped away another tear. She wasn't digging in the box to gaze nostalgically at the girl she used to be, she was looking for a particular picture—the one of her best friend Rachel and herself on the beach with their babies. She remembered that Eli, the lifeguard, had taken it right after two-year-old Battia had smacked Ari's tiny hand because he had eaten a piece of her sand cake. She and Rachel had laughed until their stomachs hurt because Battia was already acting like a little mother. "No, Ari," she had said, perfectly imitating Rachel. "It's not good for you. You'll get sick."

More than twenty-five years ago, Danielle and her friend Rachel had been neighbors in a jewellike city called Yamit, located on the coast of the Mediterranean Sea below the Gaza Strip. Although she and Rachel didn't speak to each other often anymore, they were bound together by memories in a world that conveniently forgot history. The women shared good news and bad, intertwined with reminiscing about their old friends and bittersweet memories of love and loss. They would always congratulate each other on their children's successes and be sincerely hurt if one was in pain. When they had last spoken, Rachel had commiserated with Danielle about getting old and made her laugh by saying, "Haven't you ever been to Miami? That's the way it is—old Jewish ladies have flat tushes and large saggy breasts."

Danielle looked at the picture and shook her head. How had this happened? Murder after murder as history was methodically erased. Soon no one would even remember their exquisite desert Eden. Danielle sighed, thinking of Yamit, the crown jewel of the Israeli giveaway extravaganza of 1980. It was where she and Marvin had started their family, their business, and had invested their hopes and dreams until the tragic end. Sadly, now it was just a vast expanse of sand, rocks, and dirt that covered the nefarious tunnels stretching from Egypt to Gaza.

The first time Danielle read about the labyrinth of tunnels, she had hurled the magazine across the room. According to the article, Yamit and the surrounding farming area had become a main conduit for arms. Although it was renamed the friendly sounding Philadelphia Corridor, in reality terrorists transported bombs and explosives through an underground expressway from Egypt to the murderous strongholds of the Gaza Strip, without being detected by the Israeli army. Every week the news reported more atrocities, and her soul shivered. As the mayhem and destruction became almost daily events, Danielle grew concerned for her many friends who had stayed in Israel after the Egypt-Israel Peace Treaty, which was signed in 1979 and went into effect in 1980. They rode buses, went to work, and window shopped like normal people did the world over. Although unlike normal people, they were aware that every moment brought the risk of being maimed or murdered. Danielle knew that one of the innocent men, women, or children massacred by a terrorist could be someone she loved. And then, just this morning, fate had delivered its blow in its surreal, inimical fashion.

Danielle's phone had rung just as she shut off the TV in disgust. The news broadcast was showing the macabre video of the latest Hamas terrorist, Mohammed Ali Hasan, smiling proudly at the camera before starting his day's work of slaughtering Jews. After that video was shot, he boarded a bus filled with Jewish American teenagers, shouted "Allahu Akbar," and detonated the bomb strapped around his waist. The news reported that in Gaza, people were out in the streets celebrating his martyrdom and the slaughter of innocent Jews.

Her old friend Rhoda was on the other end of the phone. She had been assigned the painful job of messenger. She told Danielle that she prayed no one would shoot her, because she had to deliver the nightmarish news that Rachel's daughter, Battia, was the tour guide of that group.

Danielle was stunned and then horrified. How could this happen? Just a few weeks ago Rachel had called with the exciting news that Battia was engaged to a wonderful guy she had met in her biology class. He worked at Hadassah hospital, and his grandparents were Holocaust survivors, who had arrived on the *Exodus*. His father had been involved with planning the Entebbe raid.

Then in an instant, everything was lost. Battia, Rachel and Natan's only child, was dead. How would they ever recover? Now they'd be planning a funeral instead of a wedding. Instead of celebrating and looking forward to grandchildren, they'd be crying and suffering from their irreplaceable loss. Danielle listened in shock as Rhoda said that one of Battia's arms was still missing. An organization of orthodox rabbis, called ZAK, was searching for all the missing parts: legs, arms, even fingers and toes, at the bomb site. If and when the missing parts were found, the rabbis would save them in plastic bags so that Battia and the rest of the victims could be buried according to Jewish law. Danielle pictured Battia's body blown apart, with pieces of her organs hanging from a telephone wire like spaghetti or melded to a car hood like a runny fried egg, and ran to the bathroom to throw up.

The horror was too painful to absorb. Rocking back and forth like an old Jew praying at the Western Wall, Danielle thought, *How will Rachel survive this? Maybe there was a mistake, and it wasn't really her Battia.* Gazing once again at the old photo of the beautiful curly haired girl sitting on her mother's lap, Danielle wept and cried out to God in despair.

For so many years the memories of Yamit had haunted Danielle. Now in her inconsolable grief, she saw her youth flash by. And it was a deluge of pain.

"Yamit!" she said aloud. "We were all so young and hopeful. Yearning for our dreams to come true, we settled land that for thousands of years stood barren and empty. From nothing more than a vision, belief, and plain hard work, we made the desert bloom. Until it disappeared in an explosion of violence, just like Vesuvius buried Pompeii. Now once again it's covered with rocks and sand, and it lives only in the memories of the people who were there. Battia, Ari, and Ilana. It was supposed to be yours, the city that we built … and the first city that the government betrayed."

Chapter 1

After surviving such a brutal attack just a few days earlier, twenty-four-year-old Danielle Katz couldn't believe she still looked the same. After examining herself in the mirror of the ladies room at JFK International Airport, she just shrugged and decided not to reapply her smeared mascara. All she wanted to do was sleep during the long journey ahead of her. Sleep had eluded her since the rape. She gave herself a last hopeless glance before walking out the door to her destiny.

Although Danielle appreciated her long black hair, big brown eyes, and enviable figure, she knew her appearance concealed an abyss of pain and shock. Even before this trauma had happened, she had felt as burnt out as volcanic ash. She recalled her father's pithy advice at that last abysmal dinner with her parents. When she accused them of abandoning her, he calmly lit his pipe and stated, "Danielle, remember that security is an illusion. You're alive. "

Concentrating on taking even, deep breaths, she made her way to her gate in the international terminal. When her flight was called, she followed the line of passengers out onto the tarmac and slowly and cautiously climbed the metal stairs, holding tightly to the railing. She tried to smile at the stewardess who greeted her with a perky, "Shalom and welcome aboard EL AL," spoken with an unfamiliar Israeli accent, but she was too emotionally spent.

She found her seat on the pristine 747 after almost tripping over someone's suitcase, which had been left in the narrow aisle while the man argued with his wife in Hebrew. Another stewardess came over to see if she was okay and provided her with a bright EL AL blanket before she went over to help the couple.

Danielle laughed silently as she watched the scene unfold. Apparently the couple was fighting over where their baby was going to sleep. Finally, the stewardess brought a big cardboard box from somewhere by the galley. The mother wrapped the baby in a couple of blankets and laid him in the box, and that seemed satisfactory to the parents.

An older woman wearing too much makeup and a bad wig was sitting across the aisle from Danielle. She too was watching the couple and their baby, and she leaned closer to Danielle to talk to her.

"It's January 1974. You would think they could do better than a box for the baby, but they did the same thing to my daughter. She ordered a baby basket. And she got a box."

Danielle didn't have the strength to reply, so she smiled weakly and hoped the lady would stop talking.

"But that's *nourishkeit*," the woman went on. "Nothing. The important thing is that EL AL is a Jewish airline. We'll be safe. That's what my son-in-law, who by the way was a captain in the Yom Kippur War ..."

That was the last thing Danielle heard. She couldn't keep her eyes open anymore and was asleep before they even took off.

Danielle was startled awake by the sounds of "Hatikva," the Israeli national anthem, blasting over the sound system as the plane entered Israeli airspace. She was cranky and stiff from contorting herself into a fetal position for the twelve-hour journey to her new life in Israel, Still she considered that hatikva meant hope, and that was all she had after what she'd been through. Maybe this was a good omen.

Gingerly peeking out of her blanket cocoon, her head throbbing from the Nembutal and black Russian concoction that she'd downed at the fiasco dinner with her parents, she thought she was hallucinating. A contingent of Hassidic men in their long black coats and shtreimel hats were greeting the day with their morning prayers. Up at dawn, they were as organized as an army of ants. She incredulously watched them scurry down the aisle to the front of the plane. Each pulled out a prayer book, seemingly from thin air, and started to pray, each at his own speed and punctuating his rhythm with swaying and nodding.

Oh shit, what have I done? Danielle asked herself. She shook her head in disbelief even as she hypnotically watched the ancient ritual. Unlike those men, her only prayer was that her sister Lauren would be waiting for her at Ben Gurion Airport in the city of Lod, just south of Tel Aviv.

Still groggy when the plane landed, she went through customs in a daze, bumping into people in the crowded terminal and even accidently knocking a lit cigarette out of someone's hand while she scanned the crowd for her sister. Then, as she waited for her duffel bag at the baggage claim, she felt her skin crawl and her stomach cramp. Out of the corner of her eye she spotted a dark-skinned man walking toward her and she immediately froze. When he got closer, she realized he didn't look like her rapist and let out a sigh of relief. He wasn't even black, just of a darker complexion than she was used to. Her mistake made her realize that the rape had changed a lot more than she'd realized. She had never been prejudiced before. When her mother had screamed at her and belittled her for bringing her friend Terry home from school with her, she had screamed back that she was embarrassed her mother was a racist. Her mother just gave her that knowing grin and calmly retorted, "I prefer realist. You'll learn."

Maybe her mother was right. She wished she could snap her fingers and life would go back to the way it had been before the rape, but wishes weren't reality.

As she grabbed her bag, she felt a stab of envy as she watched families reuniting with hugs and kisses. In her family any demonstration of affection was alien. Her mother and father had waved good-bye and wished her well as if nothing had happened. How could they abandon her when she needed them? Instead, she'd had to listen to her mother rant and rave that she was a whore and that it was her fault. Maybe she was, according to her mother's standards, but times change. Just look at what she was wearing—jeans. A few years ago she would never have gotten on a plane if she weren't wearing a skirt and sweater set.

Where the hell was her sister? Confused and surrounded by the sounds of a harsh, guttural foreign language, to Danielle everyone seemed to be meeting someone except her. She looked around to find a place to wait and noticed groups of soldiers carrying machine guns as they walked through the terminal, perusing the crowds even as they chatted and laughed. A few gave her appreciative looks that would have made her feel good just a few days ago. Now it didn't matter that one of them looked a little like Paul Newman when he played Ari Ben Canaan in the movie *Exodus*. As the whole awful experience played over and over in her head, she couldn't decide what was worse: the rape or the mental and emotional abuse perpetrated by the authorities. She still couldn't believe that the fat police sergeant had refused to look for the knife until she threatened to go to his superior, or that nasty doctor who had treated her like she was the criminal.

Now she was in a strange country where she knew no one except her sister, and as usual Lauren had disappointed her. Maybe Lauren had forgotten she was coming that day. There had to be a mistake.

Staring at the array of clocks on the wall, she become even more anxious. They looked so strange. Maybe there was more wrong with her than she'd thought. Then she realized she couldn't read them because they displayed military time in several international time zones. As she continued to search every face, she became frantic. It was apparent her sister wasn't coming. Danielle rummaged in her pocketbook and breathed a sigh of relief when she found a crumpled piece of paper with the kibbutz phone number written on it. She had to change some money and ask how the phone worked. The man at the booth gave her the *asimonim*, or tokens, as rudely as if she had asked for his life savings. It was the same despicable attitude she had encountered in the hospital.

Her fingers trembling, she dialed the kibbutz's number. She must have shouted "Emergency!" a dozen times before the receptionist understood her, and then she miraculously heard Lauren's voice.

"Where the hell are you?" Danielle yelled.

"I couldn't make it," her sister responded nonchalantly.

"What do you mean you couldn't make it? I just got off a plane in a strange country and you're the only person I know. You're my sister, for God's sake, and that's what you have the nerve to tell me?"

"Calm down. It's just too far to start schlepping. I didn't have a ride to the bus and I'm way up in the Bet Shean valley."

"Why the hell didn't you call or write to let me know?"

"I didn't know soon enough. You'll be fine. Go to the Metropole Hotel in Tel Aviv and I'll be down the day after tomorrow."

"Why two days from now and not tomorrow?"

"I'll be able to get a ride to the bus in two days. Just grab a cab and go to the Metropole Hotel. It shouldn't cost more than twenty dollars, and I'll meet you there. You can get a room to share with other people so it's cheaper. See ya soon. Love ya. I'm so glad you're here," she added as an afterthought.

Still angry and feeling lost, Danielle found a cab and, to her relief, managed to make the driver understand where to take her. As she sat in the backseat of the filthy cab, she tried to make some sense of it all. First she had been raped, and then abused by the hospital staff and called a liar by the police. To top it off, she'd been stood up by her own sister.

Resolutely, Danielle summoned all her will not to think about the last few days, while being all too aware that it was a miracle she was alive. She knew without any doubt, in every cell of her body, that if God had willed her to die, she would have. The rapist could have stuck the knife into her jugular vein and that would have been the end.

As she looked out the smeared window of the cab, she realized this was the first time she would be totally alone since the rape. A wave of nausea swept over her, and she wasn't sure if it because of the horror of the past or the uncertainty of her future.

Chapter 2

The cab driver charged too much for the ride, but she didn't even have the strength to argue. She just wanted to get a room that was clean and safe where she could wait for Lauren to show up.

She had thought arriving a month before school started would be more interesting than going directly there. After deciding to quit her monotonous government job, she had found a program that offered Judaics and Hebrew studies to young Jewish professionals. By coming early, she could spend time with her sister, who was volunteering on a kibbutz, and she could see a little bit of the country on her own. *Wrong again,* she thought.

The shabby hotel that Lauren had sent her to was near the beach, off Hayarkon Street. *Great area,* Danielle thought as she looked around. *It's on the fringe of the red light district. I'll fit right in.* But since she didn't have much money and didn't know where else to go, she didn't have much choice. Since Lauren had told her it would even be cheaper if she elected to share a room with someone else, she chose that option and prayed her roommate wouldn't be a murderer. An old man who looked like he had been sitting at the same check -in desk since the British Mandate sullenly gave her the room key. He pointed to the elevator with a finger bent with arthritis, and as she took the old, creaky elevator to the third floor, she tried to stay as still as possible. The way her luck was running, the cable would break and her crumpled body would be found on the floor of the basement.

Surprised that she made it to her floor safely, she dragged her duffel bag down the hallway and then got frustrated trying to unlock the door. Finally, after what felt like hours, the key turned. Danielle opened the door and kicked her duffel bag in. The dimly lit room contained three single beds. The mattresses were pancake thin and covered with threadbare sheets, with a gray wool blanket folded at the bottom of each bed. She silently uttered her thanks that she had arrived safely, unpacked a few necessities, and decided that what she needed more than anything was a shower. Maybe she could finally scrub off all the dirt from the last few days.

In the tiny bathroom the unfamiliar faucets turned on easily enough, but they refused to shut off. Before she could figure out what to do, water was everywhere. And it kept running, overflowing the stall and streaming through under the door onto the bedroom floor. It wouldn't stop no matter what she did. She frantically turned the faucet right, left, up, and down. And then, suddenly and miraculously, it stopped. But by then she didn't know if the flood was from the faucet or from her tears.

Chapter 3

When Danielle woke up the next morning, to her chagrin one of the other beds was no longer empty. A strikingly pretty girl with honey colored curls was bending over the side of the bed searching for her shoes. Looking up at Danielle, she announced, "Good morning."

"Hey," Danielle answered groggily. "I didn't hear you come in."

"I came in late last night and didn't want to disturb you. By the way, my name is Sarah." Danielle couldn't help but be captivated by the warmth of her smile. She felt a perceptible change in the room, but wasn't sure what it was. Puzzled, she looked around and thought it was probably her imagination, but the room suddenly looked a little brighter. It reminded her of when the rapist had been pounding her unmercifully and she thought her life was over, but then had inexplicably felt a calmness enter her. She had known she would live. She had no other explanation, but that God had answered her cry of despair.

Danielle introduced herself warily and then figured it was better to chat with someone, even a stranger, than to go round and round in her head with the same miserable, humiliating story. When she found out that Sarah was on a short break from the kibbutz where Lauren worked, she laughed with glee at such a weird coincidence. So together, like old friends, they walked over to Dizengoff Square to have breakfast. While they were meandering down Rothschild Boulevard, Danielle blurted out, "God, these buildings are ugly. They look like big boxes."

To Danielle's relief, Sarah didn't seem insulted. Instead, she laughed and explained, "Lots of people think so, but the Bauhaus philosophy of art and architecture was a great match with original Zionistic principles. It revered minimalism. The architects believed that buildings should have clean lines and provide for utilitarian needs. And look." She pointed. "All the apartments have balconies."

Danielle nodded. "Did they plan that in the original buildings in Germany also?"

"Actually, no. They were advocates of large windows."

"But look," Danielle said. Some of these windows are very narrow."

"They had to make adjustments because of the heat," Sarah said. "The balconies were a modification so that people could enjoy the sea breezes while they relaxed and took part in the street life of the neighborhood."

As they continued their walk, Danielle noticed something odd and asked, "Why are some buildings on stilts?"

"Actually, the idea was very idealistic," Sarah said. "It was to have a garden in the middle of a city right where the people lived."

Noting the concrete beneath the buildings, Danielle said dryly, "Well, it looks like that idea didn't work."

Sarah laughed, and Danielle was glad she still had her wit even after all the turmoil of the last few days.

Sarah continued to talk about how Tel Aviv became a Bauhaus-designed city, and Danielle's thoughts drifted. As Sarah explained more of how Bauhaus combined art and architecture, Danielle suddenly asked, "So Sarah, tell me honestly do you like being in Israel?"

Sarah enthusiastically described living in the Jewish country. Danielle, who had forgotten her misery for a little while, discovered a glimmer of hope deep within her. Sarah talked not only about how many of the Bauhaus pioneers fled Nazi Germany and ended up designing much of Tel Aviv, she also spoke about the centrality of Israel to the Jewish people throughout history. The stories of despair and redemption not only gave Danielle hope, but the courage to continue after surviving such brutality. There was no other choice.

That evening before Sarah left, the two young women took their shoes off and walked along the deserted beach. As they watched the flickers of light coming from Jaffa, Sarah hugged Danielle and said it was time for her to go.

Tears filled Danielle's eyes, and she was petrified she would start crying. Instead, she muttered, "I understand. Thanks for everything." She looked down at her feet and took a deep breath. When she looked up, Sarah was gone. Danielle was almost relieved, because now she wouldn't have to say good-bye.

That night in bed, Danielle tossed and turned constantly. She was up with the sun, threw on some wrinkled clothes, and impatiently counted the minutes until the café opened at six o'clock. She was the first and only customer in the hotel's dismal café, and was too preoccupied for that to bother her. The old waitress silently refilled cup after cup of black coffee that Danielle drank to keep her cigarettes company. Finally, after too many hours of brooding, she caught sight of her sister. As Lauren walked through the door, Danielle stubbed out her cigarette and ran to greet her. Lauren was so surprised by the enthusiastic greeting, she lost her balance and almost fell.

"Hey," she said, "does this mean you're not mad at me?"

"I guess so," Danielle replied with a genuine smile. After the hugs and kisses, Danielle examined her sister more closely. "You look wonderful. What a great tan! Kibbutz life really agrees with you."

Over lunch, they decided where to go first, so Danielle could see some of the country before she had to be at school. She was so happy to be with her sister, she decided to try and absolve Lauren for her blatant negligence and forget the terror she had left behind. The next morning, though, on the bus to Eilat, her façade shattered when Lauren asked the simple question, "So how are you, really?" That was all Danielle needed, and she started describing to Lauren the horror of the rape.

"When this tall, thuggish-looking black guy came at me with the knife, I thought I was dreaming ..."

She couldn't stop talking, and with each word she spoke, she felt a little more relieved. Even though she knew she was making Lauren more and more uncomfortable, she continued with her tirade.

"Those damned police actually believed it was my own stupidity that saved me. Do you believe that's what they told me? Numb and terrified is more like it. But it wasn't me, Lauren. It had nothing to do with me. It was miraculous. I truly believe that if it had been my time to die, then I'd be dead. There's no doubt in my mind."

"Enough!" Lauren exclaimed. "I knew you were being awfully quiet, but I didn't know why."

"I haven't been able to talk about this with anyone," Danielle replied. "Can you imagine how terrifying it was for me? How disgusting it was to have a violent maniac's hands all over me."

"So you flew halfway around the world to dump your baggage on me? It's always another story with you." Lauren covered her ears. "I don't want to hear it. Okay? Just look out the window."

Danielle realized that even after what she'd gone through, her sister would treat her with disdain. She would get no sympathy, she morosely decided as she tried to follow her sister's self-serving demand. Still unable to shake what had happened to her and hurt by her sister's cold response, she stared blankly out the window, missing the majestic tableau of the Sinai desert as the Egged bus wound its way down to the southern tip of Israel and Eilat. But the floodgates had been opened, and after a few minutes she continued.

"The weird thing, Lauren, is that the police couldn't find the knife. I did. Up until then they didn't believe me. They kept questioning me like I was the criminal and kept wanting more and more details about the rape." Danielle took a breath and then added with a sneer, "I think one of those fat cops actually came in his pants. That's why he wanted to hear every single detail and every disgusting thing the rapist said and made me do."

Lauren angrily pulled an American magazine out of her overnight bag, and some toiletries fell out onto the filthy bus floor. Gritting her teeth, she picked them up and then told Danielle to calm down. "And by the way," she added, "I don't know anybody from the kibbutz named Sarah." She told Danielle that she was so tired and stressed from her ordeal, she must have dreamed up this other woman. Danielle, still angry from Lauren abandoning her at the airport, felt like smacking her across the face. Tension between the sisters rose, until a live rooster flew out of someone's plastic shopping bag. It caused such a disturbance on the bus that the driver had to pull over until the bird was caught and stuffed back into the tiny Yemenite lady's bag.

"Welcome to Israel!" Lauren said, and the sisters starting laughing.

After that, Danielle decided to keep her mouth closed. Lauren was just as self-absorbed as their mother. The best thing, she decided, was simply to shut her eyes and take a nap. As her favorite heroine Scarlett O'Hara would say, "I'll think about it tomorrow."

Chapter 4

The next day, as the sisters sat on a beach, taking turns trying to find American rock and roll music on Lauren's transistor radio, a skinny young man with a big gap between his front teeth appeared next to their blanket holding two cold sodas.

"You ladies must be thirsty," he said in heavily accented English.

Amused by his ridiculous attempt at being debonair, Danielle glanced at her sister and said, "It looks like this guy watches too many old Cary Grant movies."

Still, they shrugged and took the sodas. The interloper introduced himself as Benny and asked if he could join them. Before they could answer, he made a spot for himself on the blanket and picked up the little radio. He fiddled with the dial, and the sounds of Jefferson Airplane suddenly rose from it.

"What did you do?" Danielle asked.

"It's the Abie Nathan Peace Ship," he said.

"What's that?"

"He has a ship 'somewhere in the Mediterranean.' And he plays great music and talks about peace with the Arabs."

Benny had an endearing lopsided smile and was almost as small as Danielle. Since his bushy hair and big teeth made him look almost comical, she decided he was okay. Ironically, he had appeared right after one of her rants about how lousy men were.

Danielle had noticed him a while ago, sitting with the owner of the concession stand, drinking coffee and smoking cigarettes. She knew that when she had inadvertently caught his eye, she had given him an opening. Since he looked more like a dusty clown than a snake oil salesman and he spoke passable English, her resolve not to talk to men melted away. Besides, she was a stranger in his country, and Danielle had always relied on male companionship. So, when Lauren took the Egged bus back up to the Bet Shean Valley that evening, Danielle decided to stay Eilat for a while. She suspected Benny, a stranger, would be more sympathetic to her problems than her sister was.

She rationalized to herself that he seemed nice, but the most important thing was that he was Jewish. Even more, he was Israeli and had just fought a tough war. Her grandmother had taught her that Israel was holy. When she was a little girl her grandma would tell her the story of how, after thousands of years of lying dormant, Israel arose from the ashes of the war in Europe. A Jew wouldn't do anything wrong to another Jew. So Danielle figured she would stay in Eilat for a couple of more days before going to the kibbutz in Bet Shean to spend a couple of weeks there with her sister. Then she would take a bus down to Arad and start school.

Benny certainly was helpful. He let her stay at his apartment for free, introduced her to his friends, and they went out to dinner every night. Only, she always paid. The third night they went out, Benny left her alone for a few minutes and a fat, hairy man came over to the table and sat next to her. After he lit his cigarette, he put his arm around her and said in a heavy accent, "Very beautiful."

Danielle squirmed and said, "Thank you."

"Now you come with me."

"No. What are saying? Get your arm off me. When Benny gets back, I'll tell him you're bothering me."

"What's wrong?" the man said. "I already paid."

Then it became clear. Benny was nothing but an Israeli pimp. It was unbelievable, but he planned to spend all of her money and then put her out on the street to work for him.

She got up from the table in sheer panic, knowing she had to get out of Eilat as fast as possible. She had some money in her wallet, so she'd buy a bus ticket to get her as close as she could to the Bet Shean kibbutz. She ran to the bus station and prayed a bus would be leaving soon. She didn't care if she left a few things in Benny's apartment. It was more important that she get out of town before he hurt her.

The bus dropped her off in Beer Sheva, and from there she hitched the rest of the way to Bet Shean and the kibbutz. She had no sooner arrived than her sister gave her more bad news.

"Thank God you're here. Mom just called."

"Now what?" Danielle asked in despair.

"You have to go to a doctor. She got the results from the tests they took at the hospital. You have gonorrhea."

Oh, my God, Danielle thought. *This is unbelievable. Could it get any worse?*

All she felt was numb. She had thought her life would be better in Israel, the holy land of Israel. So far all she had seen was a den of thieves and pimps. And in her fragile emotional condition, she was a prime target for every rogue looking for easy prey. She sadly thought of the beautiful antique ring her mother had bought her. It was now gone because of her stupidity. She actually had let the ring be stolen right off her finger by a thief Benny had introduced her to.

For a full week she walked into the clinic every morning at 10:00 for her daily dose of penicillin. She always cringed because the nurse looked at her like she had rolled in dog shit and tracked it in on her clean floor. She figured the nurse thought she was a whore. Every day when she left the clinic she would sit by the lake and wish she could just float away. Finally, the humiliating scourge was taken care of, and she decided to stay on at the kibbutz to recover from her personal hell.

To her surprise, she discovered that she loved the routine and the pristine atmosphere. Picking grapefruit in the cool of the morning was the balm she needed as she put the horror behind her. Before she knew it Andy, a tall thin volunteer from Philadelphia, managed to sit next to her at every meal. They ended up spending all their free hours together, listening to music and swimming in the kibbutz pool. When Danielle left for school he was the only one, besides her sister, to whom she said good-bye.

The school surprised her. In the brochure it had looked so big, but it was just a few concrete buildings containing classrooms and a couple of squat apartment buildings for the students. *One more disillusionment*, Danielle thought.

She hadn't taken school seriously for a long time. Especially after the college campuses were turned upside down by students protesting the Vietnam War. She didn't care what anybody said about the glory of the anti-war movement. She had been there and she knew it was a sham. Politics was just the cover for students doing whatever they wanted. For most of them that meant doing drugs and having sex and cutting classes. Oh sure, there were some campus leaders who really cared about Vietnam, although her father kept telling her that they were Communists. But everyone else? Girls who just a few years earlier had been petrified that their reputations would be ruined if they "went all the way" were liberated by birth control pills. Now they could smoke pot, swallow Quaaludes and have sex every night with different partners, unencumbered by the fear of pregnancy.

We were going to be different from our mothers, Danielle thought. *We were going to be equal with men. At least that's what we were told.* So why had all these terrible, horrible things happened to her? She wasn't a bad person. Even Shirah, her last roommate at the university who had come from a yeshiva—a religious school—in Brooklyn said that she didn't know anyone "so bad could be so good."

Every morning for her first couple of weeks at school, Danielle had to force herself to get out of bed as she tried to give herself a reason for living. All she had ever wanted was a family. That didn't seem to be too much to ask. So why was this all happening to her?

As she took her morning shower one day and the water pounded her body, she once more cried out to the Almighty in despair and disillusionment. "Please God, help me. I can't live this way anymore. Help me."

"The rules. The rules are there for a reason."

Danielle didn't know if the voice she heard was inside or outside. To her it sounded like both at the same time. The closest she could come to describing it was as *knowing*. She knew then and forever that the voice was real, and that she didn't imagine it or hallucinate it. When she later became pregnant and felt the first flutter of her baby, it reminded her of the elusive voice. At first the movement was so light, almost imperceptible, like a butterfly wing. But she knew the baby had moved! As the baby moved a little bit more every day, any doubt she had disappeared. That voice was like that. The voice that whispered in her ear as she cried out to God in abject pain changed her life.

So Danielle listened. She figured she had nothing to lose. She had practically no money left and had too much pride to call and ask her parents to send more. They would think, with good reason, that she was an idiot. So, as alien as it was to her, she woke up early every day and went to her classes. She found that she was eager to learn. Then, miraculously, the student service director found her a job tutoring English. She grabbed the opportunity, even though she had no idea how to do it, didn't have any books, and didn't even know rudimentary Hebrew. But twice a week she would go to her student's house, sit at his kitchen table, and struggle to translate unknown words and phrases into English.

She felt as if the dirt was slowly washing off and vowed not to cut classes or sleep with a guy just because she wanted to have sex. Soon the strange-looking squiggles and lines of the Hebrew alphabet made sounds that made words when put together. To her delight and amazement, she was actually learning something. One afternoon as she drank a cup of coffee on the balcony of the student union, she realized she hadn't felt this good in a long time. Maybe, just maybe, she would allow herself to hope for a better life.

Chapter 5

All the students at school were given small apartments, and one of her neighbors was a young married couple from New York. The girl, Marilyn, was small and brunette like herself and her husband, Hank, was twice her height with a bad, pitted complexion. They were an odd-looking couple, and every time she saw them together she would think of the cartoon characters Mutt and Jeff Sometimes when she passed by their apartment, the door was open, revealing a room filled with people. They seemed to be having a good time, playing Dylan tunes on their guitars, laughing at smart remarks and good-natured teasing. But the dark-haired wife sat in a corner anxiously gnawing on sunflower seeds, spitting out shells as fast as she put them in her mouth.

Every once in a while Danielle saw her on the way to class or in the town square. She would smile, thinking how much alike they looked. Marilyn would only nod, apparently not comfortable with the intimacy of smiling at her new neighbor, or maybe she still angry with her husband. The apartment walls were so thin, Danielle couldn't help hearing their almost nightly fights. Sometimes she would knock on the wall to remind them that they could be heard.

One night someone else in the apartment building had a little get-together. Danielle was invited, as were Marilyn and Hank. As Danielle walked around the crowded apartment with her drink, she heard Marilyn tell someone that her brother Marvin was arriving soon.

"He'll be coming with the next group of students. I'm kind

of worried because he's very depressed. His last letter was a little frightening. You know how isolating New York can be. I hope coming here will be good for him."

Then Danielle heard that voice again, the voice that was both inside her head and outside her being. "You're going to marry him."

So she waited for the next group of students to arrive. Someone threw a welcome party, and she went. But when someone pointed her out to him, and she saw a man playing a guitar in a crazed, angry way, the music totally discordant, she was appalled. *Oh, no,* she thought. *There must be a mistake.* But she knew she had to believe the voice. Besides, she wanted to. She had to believe in something.

Apparently, Marvin noticed her. The next day at break time, he made sure to lounge in the plaza close enough for her to notice him. This went on for several days. He made sure she knew he was interested, but never made any direct conversation.

Marilyn and Hank had one of their big parties. Usually there was just a lot of guitar playing and sitting around cracking jokes, kind of like a pot party without the pot, but at this one there was liquor. Danielle hadn't had a drink for a while and figured she would have more fun if she was at least a little drunk. So fixed herself a vodka and orange juice, waiting to see what would happen.

Someone grabbed her around the waist. Caught by surprise, she looked at Marvin Steinberg closely for the first time. He was good looking, with an unusual combination of blue eyes and black hair. He was more handsome than she'd expected, but skinny. When he asked her where she'd been, he made it sound as though he'd been waiting for her for forever.

So together they drank and laughed and made the silly repartee that people had been making throughout human history in different languages but that meant the same thing. He even held her head as she threw up that night and took an amazing interest in the undigested food in her vomit. She crawled into bed with the stench of vomit in her pores and the awful taste in her mouth, but at least she didn't have to make excuses about not going to bed with him.

It turned out that Marvin was very smart. He had gone to Brooklyn Technical High School, one of the four schools in New York that required applicants to pass a special test in order to enroll.

After graduation he attended Stony Brook University and double majored in philosophy and psychology. He was the second child and only son of Holocaust survivors. Every time he mentioned his parents, he would always say how crazy they were. Danielle thought that he was exaggerating and unsympathetic. She had read enough about the Holocaust to know that it was miraculous his parents had survived. She figured anyone would be a little crazy after what they'd lived through. He revealed that he did drugs, a lot of drugs, more than just a hit of acid now and then. She told herself that that had been in college. This was a different time and place and besides, love changed everything.

And it looked like he loved her. He even bought her an expensive pair of sandals because she was walking around in flip-flops. Benny the pimp and his friends had taken so much of her money that when her shoes were beyond repair, she had to use her rubber pool thongs for shoes. So when Marvin took her to the shoe store to buy her shoes, she knew that the voice had been right. This was serious. He was the one, her *beshert*. She could finally feel safe.

They developed a simple routine. They went to classes together during the day. She taught Modi, her Israeli student, English two afternoons a week. At night she and Marvin would drink some bad Israeli wine or arak mixed with water, and of course they ended up in bed. The earth didn't shake, mountains didn't move, and she didn't care. They would take walks into the desert after class and talk. Actually, Marvin would talk and talk some more. And she would listen and laugh. Nobody had ever made her laugh like he did. He had a portable cassette tape player and they would listen to his favorite group, the Grateful Dead, or to Dylan. When he became drunk and senseless late at night, he would collapse in her arms and sing the Dead's "Morning Dew." By then Danielle was spending more time in Marvin's apartment than her own.

On Saturdays they would pack up salami sandwiches and spend the afternoon watching old American movies at the desert town's only cinema. One evening after a marathon of John Wayne movies, Danielle showered at Marvin's and changed her clothes.

"Hey, let's go," she said. "I'm starving."

"Just a couple of more minutes. I have to get this powder under the cabinet before those fucking roaches invade us too. A little lick and lickity split—dead. And won't you feel grateful. Hell, you know these apartment buildings. Albert found one of those little fucks in his kitchen today. It doesn't take long for them to take over. This boric acid will take care of them. It's like roach napalm."

So while Marvin orchestrated his counteroffensive attack, Danielle told him she'd save him a seat in the dining hall. She ran down the steps and almost knocked over a tall, thin man who was on his way up. He beamed as she stumbled into his arms.

"Andy! What a surprise! My God, I can't believe it." She hoped her panic sounded like happiness to him.

"I missed you so much," he said, "that I wanted to come down and tell you that in person." He embraced her, his lips grazing her hair. When he looked at her, his eyes were bright with love and joy.

All Danielle could think was, that Marvin would be coming down the stairs any second and she didn't know what to do. She gave Andy a brief kiss, as short as she could get away with, but it was long enough for her to remember how gentle he was and how much comfort she had found in his arms. Then she took his hand and led him to the dining hall, saying apologetically that her friend Marvin would be coming down soon. Andy didn't say anything except, "Oh," but she noticed that when he dropped his fork, he took a little longer than necessary to pick it up.

As they carried their trays to some empty seats, Danielle tried to think. The best she could come up with was just to introduce the two men to each other and see what happened. As Andy and she were getting reacquainted over their dry egg salad and pita, Marvin appeared.

"Who the hell is this?" he asked.

"Marvin, this is Andy. Remember I told you about the guy I met on the kibbutz? Andy, this is Marvin, a friend I met here at WOJS."

As the men glared at each other, she told Marvin to sit down and nervously chatted, praying he wouldn't cause a scene.

"Isn't it funny that you both play the guitar? Andy was just telling me he brought his guitar but left it at the office while he came looking for me. We can go back to your apartment and play some music. Isn't that a good idea?"

Andy looked surprised but said, "Yeah, sure. I'll just go over and get my guitar and then meet you. It's a good time anyway before the office closes. So where did you say we'll meet?"

"Upstairs," she answered. "Apartment twenty-one. See you in a couple of minutes." She kissed him briefly but lingeringly on the lips before he left. As he walked out the door she said to Marvin, "I had no idea he was coming."

"What the fuck," Marvin said. "I wasn't hungry anyway."

"He wrote a song for me," she said as they went back upstairs

"You and how many other girls? You know how many girls come through that kibbutz and volunteer their services?"

"Yeah, but he came all the way down here to see *me*. You know how hard that trip is. First you have to go to Afula, then Tel Aviv, and then finally a bus out here. I can't be rude. My sister didn't even do it to meet me at the airport."

"When a guy wants to get laid, he'll do anything. My father even married my mother. That dildo head from the kibbutz had no luck after you left, so he came running to find you. Just so he could get his rocks off again."

"Well, I don't think so. But anyway, he's a really good musician, so this should be fun hearing you play together."

As they entered Marvin's apartment, Danielle wondered where she was going to sleep that night. If she slept in her apartment, she'd have to sleep with Andy and she'd lose Marvin. If she stayed with Marvin, she would definitely lose Andy.

A knock at the door announced Andy. Danielle took a deep breath before she opened it, while Marvin banged around in the bedroom looking for a pick.

Andy stood there with his guitar, smiling, still so happy to see her. *What a bitch I am*, she thought. But she let Andy in because she didn't know what else to do. She squeezed his hand before he sat down and bent his head over his guitar, tuning it. Marvin came out of the bedroom, looking triumphant that he had found a pick. He held it up, announcing like the caller at a square dance, "Pick your partner, go round and round." She winced, but Andy was so focused on his tuning, he didn't appear to hear.

"I play rhythm, man, how about you?" Marvin asked as he started to tune up.

"I play anything."

"I can see that. Oh, yes, I can. Playing hooky from the kibbutz so you can play nooky with this little girl."

Andy didn't respond, just started to play a tune. As she listened, Danielle was embarrassed for Marvin. He couldn't play. He usually sounded like a train wreck. No matter what the two men played, Marvin's guitar sounded like a tommy gun. Just rat a tat tat tat. He had absolutely no ear and what was worse, he didn't seem to know it. Meanwhile Andy could play anything from blues to the Dead. All of his songs came alive with warmth and melody. Danielle finally called an end to it.

"I have to go to school in the morning," she said. "Andy, are you ready to go?"

Andy stood. "It was cool," he said to Marvin. "See ya, man."

Cool it wasn't, but Andy was certainly a gentleman. And Marvin?

"Not if I see you first," Marvin said. "This deal didn't even go down yet."

Oh, God.

So she spent that night in Andy's arms. The song he wrote for her, just for her, was as beautiful as looking in his eyes. They were filled with adoration for her. But she didn't understand what was happening. This was a complete surprise. She had thought their time together on the kibbutz had been just a passionate interlude. She didn't remember either one of them mentioning love. Or maybe they had, but that was before she met Marvin.

Andy stayed the next day as she went to classes, and then they had dinner together. After dinner she said she had to help someone with some schoolwork and went to Marvin's apartment.

"Why are you here?" Marvin asked, not looking at her as he pretended to fix a door handle.

"I don't know. He loves me."

"So do I, my sad-eyed lady."

"I know. But you never told me."

"If it has to be said, then maybe it shouldn't. Never thought I had to. So does that schmuck know you're here?"

"I don't know. I told him I was helping a friend with some schoolwork."

"Well, good night then, little schoolgirl."

He kissed her and held her, and she could see the sadness in his eyes, and the fear that he would lose her.

When she went back to her own apartment and Andy, he told her his big news. He wanted her to come back to the kibbutz with him when school was over and get married. Apparently, he had even spoken to the secretary of the kibbutz about building a house. Danielle was shocked and told him how unexpected this was, and that she'd had no idea he was so serious about her. She would have to think about this.

The next day after classes, she said she had to take a can of tuna fish over to a friend. Even though she felt guilty, she walked directly to Marvin's apartment. She told him what Andy had said.

"Marvin, what should I do?"

They stood a little apart, looking at each other, taking each other's measure, and then Marvin spoke. He didn't say, "I love you. Please don't marry him." Or, "I can't live my life without you." All he said was, "Do what you want. It's your life."

She was stunned. Marvin was actually thinking of her. All Andy talked about was what he wanted. He'd come down here because it was what he wanted. He hadn't even called first. That made up her mind, as well as that little voice she'd heard back at that first party. The little voice that had said she would marry Marvin.

She walked back to her apartment, and with tears in her eyes told Andy that she didn't love him. She wished she had known how much he loved her before she got involved with Marvin, but now it was too late. It was a tearful good-bye. After Andy left, she went back to Marvin and told him what'd done. He held her and said, "This is the first time that I won the girl. I can't believe it!"

So that was it, but she knew that she couldn't go through this anymore. She needed something solid, a commitment. So later that week, after he found her contact lenses, which she had put in a little matchbox and left on a rock in the middle of the desert, she made a decision.

"I can't go through another love affair," she told Marvin. "If you love me, we need to get married. Otherwise I can't see you anymore. I'll be finished with classes in another month and I have to know what I'm doing."

"Marriage? Kids?"

"Of course kids. I'm twenty-four years old. I can't do this anymore. No more love affairs."

"One of the guys from school has been married awhile," he said. "Streich is married too. You know, my buddy from my building? No one ever thought I'd be next, or even last. Who would marry me? Crazy Marv or Menachem Chaim. Just a body for the soul of my mother's pop. So life goes on. Yeah, a nice Jewish girl and a crazy Jewish guy make nice Jewish babies and life goes on until it doesn't. Sure, let's get married. Why not?"

And that's how it was decided that Mr. Marvin Steinberg and Miss Danielle Katz would become joined in matrimony. Their lives would now be officially intertwined.

Chapter 6

Once the decision was made and letters were sent back and forth to both families, it became real. They were actually getting married, and Danielle could finally feel safe. Sometimes she still had nightmares about that horrible night when she was raped, but not as often as before. Her life could begin. Her new life, which would include a husband and children. That was what she had always wanted. Marvin was tough and strong, the son of survivors. It didn't get stronger than that. He would protect her and she would never be hurt again.

They chose April 10, 1975, as the date for the wedding because Marvin's year at school would be complete. They had decided to stay in Israel, but where would they live? Danielle knew she didn't want a city like Tel Aviv or even Jerusalem. Marvin said that he didn't care.

As part of their school requirements, they had both volunteered at a kibbutz in the northern part of the country, the Galil, on the Lebanese border. Danielle loved it there, but there was only one problem. The secretary of the kibbutz had taken her aside and told her that if she was interested in staying, they would love to have her. However, she would have to come without her *chaver*, her friend Marvin. When she told Marvin, he said, "Sure they'd love to have you. Every fucking guy on that kibbutz would love to have you. Do you think they didn't see your tits bouncing on the truck on the way to work?"

Disappointed that they still had nowhere to live when school was over, she read an article in the newspaper about a group of Americans that was sanctioned by the Israeli government to be part of a *garin* that was starting a new town in the Sinai. The head of the project was an American rabbi, Izzy Frankel. The group was living just a short bus ride away, in Beer Sheva, at the absorption center.

She showed the article to Marvin. "This sounds kind of interesting. The government is investing money to build a new town in the Sinai. It's supposed to get started with an equal number of Americans, Russians, and Israelis. What do you think?"

"Personally, I don't give a damn."

"Come on, Marv. Let's go see this guy Frankel in Beer Sheva. Maybe this is for us."

After calling the absorption center and making an appointment to meet with Frankel the following Shabbat, Danielle went to the market to get a bottle of arak. It was Friday night, erev Shabbat, which meant as far as Marvin was concerned, it was time to party.

The next Shabbat they got on the crowded Egged bus and headed for Beer Sheva. When they got out at the central bus station, they had to walk through deserted ancient streets to reach the absorption center. It was located on the edge of town, where they had built some new apartment houses. Danielle was nervous and hoped it didn't show. What if this guy didn't like them? Then what? She and Marvin had decided to make their life together in Israel, but she wasn't crazy about living in the city. She really liked being outdoors, and she wanted to make a contribution like the old *chalutzim,* the pioneers, but she was afraid this guy Frankel wouldn't like them. No, not *them* but Marvin. Look what happened at Kibbutz Yael. Marvin sat under the grapefruit trees smoking cigarettes and getting into arguments with everyone.

A nondescript two-story building came into view. It was typical utilitarian Israeli architecture, looking more like a concrete box than an apartment complex. After making inquiries, they found the rabbi Frankel and his wife Shoshi waiting for them in their cramped apartment.

"Shalom Aleichem," the rabbi said in a booming voice as he shook Marvin's hand. "Glad to meet you. Take a seat. Shoshi, how about some tea and a piece of cake? That sounds good, kids?"

"Thanks so much," Danielle said. "That would be great."

"Not for me," Marvin said. "No coffee or tea. I never touch the stuff."

"So kids, what brings you here?" asked the rabbi.

He wore a *kippah* on the back of his full head of gray hair, but otherwise looked like anyone else Danielle knew. He didn't fit her image of a rabbi, but the rabbis she knew weren't sitting in Beer Sheva waiting to move to the Sinai desert. Shorts and an open collar shirt showed that he was already living Israeli style.

"Well," she began, but Marvin broke in.

"We want to be part of the group that's going to Yamit."

"It's going to be hard," replied the rabbi. "Have you been down there yet?"

"No, we thought the first step was to see you," Marvin said.

Danielle was relieved that all she had to do was sit there, and Marvin would do all the talking.

"Did you need any help with that tea?" she asked Mrs. Frankel.

"No, thanks. I baked for Shabbat, so this cake is nice and fresh and luckily the kids left us some. I'll be with you in a minute."

Danielle could see that the rabbi and Marvin were getting along well. Marvin was telling him about going to school and their plans to be married in the spring, as well as their educational backgrounds.

Just as Mrs. Frankel was putting the tray of tea things on the table, the door slammed open and a small, beautiful dark-haired girl ran in.

"Rivala," Mrs. Frankel said, "come say hello to Danielle and Marvin. They came to talk to Abba about Yamit."

"Hel– I mean shalom," the girl said. "Ima, can I have another piece of cake?"

"Let the guests have first. Go wash your hands."

Turning her attention back to Marvin and the rabbi, Danielle heard the rabbi say, "So you kids fill out this paperwork and then Shoshi will bring you around and introduce you. Dror is taking a ride down there next week. Why don't you go with him and see if this is what you want. Talking is one thing. Seeing what you're in for is another."

With that last remark he got up from the couch and walked into what Danielle presumed to be the bedroom.

"Okay, man, thanks," Marvin said to the man's back just before the rabbi shut the door behind him. Then they were both left with Shoshi Frankel. Since she didn't apologize for her husband's strange behavior, neither of them mentioned it.

Riva returned. "Ima, quick, the kids are waiting for me."

Shoshi gave her a piece of cake. Stuffing the cake into her mouth, Riva was out the door with a quick, "*Lahit.*"

Shoshi looked a little distracted, and then she abruptly said, "I'll take you downstairs to the *cheder ochel*, the dining room. I think some of our garin members are still down there. This way you can meet them informally."

The sun was shining, but a gentle breeze made the unrelenting desert heat bearable. Since the absorption center was built around a central area of green space, it was filled with children running around and laughing, playing a game that looked like freeze tag. Danielle spotted Shoshi and Izzy's daughter in the middle of the group, and it brought a smile to her face.

Shoshi stopped to introduce them to a woman with bleached blonde hair. She was smoking a cigarette and talking to a short muscular man who turned out to be the Dror Izzy had mentioned.

"Rhoda, Dror, this is Marvin and Danielle. They're interested in becoming members of our garin." Shoshi turned to Marvin and added, "Why don't you talk to Dror about going down with him the next time he goes? It was nice meeting you. Keep in touch and let us know how you like our Yamit."

With that she was gone, and Danielle saw her stop by the group of children on her way back upstairs.

Dror was an Israeli who had lived in America for a while and had married an American woman named Hannah. They had two little girls, and he said his wife was upstairs resting while the girls napped. "Nu, what brought you to us here in Beer Sheva?" he asked.

Marvin again told the story about reading about Yamit in the paper, and Danielle made a mental note that he took all the credit for getting in contact with this group. Rhoda broke into her thoughts by saying that she couldn't wait to get out of the absorption center.

"Did Izzy tell you we've been here six months already and they didn't start building one house yet?"

"No, not really," Danielle answered politely. "He did say that the wheels are turning very slowly."

"Well, let me tell you, I'm getting fed up living in this little crackerjack box. I came here with three kids and it's impossible for us living like this. The walls are so thin, there's no way I can even get laid in my own house."

"Oh, I never thought of that," replied Danielle, trying not to look shocked. Was there anything else she could say? "So where is your husband today?" she added.

"That bastard? In the United States with his latest *korva*."

"Oh, I'm sorry."

"I'm not. She can have that piece of shit. Meanwhile I spent all the settlement money getting here. We better hear some good news this week."

Dror broke in. "Sharetz said they were finishing the first villa this week. You want to take a ride down at the end of week, Marvin, Danielle? It's on a beautiful site. Rhoda needs to learn patience. This is Israel."

"Patience I have, money I don't. That job at the university pays bubkahs. Well, it was nice meeting you. I hope we see you again." Rhoda took a last drag on her cigarette. "I'm expecting a visitor while the kids are outside. Shalom."

Marvin and Danielle said good-bye to her and then made arrangements to come back the next Shabbat in order to drive down with Dror.

The following Saturday Marvin told Danielle that his head felt like a hundred-pound weight and that the sound of the birds outside their window was more like reveille blasting the morning's arrival. "I really don't want to go anywhere today. I feel like shit."

"Fine," she said. "You stay here and I'll drive down with Dror and give you my impressions. Okay?"

"Never mind, my honey. Maybe if you climb back in this bed for just a few minutes more, I can find the strength to fight this goddamn hangover."

So bright and early, even though their heads were pounding from the night before, the young couple was on the bus to meet Dror and drive down to Yamit.

"Thank God for sunglasses," Danielle said. "This sun is blinding."

"My honey, God didn't make sunglasses. And the single observable proof that our Arab cousins are lacking in the brain department?"

"I have no idea, Marv."

"Did you ever notice that Arabs don't wear sunglasses? They've all burned out their optic nerves."

"Oh, come on."

"That's how your eyes are connected to your brain," he added seriously.

Danielle started singing, "'The knee bone's connected to the thigh bone, and the thigh bone's connected to the hip bone. And your eyeball's connected to your—'"

"That's it. That's why they're so stupid. They've burned their optic nerves." Marvin expounded on his latest theory, and Danielle smiled and laughed at his jokes, wondering how he'd happened to notice that Arabs didn't wear sunglasses. She hadn't.

As they neared Beer Sheva, she said, "At least this time we won't walk in circles trying to find the absorption center."

"Maybe we should take a taxi to the center, just in case we forget how to get there," Marvin said.

At that moment Danielle realized his sense of direction was really bad. She started teasing him because she knew all they had to do was walk west for six blocks, through the decrepit center of the town to the other side, where the more modern apartment buildings and houses were.

"So," she said, "you're telling me that you were able to travel the subways by yourself, in one of the biggest cities in the world since you were twelve years old, but you're worried that you can't find your way six blocks from the central bus station in this hokey place? Maybe you need a new pair of shades. It looks like your optic nerve is smoking."

She was sorry she teased him, though, because the whole way through town he didn't say a word. Not one. He pretended that she wasn't there and managed to walk just fast enough that she was always a few steps behind him. She was right about where the center was, but at least she had learned not to tease him about his lousy sense of direction.

Dror was standing in the parking lot waiting for them. "Shalom, *ma nishma*. How are you? Good to see you. And you're on time."

"You can't take New York out of a New Yorker or a bite of my Jersey tomato," Marvin said by way of greeting. "We're ready to rock and roll."

They hopped into Dror's small truck, or what was known in Israel as a tender, the men sitting up front and Danielle in back. She was happy with that arrangement. She could close her eyes if she got tired, and not have to worry about making small talk and pretend that Marv hadn't just cut her off. She could simply listen.

"So how far is Yamit from here?" Marvin asked.

"About as far as Jersey is to Manhattan, but there's no public transportation," Dror said in his heavily accented English.

"That's okay. We've got our own taxi driver now. We've been looking forward to seeing it, so drive, my man."

Dror laughed. "You're gonna love it. Hannah, that's my wife, is from New York too. The minute she saw it, she fell in love. With Yamit. Not me."

Dror was a typical Israeli driver, and once they made it out of Beer Sheva and there was nobody else on the road, he sped down the road so fast, pieces of dirt and pebbles flew behind them. Danielle listened to him talk about the gas station he had left in Queens, but mostly she just looked out the window. Beyond Beer Sheva, which was located in the Negev desert, the dry desert rock and scrub were broken up only by the green fields of kibbutzim and moshavim.

Being in Israel had changed her ideas about the desert. All her life she had assumed deserts were just endless, dull sand dunes. Until she came to live in Arad, she never could have believed the power and beauty of the ancient, eroded rocks and dried up wadis.

Dror pointed out a couple of moshavim that had been started by English-speaking immigrants and told them a little bit about the area. "Those guys grow hydroponic tomatoes and flowers. They came from South Africa and had it pretty rough the first few years, but it looks like their export business finally took off. Europe is a good market for our produce and flowers. It will only take another half hour from this point. Once we get to the end of this road, we're going to bear left and then we'll be in territory that we got in the '67 War. Did Frankel tell you that we're just south of Rafiah? There's a big Palestinian refugee camp there. There're a couple of moshavim close to the area where we're going to build, but our location … Well, Pretty soon you'll see for yourself."

The farther away they got from Beer Sheva, the more deserted the scenery became. At one point Danielle saw a man dressed in robes and wearing what looked like a white towel wrapped around his head, leading his donkey somewhere off into the distance. She didn't see houses or other cars anymore, and couldn't imagine where he was going. Finally Dror made a left-hand turn and she saw signs in Hebrew and in Arabic.

"If we continued down this road," he said, "it would take us all the way into Egypt. Yamit is part of the Sinai that we won during the war. I know Frankel told you about Dayan's plan to have a buffer zone. Our southern neighbor is El Arish. It's an Egyptian fishing village. Man, what a shit hole. I don't know how people live that way."

"It's because they don't wear sunglasses," Marvin said.

They all laughed and then were quiet while Dror turned up the news. Like all Israelis Danielle had met, he had an automatic reaction to listen in total silence while the news was on. As soon as the report was over, he would probably dissect and examine it.

"So what's the news?" Marvin asked.

"*Hakol beseder.* It's all right."

It's so peaceful, Danielle thought. Nothing marred the stark landscape except a camel caravan. About six camels walked along slowly on their knobby legs. Two women covered from head to foot in black walked alongside the animals while men rode them, as they had for thousands of years.

Almost as if he'd read her mind, Dror said, "They still have camel races out here. As a matter of fact, if you get out here really early on a Saturday, you can watch it. They bet on the camels, just like we bet on horses. "

"Do they let women go?" Danielle asked.

"Are you kidding?" Dror laughed. "They still put up their daughters as part of the bet."

They crossed a train track and continued down the road about two more miles to the Mediterranean Sea.

"Oh, my God, it's breathtaking," was all Danielle could say. Could there be any other place this beautiful? They got out of the truck and stood on the beach, gazing out over the blue water. Nothing marred the broad vista of white sand and clumps of palm trees. And then she saw the Israeli army jeep. Two soldiers sat behind a dune smoking cigarettes.

"What do you think?" Dror asked.

"A lot of fucking sand," Marvin said.

Chapter 7

Marvin stood beside the truck smoking a cigarette and said he wasn't going down to the water.

"Suit yourself," Danielle said, even though she was a little upset that he wouldn't share this moment with her. Still, as she walked to the water with Dror close behind her, she decided she wouldn't let anything ruin this day.

"I bet you look good in a bathing suit," Dror said.

She smiled over her shoulder at him. "When we move here you'll get to see for yourself."

She quickly took off her sandals and walked into the Mediterranean.

"Ooh, it's warm. Like a bathtub. Dror, this has to be the most beautiful place on earth." She splashed water onto her face and arms, loving the pungent fragrance of sand and sea. As she walked back out of the water, she said to Dror, "I'm ready when you are. Show us where we're going to live."

They all climbed back into the truck and drove up a hill, which was about a quarter of a mile from the beach, to the entrance of a building site. All she could see was sand and ancient rock marked off by barbed wire.

"We'll go see the Gingy," Dror said.

"What's a gingy?" Marv asked.

"Don't they teach you anything important at that school?" was Dror's reply.

They pulled up to a little stand that no more than a tin corrugated roof covering a small refrigerator that was powered by a generator and a gas grill. Off to the side, a hammock was tied up to a palm tree near a lean-to made of palm fronds. Sitting beside the refrigerator was a short, wiry man with bright red hair and freckles.

"Ma nishma?" Dror called. "What's up, Gingy?"

"Dror," the man replied. "I'm living. Could be a hell of a lot better, could be a hell of a lot worse. I finally got the generator. So now no complaints. You can finally have a cold drink. I see you brought me two new customers."

He pulled out three cold bottles of soda and said, "L'chaim." Dror put some coins in his hand before Marvin could even reach in his wallet.

"Nu, what's happening?" Dror asked.

"They put the first house up. It looks good. Go take a look. I'm even starting to get business."

"That's why we came down. This is Marv and Danielle. They're thinking about joining us, so I figured the best thing to do was drive them down and let them see what they're in for. We'll leave the truck here."

"Why not? The parking lot's not full," Gingy replied with a grin. "Besides, you'll need something to drink on the way back."

Dror led them around Gingy's stand and down a trail that had been made by trucks. The sun was bright, and Danielle was glad for the constant breeze from the Mediterranean. Suddenly they saw it—a little desert dollhouse.

"It's adorable!" Danielle said. "Can we go in?"

"There's no one here to stop you," Dror said. "I'm going to check out the rest of the site and I'll meet you at the Gingy's in half an hour."

"Okay," Marvin said. "But is that Israeli time or American?"

Dror just grinned and sauntered away.

"I love it," Danielle exclaimed, stepping inside. "I just love it. I hope we can do this. Look at this house. It's small, but it's got everything we need – a kitchen, a bathroom, bedrooms, a living room. This is going to be wonderful to raise a family here," she said as she ran from room to room.

"And how do I make a living?" Marvin asked.

"We'll figure it out as we go. Just look at the Gingy."

"I have degrees in psychology and philosophy. What the hell am I going to do with them here?" he asked rhetorically as he looked into the vast expanse of desert.

"Well, my philosophy is that this is a once in a lifetime opportunity. How many people get to start a city? This is like a dream." She hugged him. "Marv, you're great with your hands and you're smart. You'll be able to use everything you learned at Brooklyn Tech. It'll be fine." She added softly, "I just hope they want us."

They held hands on the way back to the Gingy's. Danielle was so happy she felt her heart would burst, but it seemed to her Marvin was lost in a maze of his own thoughts.

Chapter 8

Dror was deep in conversation with Gingy when they got back to his stand. Danielle tried to understand the rapid Hebrew, but the only thing she caught was when Gingy offered them another drink. This time, Danielle was glad to see, Marvin paid. They said their good-byes and they climbed back in the little truck.

"Now you know what you're in for," Dror said. "What do you think?"

"How are we going to make a living?" Marvin asked.

"I'll show you the blueprints when we get back. There's a section that's set aside for industry, and there's going to be a town center. The hard part is going to be getting to that point. That's what I was talking to Gingy about. Sharev wants the garin members to work for them, to help build the infrastructure, because these Arabs don't work. If we don't, we might never see this finished."

Danielle smiled to herself and closed her eyes. When she opened them again, they had reached the absorption center.

Dror took them up to his small apartment to look at the blueprints. His wife Hannah met them at the door with a finger to her lips, whispering that the girls were finally down for a nap. She led them out onto the balcony so they could talk without disturbing the children. Dror introduced Danielle and Marvin as the newest garin members to be. Danielle noted that Hannah was an interesting-looking woman. She was not actually pretty, but had an aura of practicality and intelligence. Although she was a little stocky and had close cropped rings of curls around her head, Danielle could see why Dror was attracted to her. She figured they were both in their early thirties, especially since Dror had mentioned they'd been married for seven years when their first daughter was born. Hannah had majored in journalism at NYU, and her credentials included interviewing Fidel Castro when he had been in New York. Danielle sensed that that Dror was very proud of his wife, and he still couldn't figure out why someone with Hannah's background would marry an uneducated gas station owner like himself.

Hannah brought out the blueprints and glasses of juice. As Dror explained the blueprints to Marvin, Hannah told Danielle about her two little girls and about deciding to come back to Israel. She had lived on a kibbutz for a few years when she was single and then had returned to the States.

"We met the Frankels in the United States," she went on, "when they were touring around, trying to get people to come with them. Dror made a lot of money during the gas shortage and I loved Israel when I was here before. So we figured, why not? The girls will grow up to be Israelis, and we get to live in a place that we help build."

Danielle nodded in agreement, and then Hannah asked her when she and Marvin were going to get married.

"April, although my mother is so scared that the wedding will never happen. In her last letter, she asked if we could have the wedding here next month, when they come to visit. Like I don't know why." Danielle laughed, and Hannah joined her.

"I can't believe we've been married ten years," Hannah said.

"It's hard to believe I'm actually getting married," Danielle said. "I think my parents had already given up hope. All their friends' daughters are already married or engaged. And I, for one, never would have believed I was going to marry someone named Marvin."

A cute little girl about three years old with blonde curls toddled over to Hannah. Hannah gave her a hug and sent her over to Dror. Dror picked her up and raised her far over his head. She giggled and shrieked, "Abba, Abba, put me down."

Dror put her down, and Marvin said it was time to go. Hannah and Dror told them to come to the next meeting so that everyone could meet them. After that, there would be a vote about their acceptance. They made arrangements to be back at the absorption center Tuesday evening. As they stood outside saying their good-byes, Rhoda joined them and announced she had just gotten a job as a secretary for an American company.

"Everyone keeps saying patience, but I'm starting to get worried. I haven't seen anything being done. Oh, well, at least I'll have work if this doesn't happen."

"One of the houses is finished. We saw it today," Danielle said to make Rhoda feel better.

"You did? Nobody told me. That's great. I guess Izzy was saving the news for the meeting. Wow! That's made my day. The only thing that could be better is getting laid by my twenty-four-year-old boyfriend." She smiled, gauging their reactions as she took a drag on her cigarette. "He thinks older blonde American women are sexy." She studied her cigarette as she asked, "Is it true that sex is better when you're happy?" Before anyone could speak, she answered her own question wistfully. "Maybe now I'll get to find out."

Danielle and Marvin caught the last bus from Beer Sheva to Arad, and Marv described to Danielle the plans that Dror showed him. "The city will be built in three stages. During the first stage, they'll put up two-story apartment buildings. Some of the apartments will have two bedrooms and some will have three. There's also going to be some villas, or houses, just like we saw today."

"Oh, God, Marv, I hope they like us enough to include us."

"Well, the government is setting aside enough housing for thirty-five American couples, thirty-five Russians, and thirty-five Israelis. Dror told me they're still trying to make the American quota. The cool thing is, this is the first planned city Israel has attempted. Part of the design is to have a road around the city, which allows for parking lots behind each of the apartment complexes. But no traffic will be allowed inside the city. Everything will be connected by sidewalks and walkways."

For the first time since Danielle had met him, Marv looked contemplative and serious. The New York veneer of sarcasm and cynicism had disappeared. She kissed him on the cheek and said, "I hope they like us, because I think this is going to be great."

"My honey, my baby, I think you're right," he said as he gave her an enveloping hug. And Danielle saw a brand new look in Marv's eyes. At first she didn't recognize it, and then she realized what it was. It was hope.

Chapter 9

Tuesday's meeting was over. The vote had been taken, and Marvin Steinberg and Danielle Katz were official members of the Yamit group. The next day, they went to their favorite falafel stand after class to celebrate the good news.

"I was so afraid they wouldn't take us," Danielle said.

"Beggars can't be choosers," Marvin said. "It's not as if people are lined up outside Frankel's door, asking to live in the desert, surrounded by Arabs. They're lucky they have us."

"I guess you're right, Marv. I never looked at it that way. I was just worried that they wouldn't want us."

"Why wouldn't they want us? The Frankels are alter kockers. They're old. They must be close to forty. So are Dror and Hannah. Then they have that nymphomaniac divorcee who'll fuck anything with a circumcised dick and her three rotten kids, and to top it off that guy with the withered arm. They need some healthy young blood."

"I'm really glad we can show my parents where we're going to live when they come next month," Danielle said. Then she added, "Although, I don't think they're going to like it too much."

Danielle started biting her fingernails again just thinking of the upcoming visit. Her parents would have to digest a lot of information in a very short time. First, they'd meet Marvin, who was a little weird. She knew that. The good thing was that he fit the profile. He was Jewish, from New York, and had a college education. Those details were what was important to them. For her, Marvin had an added benefit. He was terrific with his hands. It turned out that he was one of those guys who could fix anything, and she found that very sexy. Besides, nobody ever made her laugh the way he did. He had a way of reducing everything to its most basic ironies. Her only concern was his drinking, but she told herself it would stop. They were both young and Marvin just liked to party. That was normal. Once they were married, the drinking would stop. Besides, she would remind herself, she finally felt safe. One night she had made him swear he would be financially responsible for her and their future children forever. That was what she needed. It was a relief that she had someone strong to love and protect her. The world was too difficult for her to handle alone. She couldn't go through another rape, another rip-off, another betrayal. Anyway, she wouldn't even know how to start to make a living. Even though she had a degree in elementary education, teaching was the last thing she wanted to do. Besides, she had heard that voice.

She knew her father was impressed that Marvin had gone to Brooklyn Tech. Her father was a graduate of Bronx Science himself, so he knew how tough the standards of those schools were. Mainly, though, her father seemed relieved she finally was getting married.

When her parents, Solomon and Helen arrived, they first did some sightseeing in Jerusalem and Tel Aviv, and then they made their way to Beer Sheva. From there the next stop was Yamit. They had rented a small yellow car, and they headed out on the same road they had traveled with Dror a month earlier. Although her mother didn't say anything, Danielle could feel the tension rise as they drove down the arid, deserted road. Suddenly a plane swooped down low, looking as if it would crash into them.

"Solly, Solly," Danielle's mother said. "What's going on?"

Her father immediately stopped the car. Instantly a jeep with four soldiers armed with Uzis pulled up next to them.

"Oy gevalt, oy gevalt!" Danielle's mother said. "We had to come here?"

Her father explained to the soldiers where they going. One of the soldiers said they had taken a wrong turn and sent them back to the right road to get to Yamit.

"It's all right, Helen," Solomon said. "Everything's okay. We should be there in about ten minutes."

Danielle was familiar with her father's soothing tone. Although he'd had to do it every day for twenty six years, calming his wife was the only undertaking in his life that he hadn't succeeded at. Danielle couldn't count the number of times she had watched this scene play out. Anything that disrupted the perfection of her mother's universe would result in anxiety, migraine headaches, or screaming. It didn't matter if it was spilled milk on a freshly washed floor or a plane swooping down at their windshield in the middle of the Negev desert. To Helen Katz, it was all the same catastrophe.

"We must have turned onto some unmarked airstrip or something," her father said, "because we weren't supposed to be on that road."

"Sorry, Dad," Danielle said. "It must be the next right-hand turn. I told you to turn too soon." She braced herself, preparing for an onslaught of recriminations from her mother.

It came on cue. "You have to go live in the middle of the desert? You couldn't live in Tel Aviv or Jerusalem like a normal person. We're lucky the plane didn't crash into the windshield."

"Helen, calm down. The plane wasn't going to crash into the windshield. They were just checking us out. The soldiers were very polite and they all spoke a little English. It's okay. We'll be in Yamit in about ten minutes."

Sitting in the backseat with Danielle, Marvin squeezed her hand. She was about to cry, and he whispered in her ear, "All your mother needs is a hit of acid to straighten her out."

The thought of that made Danielle smile.

They drove about another three miles and reached the next turn. When they crossed the railroad tracks, Danielle knew they were on the right road and sighed with relief.

"Isn't it strange that that these tracks are in the middle of nowhere?" she said, hoping to break the tension.

Her mother just looked out the window and ignored her daughter, and Danielle could see the muscles in the back of her neck tightening.

Uh-oh, she thought. *She's got a migraine coming on.*

Her father, who was a history buff, had an answer as he knocked the cold ash of his pipe into the ashtray. "It's possible those tracks are from when the Brits were trying to get a foothold in Egypt. There was a railway line that was built in three phrases starting in 1916. Later it extended to Rafiah when Egypt was going up against the Ottoman Empire."

Her father kept driving down the road until they came to the beach. There they all climbed out of the car, grateful to breathe fresh air and stretch their legs.

"It's so close," Danielle said, gesturing to the water. "I'll be able to walk here from the house. Isn't it beautiful?"

"The Jersey shore is beautiful too," her mother muttered. "Why can't you live there?"

"Mom, this is Israel. This is where I want to be. This is where I want my children to grow up. Can't you tell how happy I am?"

"Happy? Happy? How many times do I have to tell you, Danielle? Only retards are happy. Do me a favor, just be healthy."

"Okay, it's a deal. Now, Mom, take off your sandals. Come on, show off those beautiful polished toenails. That's right. Isn't the water wonderful? It's a perfect temperature!"

Danielle managed to coax her mother to stand in the Mediterranean Sea. Both women allowed the breeze to caress their bodies as they watched the birds fly low, squawking to one another that there were new inhabitants on their beach. They stood there, the water lapping at their knees, bathing their arms and faces with the salty water. Danielle had never seen her mother so relaxed and pleased.

It was a good omen.

Danielle and her mother turned and walked back to the men, who were waiting under a grove of palm trees.

Solomon had lit his ever-present pipe, and he gestured with it as he spoke. "I was just telling Marvin that Napoleon must have walked on this same beach when he fought in Egypt". He puffed on his pipe and then added uncharacteristically, "This really is nice. I've never seen sand this white."

"Ready to see where the town is going to be?" Marvin asked.

"Let's go," Solomon said. "Did you say it's walking distance?"

"Solly, it doesn't matter," his wife said. "Don't leave the car. We'll drive."

They piled back into the car and drove up the hill. Across from the gates to Yamit stood a hut that appeared to be made out of twigs and mud. Outside was a clothesline and a donkey tethered to a palm tree. Marvin pointed out the small hole in the roof that would allow smoke to escape.

"They still make fires out of camel dung," he said.

"And they're going to be your neighbors?" Helen asked disdainfully.

"Not for long, Mom," Danielle answered.

"How do you know?" her mother asked.

"Because they're nomads!" Danielle and Marvin said at the same time, laughing.

Gingy's tin hut was locked up tight. Marvin commented that he'd put a barbed wire fence around the generator and a solid lock on its door.

"I wonder who would steal anything all the way out here in the middle of nowhere," Danielle said.

"Nomads, my honey, nomads. Why did you think they're always moving? Looking for better pasture land? Where's the pasture? This is a fuckin' desert."

Danielle could almost feel her mother clenching her teeth at his language. Well, she knew he didn't mean anything by it. It was just the way he talked, and she figured he must feel pretty comfortable with her parents not to censor himself.

"Hmm, I guess you're right," she said, musing once again that Marvin always thought of things that she didn't think of.

They followed the same dirt road and came to the same little house they'd seen the first time they came there. This time they could see fresh holes dug farther down the road.

"Stop the car, Daddy, this is it."

Her father stopped the car, and Danielle and Marvin quickly opened their doors and hopped out.

"Aren't you coming, Mom?" called Danielle over her shoulder. Her mother was sitting as still as one of the eternal desert rocks.

"Coming? Coming? I'm not stepping out of this car. This is the craziest thing I ever saw in my life. Danielle, there's nothing here! This is plain meshuggeh."

"Ma, I'm telling you, in five years we're going to have everything: schools, synagogues, and businesses. There's going to be grass and there's going to flowers. It's going to be wonderful, I swear."

"You are a meshuggeneh. And I'm not getting out of this car."

"I might be a meshuggeneh," Danielle shouted at her mother, "and you don't have to get out of the car. But this is *my* life, not yours." She ran to catch up to Marvin and her dad.

Even though she went back and apologized to her mother, Helen Katz never got out of the car, and she didn't say one word the whole way back to the hotel.

Chapter 10

Danielle's parents returned home, and Helen started planning her daughter's wedding. Danielle read between the lines of her mother's letters that although both of her parents were relieved their daughter was finally getting married, they didn't know what to make of the Yamit nonsense. There was nothing there except sand, her mother wrote. They figured it was another of Danielle's mishegas, her craziness, and that she would eventually come to her senses. Her mother's letters continued to encourage her to return to the United States as her sister Lauren had.

When they were finished with school, Danielle and Marvin obtained single living quarters at the absorption center. Since they weren't married, they were forced to share a single room meant for one person. It came supplied with only two things: a twin bed and a small refrigerator. It was so small, there wasn't even room for a kitchen table. A Formica ledge that jutted out from underneath the window served as best it could. A tiny bathroom was allotted for their personal use.

"What a way to live!" Danielle said one day. "But at least it won't be for long. When we're married we'll be able to move across the street to the main center. It should be a little better, and maybe, with a little luck we'll be Yamit soon after that."

They had just come back from the weekly garin meeting, where they had voted that the men should start working for Sharev so the work could get completed faster. It would also show the Israeli government they were serious and had a commitment to this project.

"Where are the Russians?" Danielle asked Marv. "I thought they had some people involved with this too?"

"The closest that I can figure is that they're in another absorption center. This will be way cool if we're able to live in houses that we built with our own hands. Come over here, my honey, my baby, and let's have a drink to celebrate a good decision. L'chaim."

After Marvin and Danielle toasted each other, she watched as Marv guzzled drink after drink and slowly spiraled into an incoherent rant about his family. He started with the saga of how his father had tricked his mother into going to the United States instead of Israel. Then he told her a new story about how the Nazis had killed his uncle Iggy, the boxer, for beating the Aryan contender in a match for a slot the 1936 Olympics. The last story that she could follow was about how he and his sister would play hiding from the Nazis, instead of cowboys and Indians, when they were growing up.

She held him in her arms, curled up and crunched together on the narrow bed that was meant for one person. She was uncomfortable but was afraid that if she moved the wrong way, he would take that as an insult. She just tried to breathe normally while she prayed he would fall asleep soon.

Since there was no television, the only other sound came from the tape on his cassette recorder. If she listened carefully through the noise of the worn-out tape, she could make out the Grateful Dead singing "St. Stephen." As she lay there, she wondered if she was doing the right thing. She quickly chased that thought away as she remembered the voice.

That voice had told her she was going to marry Marv. No matter what happened, at least she would have Yamit.

Chapter 11

The men started working the Monday after the vote, and noisily left the parking lot before the sun was up. Danielle made a fuss kissing Marvin good-bye, but before the week was over she decided that even though it got a little lonely, it was much easier to live in the tiny room by herself. During the following weeks, all the men who were physically able stayed in Yamit and worked putting the prefabricated houses together. Izzy, Dror, Marv, and a crazy drunk, Mickey Barker, would drive down there at sunrise on Sunday mornings and then return to the absorption center Friday afternoons in time for Shabbat. The men set up a makeshift dormitory in a house that was already finished and used a generator so that they could cook, although most of the time they ate at the Gingy's. According to Marv, one whole section of the town was almost done.

In the meantime Danielle spent her days at Ulpan learning Hebrew and her evenings chatting with the women and working on a blue and purple afghan for their new home. When another Friday arrived, she started looking forward to Marv coming home. She went to the small corner store and bought a roast chicken and some fresh vegetables for a salad, so they could have a private dinner instead of eating in the communal dining hall.

Right after she had finished showering and thrown on some clean clothes, Danielle heard Marvin at the door. She ran to open the door, excited that he was home, but as soon as she saw him she knew he had already started drinking. She wasn't sure if it was in the tilt of his head or the grin on his face, but whatever it was, it was subtle enough to fool everyone but her. He appeared totally unaware of her disappointment and gave her a big hug, swinging her around, obviously happy to be home.

"My honey, my baby, soon you're going to be my wife, my life. We finished. The first section is complete. It's hard to believe. We did it!"

"Wow, one giant step closer." Danielle spoke sincerely, but she was also concerned when he pulled a bottle of arak out of his bag.

Marvin must have seen her looking at it, because he excused himself by saying,

"Mickey and I drank some beers at lunch to celebrate. The rest of those guys are so straight, they make a level look crooked."

"Nothing bad happened?"

"It depends on how you define bad."

"Just tell me what happened," Danielle demanded.

"Well, Izzy thinks he's the king. Not only that, but he thinks he knows something about construction. The guy went to rabbinical school, for God's sake. Mickey's been working construction his whole life. It doesn't take a genius to figure out who knows more about building."

"Nu? So tell me."

"Well, Mickey said a wall he had put up was straight, but he didn't use the level to make sure, and Izzy called him on it."

"Well, isn't he supposed to use the level, to make certain."

"Mickey knows what he's doing. He said all he had to do was eyeball it."

"Was he going to eyeball it before or after his eyeballs started rolling around his head?"

"He may drink, but so what? Does it mean he doesn't know what he was doing?" Marv asked a bit too defensively.

"So it sounds like you took Mickey's side in this argument."

"Hell, yes. You know Izzy is a pompous ass. So Izzy told Mark to check the wall with the level, and guess what?"

"It was straight."

"Right. So of course we all started laughing."

"That's it?"

"Well, then I called him an old man and told him the reason his paycheck bounced was 'cause he didn't know shit about building. And that's when he threw the level at me."

"Izzy threw the level at you?" Danielle said, her voice rising. "I can't believe it." She took a deep breath and added more rationally, "You look okay, so I guess he missed. I'm just astounded. I never thought he'd do that kind of thing."

"You're so naïve. You think because he's a rabbi he has to be a good guy," Marv said derisively. "The problem with you, my honey, is that you never watched enough television."

"Did his check really bounce?" Danielle asked, ignoring his insults.

"Hell, yes, and his was the only one. Man, you should have seen how pissed off he was." Marvin grinned. "Maybe the Ministry of Housing is trying to tell him something that I already know—he's worthless."

"But, Marv, we wouldn't be here without Izzy. What the hell is Mickey Barker but an everyday trailer park lush? I can't even believe that guy is Jewish. His wife Myra spends her life running back and forth to the supermarket with shopping carts full of bottles."

"Nobody's perfect. But I know this. Never take the side of the tiger. You'll get eaten anyway."

That's what she liked about Marv. He called it exactly like he saw it, and the weird thing was, he was usually right.

"So now just forget about it and let's make a toast," Marv declared. "To us and to Yamit. L'chaim."

Since she figured she might as well join him, instead of watching his descent into incoherency, Danielle toasted their future. And once again, on that cramped bed, their bodies found each other. After what seemed like hours of giggling and making love, she fell asleep, glad to feel safe and loved.

When she woke up a few hours later, Marv was coming out of the bathroom drying his hands.

"Marv, you ready to eat? I bought a roasted chicken today."

"I know. It was delicious."

"Oh, you ate already? You should have woken me up. I'm starving."

"Sorry, there's nothing left," Marv said sheepishly as Danielle's eyes focused on the bones of the carcass. "I ate it all."

She rubbed her eyes and said unbelievingly, "You did what?"

"You heard me," he said gruffly. Then, as if it could explain away his behavior, he added, "I was hungry," Without another word he climbed into bed and pretended to fall right asleep.

Danielle turned over onto her stomach and cried. That was when she realized, without a doubt, that she was making a big mistake, but she didn't know what else to do. She loved him. Besides, the voice had said this was the man she was supposed to marry, and he kept her safe.

Chapter 12

The wedding was over, so Mr. and Mrs. Marvin Steinberg were allowed to reside at the main absorption center, which was set aside for married couples and families. They were both glad to be back in Israel after their wedding, even though their honeymoon had been so miserable, Danielle didn't even want to think about it. Marvin had gotten so drunk at their wedding, he had started a yelling match with one of the musicians. One of the other band members called the police, and when they arrived, in full storm-trooper mode, they threatened to take him to jail if he didn't calm down. Thank God almost all the guests had left by then, but her parents had been there and seen what an ass he had made of himself. To top it off, after he ruined the whole evening and embarrassed her, he still expected to have sex. Now that they were back in Israel, Danielle refused to think about it. She knew he loved her. It would get better. It had to.

Even though they had to share an apartment with Jeannie and Yossi, who were definitely not a good fit with them, it was better than the singles housing they'd had before. Yossi seemed okay, and he was working hard with the rest of the guys to get Yamit built, but Jeannie was a huge hypocrite. She pretended to be a Zionist, but Danielle knew better. She heard Jeannie crying and fighting with her husband almost nonstop, when he was home, because she wanted to go back home and live in the States. She had to give the two of them credit, though. They put on a good show in public.

She heard from the grapevine that Jeannie came from a very wealthy family. Danielle figured that if that was true, living at the absorption center must be hell for her. It was bad enough that they had to share a kitchen, but the bedrooms shared a wall and the walls were paper thin. They knew too much of each other's business.

Danielle struggled to be patient because she knew the uncomfortable living arrangements wouldn't last forever. Sooner or later they would be in Yamit.

Unfortunately the group had already lost a few couples because the project was taking longer than they expected. Others just couldn't take the fighting among the group members. What had that blind guy, Kolodin, said the night before? Danielle had to laugh when she thought of it. Marvin, doing his impression on the way home, had been cruel but decidedly accurate. Kolodin had stood up, shaken his cane at everyone around the room, and shouted, "Enough! Enough already! Stop raping flies!" She had heard at breakfast in the communal dining room that morning that he and his wife were making plans to leave. Other couples, like Dror and Hannah, had been in the absorption center for almost a year.

Although almost everyone thought the weekly meetings were senseless and accomplished little, at least they kept their minds on the goal. So week after week everyone showed up. Rhoda acted as the secretary and Izzy, the president, was a stickler for the meetings to be run by Robert's Rules of Order. It was an exercise in the absurd.

Jeannie and Yossi and Danielle and Marv were the only childless couples. Danielle wished she got along better with the other couple. Yossi seemed to be a yes man to Izzy, and that was anathema to Marv. Marv thought Yossi was a putz. Actually, Danielle thought Yossi was very nice. He just wasn't street smart. In fact quite the opposite. He was clean-cut, didn't do drugs or alcohol,and had graduated from the University of Pennsylvania. Since her spoke Hebrew very well, he had applied for a job as a journalist at the *Jerusalem Post*, the English language newspaper, and was waiting to hear from them. In the meantime, he worked at the site with the rest of the men. Jeannie was teaching English, and she hated it. Actually, she hated everything about living in Israel. Danielle thought she especially hated her husband.

Everyone was getting frustrated and irritable. Every day there were more excuses from the government as to why they couldn't move in, but Danielle and Marvin, along with a handful of others like Rhoda, Rivka, and of course Hannah and Dror, were sure it was going to happen soon. Too much money had been spent already, and besides, they wouldn't be working on the foundation of the town center if it weren't going to happen. They were hopeful that before long they'd be in their new homes. And Rhoda, in her official role as secretary of the American garin, was sleeping with every government official that she could. The men liked her because she was blonde, zaftig, and easy, and she liked them because they made her feel sexy and she thought she had the inside track on what was going on.

According to her announcement at the last meeting, they would be in by the end of the month. In addition, Moshe Dayan, the Minister of Defense, had promised that Yamit would never be returned to Egypt. It was a measure that Golda Meir had believed in and had resolutely convinced the rest of her government. Although the Northern Sinai was located over the green line, it now unequivocally belonged to Israel. Dayan believed that the country needed to have this ring of settlements as a security zone between Egypt and Israel proper.

Most of the settlements were either moshavim or kibbutzim. Yamit was the only town that was planned for the region. It would be a center for business, so that the moshavniks and kibbutzniks could do their shopping and banking without the inconvenience of driving all the way to Beer Sheva. Everyone hoped the beautiful beach would draw tourists from inside Israel as well as from all over the world. Dayan stated to the garin, the Knesset, and the newspapers that the land would never be returned. The garin members believed him.

Danielle thought it was ironic that even though the blueprints planned for a synagogue, not one of the garin members was religious. It was particularly strange, because Izzy Frankel had been the rabbi of a big conservative synagogue in Cincinnati. Danielle knew they kept kosher, and Shoshi always lit candles and made her own challah for Shabbat dinner. Although who knew? Maybe they went to Shabbat services, but how would she or Marv know? They were both totally secular, the kind of Jews that went to High Holiday services, ate bagels and lox in the United States, and falafel and pita in Israel.

She had to admit, though, she hadn't even known it was possible to be Jewish without keeping kosher until she came to Israel. Her maternal grandmother came from an Orthodox family that had started its own synagogue when they arrived in the United States, and she kept a kosher home. Her uncle still wrapped his tefillin and prayed every morning while Grandma listened to the rabbi on the Yiddish station beg for donations for all the poor Jews. Her grandmother always sent money, even if it was only a few dollars.

Once her mother married, she rebelled against all the boiled chicken and rituals. No more candle lighting, no more synagogue, no more rituals for her. So the only thing the family had left was a kosher kitchen. Her mother was scrupulous in using the right set of dishes with the proper food, and would only allow kosher products on her shelves and in her refrigerator. Unless, of course, they went out to dinner. Then they could bring back a doggie bag of unkosher food even shrimp or lobster, but they had to eat it on a paper plate. Now Danielle was being introduced to the Israeli version of kosher: kosher food in nonkosher kitchens. Here you bought kosher food, which was the norm in the stores, but you didn't have to have separate dishes and silverware for milk and meat. Kosher food was apparently enough.

One beautiful clear morning, after the men had set off for their work week in Yamit, Danielle left her apartment to meet Hannah. She was excited and nervous because she was going to learn how to drive her new car. Even though she had driven since she was seventeen, driving a standard stick shift was a skill she had never learned. Since she and Marv were new immigrants, they didn't have to pay taxes on big item purchases. So they decided to buy a car with gift money from their wedding. Although they wouldn't need a car inside Yamit, it would be a necessity to go anywhere outside the town. Marv had promised to teach Danielle how to drive it when he came back for Shabbat, but she couldn't wait a whole week.

When she reached her friend's, Hannah greeted her with a smile and asked if she was ready.

"Ready as I'll ever be. I'm a little nervous. I've never even tried to drive a stick shift before, and my girlfriend got in an accident the first time she tried. She lied and told her boyfriend she knew how so she could drive his new Mustang. Isn't it hard?"

"Once you get used to it, it's easy. I don't even like automatics anymore. It's like you're not even driving."

"What if something happens to the car? Marv would kill me."

Hannah just smiled and said, "It's your car too. Right?"

Danielle looked straight into Hannah's eyes, and any anxiety about Marvin disappeared. Hannah was absolutely right. Half of everything was hers. He would have to get used to that. She wondered if she could ever be as confident and capable as Hannah. She seemed so together and appeared to know everything, and Danielle felt ignorant and incompetent in comparison. Of course, Hannah had the lesson all planned out. First she would drive the car so that Danielle could get the feel of it and Hannah could show her what to do.

So Danielle sat in the front seat of the little VW Passat as Hannah drove down some side streets that had little traffic.

"You always start in neutral," Hannah explained, "and then push in the clutch. Put it in first and then let out the clutch slowly as you accelerate. As you pick up speed, you can hear the difference in the motor and that's when you switch gears. Once you're going about ten to fifteen miles an hour, you put it in second. Third gear is about thirty-five miles. That's what you'll be driving on most of the roads in the city. You can hear the motor needing to switch gears. The important thing is to let your foot off the clutch quickly, but you'll get the timing down."

"It sounds like so much to learn. You make it look so easy," Danielle said admiringly.

"I always liked to drive. Don't worry. This gets easier the more you do it." She grinned. "Kind of like sex."

"Okay," Danielle said. "I have to believe you. But what if I stall?"

"So, you stall. Don't worry." Hannah patted Danielle's knee. "It won't ruin the car. Now, it's your turn." She pulled over and shut the car off.

They switched seats, and Danielle started the car. She put it in first gear successfully, smiled, and then changed to second too quickly. The grinding sound went through her whole body.

"Hey," Hannah said, "I have a great idea. I'll just put my hand over yours so I can guide it into gear and you can feel it better."

"Sounds good," Danielle said.

They continued that way for a while, stopping, starting, and driving, and then Danielle said she felt comfortable enough to try by herself. Even though she was glad to get Hannah's hand off hers, it had made her feel more secure. They drove around for about half an hour, laughing and talking, and then Hannah said she had to pick the girls up at their nursery school.

Danielle turned the car around, toward the absorption center. "I felt good doing this. I felt more like myself again. Like I was a person. Thanks."

"It was fun," Hannah said, and then added confidentially, "You know, marriage offers a lot of independence. I know it must be hard to believe, but I find the longer I'm married, the more independence I have."

"I sure hope I feel that way in ten years," Danielle said as they got out of the car.

After they said their good-byes, Hannah walked one way to pick up her girls while Danielle went back to her apartment. On the way she thought about the drive and that she would practice more so that she could show Marv when he came back Friday night. She was proud of herself and she wanted Marv to be too. She didn't want him to think she was just a little bimbo that would do whatever he said.

Funny thing, even though she liked Hannah, she never felt comfortable around her. Not only did she feel incompetent, which she could chalk up to age, but she felt Hannah was watching her. Still, Hannah and Dror were the best friends they had here. Age and experience would make a difference, and she could learn a lot from observing Hannah.

She climbed up the one flight of stairs to let herself into the cubicle that masqueraded as their apartment. She had put water on in order to make some instant coffee, when she heard a knock on the door. Figuring it was one of the neighbors, she went and opened the door. She was surprised to see a stranger, a skinny girl with straight black hair and a nervous smile.

"Hi!" the woman said. "I hope I'm not interrupting you, but my name is Rachel and my husband and I are thinking of moving to Yamit."

Danielle smiled. "That's great! Come on in. I was just having a cup of coffee. Want some? Or tea perhaps?"

Finally, she thought. *Someone my age who looks normal.*

"Coffee will be fine," Rachel said.

And that was the first time, but certainly not the last, that the two would have their afternoon coffee klatches, which cemented their relationship through the years.

For the next few months Rachel and her husband Natan came down from Tel Aviv, where they were living, to stay informed of what was going on and to develop a relationship with the garin members. It turned out that Rachel was really smart. Not smart like Marv, who could debate and argue about anything, but smart in something that Danielle had never understood—math. As a matter of fact, Rachel had gone to Cornell and, against her parents' wishes, dropped out when she was just a few credits shy of graduating with a master's degree in math. Apparently her parents were still furious with her and thought she was ruining her life because she had married an Israeli who not only hadn't go to college, he hadn't even finished high school.

Danielle, however, thought the story was so romantic. The summer before she was supposed to finish her degree Rachel volunteered on a kibbutz. Natan met her when he went there to visit his aunt and uncle. It was love at first sight and Rachel, who considered herself the epitome of a skinny nerd, couldn't believe that such a handsome guy could be attracted to her. Since she couldn't speak Hebrew too well, she told Natan that if he wanted to get married, he would have to learn English. The amazing thing was that he did.

"So," Rachel said as she finished telling Danielle the story, after the couples had known each other for a while, "we got married here, because his family is so big, and even though my parents came, they're still angry. In every letter they let me know that he is the biggest mistake of my life. The second biggest is going to Yamit, which of course, they say, I wouldn't have made if I hadn't committed the first one."

"I know what you mean," Danielle said. "In every letter I get from my father, he seems to be more and more upset that we're not 'doing anything.' In the last one he said it seems that we're 'waiting for Godot.'"

"But," Rachel said with a twinkle in her eyes, "I think maybe my parents attitude is going to change soon."

"Why? Did Natan just win a million dollars or something?"

"Close" Rachel smiled her perfect smile, which was the handiwork of her orthodontist father. "I'm pregnant!"

"Oh my God!" Danielle exclaimed. A baby! The first Yamit baby! She came around the table in order to hug Rachel and wish her mazel tov.

As the women were hugging and laughing, the front door opened and in walked Marv and Natan. They had gone out to a wadi with a couple of other guys for target practice.

"Man, I thought Izzy was going to hit me when I got three bulls eyes in a row," Marv said, boasting.

"Who cares?" Danielle said. "Rachel's pregnant."

Chapter 13

It was hard to believe when moving day finally arrived. The first group of Yamitniks was finally going to move into their new homes. Rhoda, in her capacity as secretary for the garin, asked the manager of the absorption center if they could use the communal dining room for a little party to celebrate their imminent departure. The manager agreed, but only because he was so happy to finally see the crazy Americans leaving. Every one of the garin members, including the children, was jubilant.

They had all spent the last few weeks choosing and making arrangements for their homes. Of course there were fights about who deserved to live where, even though the homes were assigned according to the government criteria. The size allotted to each family depended on the number of children. If a family had more than one child, the government granted the family the right to buy either a three-bedroom apartment or a villa with a small plot of land. Hannah and Dror bought the very first house that had been built, the one that Marv and Danielle had seen the first time they went to Yamit.

Rhoda, Rachel, and Danielle were thrilled that they were going to be neighbors, for they each had bought apartments in the first block of buildings. They were the original multifamily houses, so they were close to the entrance and faced the Mediterranean. Marvin had worked on that particular block of housing and could testify to the quality of the work. Besides, it was a matter of pride for a man to be able to live in a house he had built. In addition, both Marvin and Natan were adamant about getting a good view of the beach. They knew from the blueprints that the first group of buildings would be the only ones with an unobstructed view. As the town grew, newer buildings would face each other.

The first group of buildings each consisted of six average-sized apartments. The ones on the top floor were seventy-five square meters and the ones on the bottom were ten square meters more. Although they were prefabricated, brought down from Tel Aviv by truck and all looking the same, the walls were fortresslike and made of almost half a meter of reinforced concrete. Each of the upstairs apartments had a small *merpeset*, or balcony, while the downstairs apartments had backyards. Every block of buildings was built around an open square that would someday grow grass and even flowers. Hidden in the corner of every square was a bomb shelter that Danielle noted but didn't want to think about.

According to the housing agency, since Rhoda had three children she was entitled to one of the bigger downstairs apartment. Rachel and Danielle bought identical apartments on opposite ends of the block, overlooking the villas. The two bachelors of the group, Rich and Gene, were allowed to live in housing set aside for single people. When they married, they would have the chance to buy a house.

Everyone from the garin, including the smallest children, was meeting down in the dining hall to schmooze, eat, and celebrate. But Danielle and Marvin hadn't left yet.

"Marv, let's go. We're late. I can hear music already."

"Late, schmate who cares? My honey, my baby, this is it. This is the last Saturday night in this shithole."

"I know, Marv, that's the point. I want to go celebrate with our friends."

"Friends? I'm your only friend, Don't be a fool. Did you forget already how everybody's been fighting? It's too bad that you calmed Rhoda down before she scratched Rivka's eyes out over the apartment she wanted."

"Rivka is too classy for that."

"Nothing like two old yentas scratching each other's eyes out." Marv chortled and took a last gulp of arak.

"Enough already Marv. This is a happy occasion. Please don't ruin it. As a matter of fact, I'll go downstairs and you can come down when you're ready."

Since she didn't want Marv to know she was upset, Danielle walked out nonchalantly, pretending that nothing was wrong. *He's been good,* she told herself. *It's not like he's drunk all the time.* She thought of Mickey's wife Myra Every Friday Danielle saw her at the supermarket buying half a dozen six packs of Nesher beer, and every Sunday, when the men returned to Yamit, she saw Myra bringing back the empty bottles. Lost in her thoughts, she almost bumped into Rachel, who was wearing a maternity outfit for the first time.

"Oh my God, you look beautiful," Danielle said as she hugged her friend.

"Thanks. I think this is a let's make up present," replied Rachel with a big smile.

Danielle glanced at Natan. "Oh. Did you two have a fight?"

"No, he didn't buy this for me. Come on, you know him better than that." Rachel looked at him lovingly. "I got a package from my mom today with three beautiful maternity outfits and a letter."

"That's great, Rach. Now you'll feel so much better about the move. Thank God for babies."

"Where's Marv?" Natan asked in his heavily accented English

"Oh, he'll be down in a minute," Danielle answered. Silently she added, *I hope he doesn't make an ass out of himself.*

The three of them walked into the familiar drab dining hall and were surprised that it was draped in blue and white crepe paper with balloons fastened to the ceiling.

"It looks like somebody worked hard to make this place look festive," Danielle said.

One of Rhoda's children was walking out the door and overheard the compliment.

"Thanks," he said to Danielle. "Did you see the sign? We made that too."

"Wow, you guys worked hard. I especially like the blue glitter on the star, and the lettering is so neat. It looks great."

Izzy stood at the front of the room with a microphone in his hand, and he started to sing "Hine Ma Tov." Everyone linked arms and joined in the singing.

When that song was done, Gene started playing a medley of Hebrew and English songs on his accordion, and again everyone joined in. Danielle looked at all the happy faces around her and was so thankful she had found this group of people. Suddenly Gene broke into a lively horah, and Rachel grabbed Danielle's hand.

"Are you sure …"

"Of course I'm sure. I'm pregnant, not sick. Let's go."

The circle got bigger and bigger. Then Shoshi led the group around the room, like a Jewish conga line, with all the women, children, and some of the men behind her. Before long everyone was exhausted and the dancing and singing started to wind down. People lined up at the buffet table to snack on pita and hummus, egg salad, tabouli, and eggplant salad. Suddenly Danielle felt an arm wrap around her waist and smelled Marv's alcohol breath on her face.

"My wife, my life, come dance with me."

"Marv, Gene is done playing. Come eat something instead."

"I'm tired of this damned hummus and pita stuff. What I want is a good ham sandwich."

He spoke with just a bit of a slur in his voice, so he wasn't too drunk. Danielle figured no one would notice.

"Do you like green eggs and ham?" she asked to divert him.

"No, I hate green eggs and ham," he said in a singsong voice.

"How about some fresh baked bread?" She pointed at the challah on the table.

"Fresh? Fresh? Is that what you said?"

"How about a bite of cheese?" she added.

"All you need to say is please." He laughed. "Hey, I brought my guitar down here. I'm gonna go tune up."

Danielle sighed as he walked off. Another disaster averted.

Izzy picked up the microphone again to make an announcement. "Everyone, quiet please. Some of you might not know this, because she's too modest to talk about it, but one of our very own garin members sang with her hometown opera company."

Danielle looked around, as did many of the others, trying to figure out who it was. Rachel gave her an "I don't know either: look.

Izzy went on, "Who knows? With God's blessings, maybe she'll be the driving force to start our own opera company in Yamit. Rivkala, come on up here. How about treating us to one of your favorites?"

Everyone applauded as Rivka smiled and took the mike from him. Gene strapped his accordion back on as she started the Israeli classic, "Jerusalem of Gold." Everyone joined in on the chorus. When the song was over, everybody applauded wildly and then started to move outside. The celebration was over. Tomorrow they would spend their first night in Yamit. Danielle kissed Rachel and said good-bye to Natan. They were leaving to spend the night with Natan's sister, who lived nearby.

Then Danielle heard Marvin's guitar. He was sitting around with the older kids, completely oblivious that all the other adults were leaving.

She would have to wait for him, she realized. If she went upstairs and left him alone, she'd be petrified that he'd do something embarrassing.

Just then Rivka came up and gave her shoulder a squeeze. "Some men are just immature. They're like kids. Believe me, I know. I was married to one just like that."

Danielle's forced smile felt like a grimace, but she nodded. To change the subject she said, "Rivka, what a terrific surprise. I had no idea that you sang so well. It was beautiful."

"Thanks. Come on, let's get our kids upstairs. We have a big day ahead of us tomorrow."

Chapter 14

Danielle didn't know about anyone else, but for her the beginning of Yamit was almost surreal. Here they were, the *chalutzim*—the pioneers—finally at their destination. Now what were they supposed to do? Marvin had warned her, before they left Beer Sheva, that there wouldn't be any utilities for the first week or so. Hard to imagine in 1975 not having gas, electric, or water, but the funny thing was that she didn't mind. Actually, she felt like she was doing something important, and that their presence there had meaning.

Luckily, she and Marv had bought a Coleman stove and lantern before they'd left the United States after their wedding. At the time she didn't have a clue why they needed it. She just figured that Marv knew more about stuff like that. So, in planning for the move, she had left the details to him and she wasn't disappointed. Thanks to Marv's planning, they had stocked up on supplies in Beer Sheva before they came down. Something in his survivor genes must have kicked in, because he demonstrated how resourceful he was. He took charge of their water supply and was compulsively frugal with its use. He made sure there was enough for them to cook stew on their propane stove for dinner, and have enough left to wash up and make morning coffee.

Then Marvin had to go up to Tel Aviv with Dror to get their furniture and appliances. They had been shipped over from the United States and had been sitting in a container ever since. The two families rented a truck together, and it seemed to Danielle that all these people were like her new family. It looked like everyone in the garin was helping one another. She hoped it would be this way forever.

————————

Originally, Marvin was going to be partners with Dror in a garage that repaired army trucks, and they were both disappointed and concerned when the plans fell through. Everyone in the garin was counting on the government's promise to offer them grants and low-cost loans in order to start businesses. Government ministers like Shlomo Avni and Elchanon Ishai were working with the settlers, trying to figure out which businesses would be successful.

In the meantime, Marvin got a job working for Makoret, the Israeli water company. Even though Yamit had wells, the company piped down water from Lake Kinneret, located in the northern part of Israel, to Yamit and the rest of the settlements at the country's southern tip. Marvin's job was to turn the town's water valve on in the morning and off at night. In addition, he had to monitor water usage to make sure people weren't wasting the town's allotment. Most of the time, though, he patrolled the construction sites with a big wrench attached to his belt, happier than he had been in a long time.

More people, including Russians and Israelis, slowly arrived at the modern-day frontier town. Sometime during the first month, Izzy, Shoshi, Gene, and Rhoda went to a meeting of the Interministerial Council in Tel Aviv. They came back with two interesting pieces of news. The first was that Moshe Dayan was coming down to speak to the Yamit settlers. The second was that Shlomo Avni, head of Rural Development, had propositioned Rhoda.

A few days later, Danielle and Rachel were having their afternoon coffee, talking about Moshe Dayan arriving that evening to speak at a town meeting.

"I can't believe we'll be seeing Moshe Dayan in person," Danielle said. "He's a living legend."

"I think he's very sexy, don't you, Dani?" Rachel asked. "Especially with that eye patch."

"A hell of a lot sexier than Shlomo Avni," Danielle said, grinning as she got up to get more cookies for them both.

She still had trouble believing the story that was going around about Rhoda and Shlomo Avni, who looked old enough to be her father. She told Rachel she was shocked that a grown woman, a mother of three, would announce to anyone who would listen that he had stuck his tongue in her mouth. According to Rhoda, when they were getting ready to leave the meeting, he had grabbed her and asked if she wanted to go someplace so they could be alone.

"It must be the Helen and Solomon Katz upbringing," Danielle said to Rachel, "but bragging about an old drunk wanting to go to bed with you is ..."

"Gross," Rachel finished.

"Uncouth," Danielle added.

"Disgusting!" they both said together, laughing.

"But what's more disgusting is that she probably will," Rachel said, suddenly serious. "She wants a restaurant on the beach and she'll do anything to get it." Almost as an afterthought, she added, "As a matter of fact, she and Natan may go in as partners."

"That sounds like a good idea. Well, just as long as he doesn't have to go to bed with Shlomo Avni too."

And as long as Natan doesn't have to go to bed with her," Rachel added, only half joking.

"You've got to be kidding. Besides, Natan isn't young enough for her ego to be massaged or powerful enough to mask her insecurity. So from where I'm sitting, you have nothing to worry about."

"Thanks, Danielle. I know you're right. It makes me feel better to hear you say it. Being a giant incubator certainly doesn't help in the ego department."

"What are friends for?" Danielle answered. "I'll see you tonight. By the way, do you want to make a bet that she tries to spend some time alone with Moishala?"

"No thanks. I only bet when I know I'll win." Rachel walked out the door. "*Lahit*. See you later."

————————

That evening, Danielle looked around at everyone gathered for the town meeting and was surprised to see a few people she didn't recognize. She knew some of the Russians by sight, and several of the Israelis too. Doing a quick headcount, she guessed more than fifty people were there.

She nodded and smiled at two of the Russians she recognized. Here in Yamit, she was learning that people tended to stay with their own kind. It was totally against the philosophy promulgated on college campuses by student activists, that all people were alike and were all brothers. It might be true, but as a stranger in a still unfamiliar country, she felt more secure with other Americans.

Maybe it had to do with learning the language, but she had observed that she was like the other new immigrants. When she was out on the street, she spoke Hebrew, but in her own home and with her friends she spoke English. The Russians did the same thing. She guessed it had something to do with everyone's comfort zone. People who shared a similar culture tended to hang around together. Within the garins, of course, there were smaller cliques based on similarities besides culture.

As she looked around, she was surprised to see that the Gingy had enough chairs to seat everyone in his outdoor café. Then again, he was the kind of guy who always got things done. Izzy, the president of the American garin, and Anton, the president of the Russian garin, each had the honor of sitting under the awning with Moshe Dayan. Just as Izzy introduced their honored guest, she saw Marvin walking toward her where she sat in the back.

"Izzy's Hebrew is excellent," she whispered to him.

"So what? I'll be right back." Holding his camera, he started walking to the front.

Everybody clapped as Moshe Dayan came up to the microphone. Danielle had to listen carefully to translate what he said, but it seemed to be a pep talk about how important this town was for Israel and the surrounding settlements. In the meantime, she lost track of Marvin.

It was hard to believe that Moshe Dayan, one of Israel's most renowned heroes, had come to speak to them, in order to reiterate that the government would never give any of the Sinai back to Egypt. He concluded his speech by stating that everyone should forge ahead with business plans, secure in the knowledge that Yamit had the full backing and support of the government. Lost in her reverie about this historical moment, she was startled when she felt a tap on her shoulder.

"I think I got some good photos," Marv whispered.

"Great," she whispered back, and then placed her finger on her lips so that Marv would be quiet.

"He doesn't," he added.

She didn't have any idea about what he was talking about, but just nodded and tried to ignore him. In a few minutes everyone starting applauding and standing up, so she figured she could ask Marvin what he was talking about.

"So, what were you talking about? He doesn't have a what?"

"An eye. He really doesn't have an eye behind that patch."

"What! Of course not. How do you know?" She suddenly realized that Marv had done something weird during his photography journey to the front of the café.

"Well, if you noticed I walked around to the side. When I got up to the front, I walked right behind him. I got close enough to see that he had nothing but a hole behind his patch."

Danielle laughed so hard, her whole body shook and absolutely no sound came out. She just shook her head in amazement. No one in the world would have thought to look except Marvin. It didn't even matter if he was exaggerating or even telling the truth.

Chapter 15

It was spring almost a year later and Yamit was starting to look like a town. Green grass added a startling contrast to the desert's bleak and overpowering terrain. To Danielle, it really was miraculous. Just like in the songs and ancient stories, the Hebrews were making the desert bloom. Even though it wasn't as heroic as pushing back swamps, as the original immigrants had had to do, it still made her feel like a pioneer. Moshe Dayan himself had said that they were doing a mitzvah for Israel.

Bushes and colorful flowers were also starting to blossom. The plans called for each group of buildings to have green space outside and a big sandbox for children. The central sidewalk, which started right outside their door, would be completed when the third stage of building was finished and it would go all the way through the town. It was made of tiles and ran straight through the town's commercial center. Although they had to walk down a hill to get to the beach, the town itself was flat. When she realized how the town was going to be laid out, Danielle got even more excited. The town would be perfect for bike riding.

The next time she went to Beer Sheva with Hannah, she told her that she really wanted to get a bicycle.

"Ask and you shall receive," Hannah said with a big smile. "My friend Annie is going back to the States and has a bike she wants to get rid of. You want to stop over there and see it?"

"Sure," Danielle replied. "But, Hannah, when are we going to have a store in Yamit? This driving back and forth to Beer Sheva is very time consuming."

"Sooner than you think. You know my neighbors, the Barchovskys?"

"The Russian family with that cute little boy?"

"That's the one. They're going to open the grocery store in about two weeks. They just finished negotiations and signed all the papers. So, if everything goes well, we'll soon be buying our eggs and milk down the block, instead of driving twenty five kilometers."

"That's great!" Danielle said. "So where is it going to be?"

"I think the deal is that they're going to open in one of the empty ground floor apartments. Then they'll get a space when the commercial center is finished and we'll have a real supermarket."

After they finished their weekly shopping, they drove over to a street that was close to the university. Hannah parked in front of a house, and the two women walked up the dirt path. Hannah called "Hello" as she knocked two times and then opened the door. Annie, a young woman about Danielle's age, was on her knees in the middle of the living room, trying to cram a sweater into a duffel bag.

The young woman, mumbled something in return, but otherwise ignored them as she continued to push the sweater into the already full duffel bag. Without looking up, she asked dully, "Hannah, what are you doing here?"

"We were in the neighborhood and I figured why not?" She hesitated and then added, "By the way, this is my friend Danielle. She's looking for a used bicycle and I knew you had one for sale."

Danielle smiled and said hi, even though she felt really uncomfortable. Annie looked up and smiled an obviously phony smile, pretending to be pleased to meet her, but Danielle knew she wasn't.

"You know, Annie, there's a trick to packing," Hannah said, either ignoring Annie's attitude or unaware of it. "You have to roll everything up and stuff as much as you can into something bigger. My aunt, who's a world traveler, taught me. You want to take some stuff out and I'll show you what I mean?"

"Yeah, well, thanks, but I'm just about done."

Danielle was not surprised that Hannah knew the best way to

pack. She seemed to know the best way to do everything. When she was around Hannah, she felt so young and awkward, but she was always eager to learn something new from Hannah. Like the trick Hannah had showed her about laundry. The older woman told her that if she didn't have time to fold it and put it away, just stick it in a backroom and close the door. Once she said that, Danielle wondered why she hadn't thought of that. Having the living room and kitchen clean and neat was important, not some room no one would ever see. Of course, her mother would have a coronary if she heard Hannah's advice. Her whole house was always perfect.

"Why don't you just take the bicycle?" Annie said to Hannah.

"You're sure? I know you can use the money," Hannah replied.

"It's not money I want. You know that."

"I know. I'm really sorry. Please believe me," Hannah added softly. Danielle wondered what had happened. Maybe something had happened to Annie's parents, or maybe her boyfriend had left her. She looked miserable.

"Please just take the bicycle from the backyard and go," Annie said. "I can't stand this anymore."

Hannah kissed her softly on the cheek and then went out the front door. Danielle thought Annie was going to cry. The woman suddenly addressed her.

"Danielle? That's your name?"

Danielle hadn't thought Annie was aware of her, even after Hannah's introduction. "Yes," she answered.

"Are you married?"

"Yes."

"That's good. I sure wish I were. Maybe this would never have happened."

Danielle said good-bye and met Hannah at her truck. Hannah had already put the bike in the back and was ready to go. Danielle noticed that Annie didn't come out to wave good-bye, and Hannah was awfully quiet. Since she didn't like to pry, she didn't ask Hannah anything about what had just occurred. Before long Hannah started telling her about the funny things her daughter, Tzippi, was doing and how much she appreciated Dror.

"You know, Hannah, I think it's time Marv and I started to have kids too."

"So?"

"Well, it's scary and …" Danielle took a deep breath. "How do you know when you're ready?"

Hannah laughed. "The truth is, no one's ever ready. You just make a decision and that's that."

Then they were both quiet. Danielle thought about how weird Annie and Hannah had behaved with each other and about how nice it would be to start a family. She had no idea what Hannah was thinking, she just knew she didn't look happy.

When they got home, Marvin was sitting on the porch drinking a beer. He waved when he saw the truck and met them in the parking lot.

"What did you get?" he asked as the women unloaded Danielle's groceries.

"A bicycle, Marv."

"Cool."

"Very cool. And it's not just a bicycle. It's a Schwinn. I can't believe it. Hannah's friend is leaving the country and she just gave it away."

Marv grabbed it from the back of the truck. They both waved good-bye to Hannah, and then Marv jumped on the bike before Danielle could stop him.

He called back over his shoulder, "Last one to the house is a rotten egg."

"First one is a whole dozen," she answered in a singsong voice.

By the time she rounded the corner, carrying the groceries, Marvin had parked the bicycle under the stairs and was walking back to her.

"You came just in time," he said. "I have to go to Rafiah to put my check in the bank."

"So I'll go with you. I've never been there."

"I don't know." He hesitated and then changed his mind. "Okay, but stay close to me. Don't go wandering off by yourself."

"What's the matter? Are you afraid an Arab is going to grab me and throw me on the back of a camel?"

Marv looked a little sheepish as he answered, "Of course not."

"Marv, if one does I'll just start singing 'Midnight at the Oasis.' Little Tzippi thought that was me, not Maria Muldaur, on the album cover, by the way."

"Yeah, yeah, yeah. Let's put the groceries away and go. And if I hear anyone singing, 'I'm the Sheik of Araby, I got me Jew cunt, so come and see …'"

Danielle laughed. "Don't be ridiculous. We better start moving before the bank closes."

They got in the Passat together, and after Danielle lit her cigarette, she told Marvin about her day and how weird the scene with Annie and Hannah was.

Marvin answered without hesitation, "Hannah's a dyke."

"What the hell are you talking about, Marv? She's a wife and mother."

"I keep telling you my wife, my life, you never watched enough television."

"And you must have watched too much. You're always looking for the worst in people."

"I didn't have to watch television. Remember, I was born to a pair right out of the Great Loony Bin of World War II. So guess what? On the topic of the quirks of human nature, I'm usually right."

Danielle had never heard anything so ridiculous. She took a couple of deep drags on her cigarette while she stared out the window, thinking what a lousy attitude her husband had. Maybe that was why he drank. When they had a baby though, he'd be a dad. He'd have to grow up.

Marvin distracted her by putting a Grateful Dead tape into the cassette player, and they both started singing "Sugar Magnolia." As they drove along the deserted road, Danielle wondered about the best time to broach the subject of getting pregnant. Rachel was due any day, and it would be great if they had kids that were close in age.

About ten minutes after they passed the main junction, they turned onto the road that went through the center of Rafiah. It was an old Egyptian city located in the northern Sinai, part of the land that the Israelis had gained in the 1967 war. All the towns that were considered part of the Gaza Strip had belonged to Egypt. It was apparent the area had been terribly neglected and run down over the years. They parked down the street from the bank and started walking to it.

Danielle was overwhelmed by the squalor around them. She felt like she had entered another universe where time was suspended. The buildings and streets looked ancient, as if they had been there since biblical times. Dirt and more dirt covered everything because the street wasn't paved, and it seemed as if every building was a memorial to ancient battles. She had never seen anything like it. All of the old stone buildings were full of bullet holes. She couldn't understand it. Why didn't they fill in the holes and pave the road?

"My God, Marv, how do they live like this?"

"I don't know, but now you know why I didn't want you to come. Just act normal, don't stare, and don't give money to anyone."

As they continued down the street, Danielle was shocked by all the women covered from head to foot in their black chadors. A row of them sat on the curb outside the bank, like crows sitting on a telephone wire. The folds of their garment were caked with dirt from the street. Black flies buzzed around the babies they held in their arms, and they sat immobile and oblivious to the filth, as if they were just part of the scenery. Danielle stared at a mother who totally ignored the fly that had just landed in her baby's eye.

"Marv, look at that. That fly could lay eggs right in the baby's eye. It hurts me to even look at it."

Marv gruffly replied, "So don't look."

He opened the door to the Bank Hapoalim, an Israeli bank, and let Danielle in first. She stood in the doorway for a moment, feeling something was wrong before she could see what it was. Then she whispered to Marv that she was going to stand outside and wait for him.

"No," he said, "stay here with me."

"No way. Look, I'm the only woman and I'm wearing shorts and a T-shirt. I feel like all those men are eating me up with their eyes. I'll stand right outside." She added, "With the rest of the chattel."

She stood outside the building with her body pressed up against the wall, hoping no one would notice her. Why the hell were those women sitting in the street and letting filth and flies contaminate their babies?

Along with the women she saw quite a few men. Many of them were dressed in one-piece garments, called djellabas, that looked just like nightshirts. They reminded her of a picture she saw once in a book of nursery rhymes. A character named Wee Willie Winkie ran from house to house dressed in his nightshirt and holding a candle. Now there was a whole city of these characters. Many men sat in cafés drinking tea or coffee, their heads covered with keffiyehs to protect them from the sun. Some rode through the street on donkeys, their wares strapped across the animals' backs. Others drove by in old cars, especially Mercedes Benz. Maybe Marv was right about the shades, because few of them wore sunglasses.

No one even nodded to the row of women sitting silently. It was as if they were invisible. Of course, the only part of them that could be seen were their eyes. Danielle wondered what they were thinking. Were they aware that there was a different way of life? Did it bother them that they were sitting in dirt and that their babies had flies buzzing around their heads?

Lots of little boys were also riding bicycles up and down the street. Most of them were dressed in a version of the men's djellabas, except theirs were in two pieces, so that they looked like pajamas. She didn't see any young girls running and playing; the only females were the ones sitting at her feet. When she started to feel hot and thirsty after standing so long in the Middle Eastern heat, she didn't complain to herself. She just looked at the silent black row in front of her and felt better. The mystery was how they did it. How could they wrap themselves all in black in this unrelenting sun?

Danielle was just congratulating herself on remaining invisible when a raggedy urchin about ten years old walked up to her with his hand outstretched

"Money, miss," he said.

She tried to ignore him by looking the other way. But he just stood there, and finally she decided she didn't care what Marvin said. She gave him all the coins she had in her pocket and his smile, although sullied with rotted teeth, seemed heartfelt and grateful as he said, "Allahu Akbar."

She decided it didn't matter if he was a professional con artist, or if his father had sent him over to get money from the rich Jew lady. Anyway you looked at it, she wished she had more to give him. It was amazing. Two years earlier she had been sitting in a drab office on the other side of the world, unaware that this town existed. She had survived rape and degradation, and, thank God, had come out of those experiences whole and alive. Now she was standing here in the middle of an ancient town where time seemed to stand still, waiting for her husband to come out of the bank. It was almost surreal. She was so thankful she had taken the risk of leaving her parents' suburban dream. She just hoped her own dream didn't turn out to be a nightmare.

Marv walked out of the bank. "Okay," he said, grabbing her hand. "Let's go."

As they walked back to the car, Danielle noticed the little boy she'd given money to was following close behind.

"Shit, don't turn around," Marvin said. "There's a little towel head following us."

"Don't you feel sorry for these children? Look how they live."

"Not our problem. They get plenty of money from the UN. I'll go around the other way and show you the refugee camp."

So they got in their car, just as the little boy passed them and walked over to a man sitting at the one table outside a store. Two other men, who were playing backgammon, sat with him. Danielle had noticed them when was waiting for Marvin. *Had they been there all day?* she'd wondered, *What did they do for a living?* As she closed her door, she heard them all laughing and got chills up and down her spine.

Marv started the car and crawled down the street. It was the first time she'd been glad he was such a slow driver. If, God forbid, he hit anyone, an accident could turn into an international incident. They turned a corner, and Marv gestured with an exaggerated flourish.

"So my wife, my life, here it is. The infamous Palestinian showplace. Excuse me, refugee camp."

"It doesn't look any worse than the rest of the town," Danielle said. "The only difference is that it's behind barbed wire."

Marvin pointed out something she hadn't noticed. "Look at all the antennas. Every single fucking house has a TV antenna."

"Marv, you're right. That means they all have televisions," Danielle said incredulously.

"That's right. They just like to live in shit. They get plenty of money from UNRWA. Who knows what they do with it?"

"Why are they in the camps to start with?"

"Their own people use them as pawns in order to make us look bad. The UN put them there because the Arabs didn't want them, and guess what? That's where they'll stay. No Arab country wants them. Remember the Black September massacre in Jordan. Did you know that most of these guys made as much money as we did in building Yamit, and on top of it didn't have to pay taxes?"

"Marv, slow down. I don't know much about this. Remember, I didn't even go to Sunday school. Tell me the whole story."

"Well, you know my aunts and uncles came here before the war. My mother was the youngest and was in Poland when the Nazis came to power. You met my uncle Tsvi and aunt Pinina. They settled here in the thirties. By the way, I think he was one of the first pilots. Anyway, as soon as Israel was granted its independence in 1948, the Arabs declared war."

"I think the bullet holes in these buildings have been here since then," Danielle said.

"No shit. The territory had been divided into two parts by the UN. The smaller part was given to us and the bigger part was for the Arabs. Well, the Arabs wanted all or nothing. So their leaders called for a war to annihilate us. We ended up fighting five countries—and we didn't even have a regular army yet!"

"What countries?"

"Jordan, Egypt, Syria, Iraq, and Lebanon. They thought they would decimate us. But they didn't, and we gained more land. They're rotten losers. So in order to make us look like the bad guys, no Arab country took in the refugees after the '48 war. They let them live in their own piss and shit to make Israel look bad."

"Why would they do that?"

"My wife, my life, wake up and smell the coffee. It's called anti-

Semitism. People hate Jews. So it's always easy to make us look like the bad guys."

"But where did all the refugees come from?"

"The Arab League was made up of the countries that fought us. They swore they would destroy every Jew and announced that all the Arabs who were living here had to leave in order to get out of the way of their armies. They told them they would be able to come back after they won the war. As a reward, they'd be able to have any Jew house they wanted. "

"Oh, now I understand a little better. Wasn't Egypt an ally of the axis power during World War II?"

"Uh-huh. Why?"

"I think I read Nasser was a Nazi. Wasn't all this part of Egypt? We just gained this land in the 1967 war. It's obvious that it's been neglected for a long time. I can't help thinking of that lady I was talking to in Tel Aviv. Remember that nice-looking blonde we sat next to on Dizengoff Street? Her husband works for an oil company and he's always given the choice whether to stay in Cairo or Tel Aviv, and guess which one he picks?"

"I think I know the answer—since we were talking to her on Dizengoff."

"Okay, wise guy, quit it. She said Cairo was just terrible, not a place for an American to live. If this is any indication, I can see his point. By the way, does Israel fund the refugee camps?"

"It comes out of UN funds. In case you still don't get the whole picture, guess what? Arab nations contribute bubkahs. European countries and the US basically maintain them. I know that right after the'48 war Israel, unbelievably, gave something like $3,000,000."

Danielle was starting to get tired. "Let's go home. This is making me sick."

"If you think you're getting sick now, just wait. We're going up to my folks tomorrow."

"Shit."

Chapter 16

It couldn't just be a coincidence. Danielle noticed that every time they went up to Jerusalem to visit Marvin's parents, they both got sick. It wasn't the kind of sick that let you to stay in bed or made you go to the doctor. It was just a vague, queasy feeling and a lethargy that kept them in bed longer than usual. Then they would both look at each other, sigh, grumble and go take an aspirin. Then finally drag themselves out of bed to get ready for the day.

Much to Danielle's surprise, soon after they got married, Marvin's parents bought an apartment in the Rehavia section of Jerusalem. At first, despite her new husband's adamant protests about the move, Danielle liked the idea. She would have preferred her own family, even with their cold aloofness, but she figured it was better to have some family around. She had only met Tosha and Fredreich Steinberg a few times, and her impression was that they were both a little weird. She figured, though, after what they lived through during World War II, they were entitled.

After his mother had called to tell them that they were moving to Israel, Marvin had slammed the phone down and said, "Shit, I knew this would happen."

"How did you know?" Danielle asked.

"She's always wanted to live here. Since her older brother and sister were part of the early Zionist movement and made aliyah before the war she planned to come here too."

"So why did she go to the United States instead?"

"My father tricked her."

"How? Tell me that story again. I forgot."

"He bought the tickets. He told her they were going to Israel, and the next thing she knew she was looking at the Statue of Liberty. She's never stopped crying. He got what he wanted, got off the boat, kissed the ground, and promised her that *someday* they'd move to Israel. It looks like fucking 'someday' is here."

Danielle started singing "Someday Someday" to the tune of The Mamas and The Papas' hit song "Monday Monday" to try change Marvin's mood. Instead, he poured a glass of arak and told her the story of graduate school.

His parents had wanted him to live at home and continue his education by going to graduate school. Against their wishes he started working at John Jay College and moved into in his own apartment in Manhattan. According to him, they had wanted him to continue his education so badly they used their apartment and personal lives as bargaining chips. They told him that if he moved back, they would stay in their bedroom and not come out when he was home. They added that in their eyes, the apartment was now his. It was their gift and they would stay out of his way. He still refused.

"That's crazy," Danielle said.

"Crazy? You don't know what crazy is. " Marvin paused to drink another shot and then continued. "My mother thinks I'm her father."

"What!"

"Ever since I can remember, my mother would cry and tell me I was so good and so brilliant because I was the incarnation of her father, Menachem Chaim. He was supposedly this tzadik whom the whole town revered. He also had this big farm and made pickles."

Danielle laughed and then said she was sorry.

"You think that sounds funny? Listen to this. When the Nazis came into that town, they kept him alive just because they liked his pickles. Then one day his delivery didn't arrive and they came to the house and shot him. It was Rosh Hashanah."

"Oh my God! But what did that have to do with you being the incarnation of him?"

"Who the hell knows? I'm going down to the workshop."

———————

Once Danielle was pregnant, she and Marvin went up to visit his parents once a month. Now that she knew them better, she agreed with her husband wholeheartedly, that once a month was more than plenty. From the moment she and Marvin arrived, they became prisoners. They felt smothered and weren't left alone for a minute. In addition, Danielle noticed something even odder. It appeared that being around Tosha exhausted her. She had read a book years ago about energy vampires and decided that Tosha was one of those. There was no other way to explain it.

Every visit would start the same. Marv, the coward, immediately feigned exhaustion and went into the guest bedroom. Danielle would sit at the kitchen table to be polite and listen to the horrific family stories that Marv had grown up hearing and knew better than nursery rhymes.

Even the apartment was odd. Entering it was like walking into the inside of a wrapped package. Every room was decorated with a different color of shiny foil wallpaper. Danielle knew that this style was the rage in the United States, but just like everything Marv's parents did, it was a little off. They had wallpapered every centimeter of wall space, in every room and in every nook and cranny, including the inside of closets.

The living room walls were cherry red with appliqués. It was so shiny, Danielle tried to focus her attention on whoever was talking. Otherwise she would get sick looking at a whole wall of her own image. She told Marv that it looked like a whorehouse in some bizarre dimension. Marvin shrugged and told her that that bizarre dimension was where he'd grown up. He added that she should keep her sunglasses on or come and take a nap with him, and then she wouldn't notice it as much.

———————

This visit started out no differently than the others. Ten minutes after they arrived, Marvin yawned and complained how tough it was at work and headed for the bedroom. Tosha put on water for instant coffee and then unexpectedly said she had to go downstairs. She asked in her thick European accent if Danielle minded, but she had to go visit her friend Sasha who was sick. Even though Danielle was astounded that Tosha had a friend, she was even more relieved that she didn't have to be with her all afternoon.

"Of course," she said, "Go." She hoped that she didn't sound too excited.

Before Tosha left, she put coffee and some rugelach on the table for her daughter-in-law and introduced her friend Sasha by way of a story. It turned out that Sasha was a camp friend who had come to Jerusalem right after the camps were liberated. They had been together at Auschwitz and had kept each other alive.

"One time," Tosha said, "I was sick in the infirmary and they had a selection from our barracks. You know what's selection?"

Danielle looked at her mother-in-law, picturing her as a teenage girl, and tears came to her eyes as she said yes.

"If you were in the infirmary when they did selection, then you vent automatically to the gas chambers. They kept you there, lying on a board with a sheet, naked. I guess they figured no one needs clothes when they're dead. I had such swollen feet I couldn't stand, so I was in the infirmary. Sasha ran to the infirmary and threw pebbles at the window to get my attention. She waved her hand for me to come and mouthed 'selectcia.' I jumped out the window and made it in time to line up."

Danielle wiped tears from her eyes. "Did you have time to get dressed?"

"No, *mein Kind*. It was not necessary. Everyone was naked for selection. They walked us around like animals, naked, and then they chose."

"How about everyone left in the infirmary?" Danielle asked, noticing that her mother-in-law's eyes were watering and her voice was choking up.

"Dead. Everyone dead. So now I go to Sasha, who once again helped. When Fredreich and I were looking for an apartment, it vas *beshert* that von vas right here in Sasha's building."

Danielle said she was glad for them both and meant it. Meanwhile, she knew that "camp friend" would have a totally different meaning for her now. She wasn't sure she wanted to get used to the new meaning, but she knew her mother-in-law had lived through horrors that were indescribable. She hugged her swelling belly and was glad that the new life inside her came from survivors. It was her revenge on the Nazis.

Tosha called Fredreich to come to the kitchen and have coffee with Danielle, and then she kissed Danielle good-bye. Danielle felt so uncomfortable when she did that. Her family was not demonstrative. Hell, she didn't remember her mother ever hugging or kissing her, so she didn't understand this. Why would Tosha kiss her good-bye just to go downstairs? It felt so damn phony. Everything Tosha did felt phony, except when she was crying.

Suddenly Danielle had an epiphany. Tosha was simply a shell. There was absolutely nothing inside. She had been drained of all emotion years ago. Every gesture, every smile, and every tear was just an imitation of what she thought she was supposed to feel.

Fredreich appeared at the far end of the table, cigarette in hand, looking very dapper as usual.

"Danielle," he said her in his German-accented English, "do you know why I detest this apartment?"

"No, Fredreich why?"

"Because a civilized man must have his own bathroom. I ask you." He paused dramatically for a drag on his cigarette. "Isn't that correct?"

She smiled at him and said, "Absolutely."

Fredreich didn't bother her as much as Tosha. Actually, she found him quite amusing. He looked like he had just stepped out of an Austrian café circa the 1930s. He was always impeccably groomed, wearing a crisp starched shirt, a tie, and of course dress slacks with a pressed knife pleat. This was in his own living room. When he stepped out, even to go the grocery store, he would add the matching suit jacket and complete his ensemble with a cap.

"Danielle, would you mind if I tell you something in confidence?"

"Of course not, Fredreich," Danielle was starting to feel like his straight man. He took another drag on his cigarette and said, "I met my wife in Sweden, you know, after the var."

"Yes. Marvin told me."

"She was so beautiful. I must tell you. That is the truth." He added in a stage whisper, "I have had many women."

Danielle giggled. He had said this before, and she never knew if he was telling the truth. It always sounded so absurd.

"Don't laugh, Danielle. It is true. Remember, I was not a married man for my whole life. With her blue eyes, blonde hair, and, yes, I must say if you don't mind, her beautiful figure, my Tosha looked like a porcelain doll."

"It's okay, Fredreich. I get it. You were a young man in love."

"And this is what I must tell you." He sighed deeply. "My Tosha is still beautiful," He took another drag of his cigarette and lifted his eyebrows theatrically before he continued. "She is loyal. She is thrifty. But if I had to do it over again, I would never"—and he banged his hand on the table for emphasis—"never marry a girl from a concentration camp." After his confession he finished his cigarette and said, "I cannot drink this coffee. It is like water mixed with a little dirt. Come, let us go for a walk." He went to the closet and got his suit jacket and his cap.

Danielle was still in shock and had no idea how she was supposed to respond to his declaration. So she decided the best thing was just to say, "Okay , let's go."

She didn't mind going for a walk with Fredreich. It was like stepping into a movie set of Austria before the war. He held her arm as they walked down the street to the little café that was open on Shabbat. As they strolled down the street, he would smile and actually tip his hat at nice-looking women. Most of them were so surprised, they smiled back. Danielle never saw him as happy as when he was acting the part of the boulevardier.

"Danielle," he said, continuing their conversation, "allow me to explain. A beautiful woman is a work of art. And I, my dear, am a connoisseur. But do not misunderstand me. I would never, never do anything to hurt my Tosha."

Danielle smiled uncomfortably and said, "Of course." She really didn't know whether to believe him or not.

"You see, Danielle, when I was in Siberia during the war, I was in charge of the black market. Oh, the women they liked me very much, and I would always give them a present of chocolate or silk stockings. The important thing was that I always made a woman feel special."

"I guess you had a lot of girlfriends, Fredreich?"

"Of course. The important thing was that I was always respectful and used a condom."

Danielle couldn't believe what she was hearing. Was this his idea of humor? She nodded as if she understood and thought about how strange this was. Was this how people talked to their daughters-in-law? She had grown up in a house where her mother would spell the word *shit* if she got extraordinarily angry, and her dad chastised her for using the expression "pissed off" as unladylike. She was starting to understand how Alice had felt in Wonderland.

They stopped at the café that was located at the bottom of the hill. Fredreich pulled out Danielle's chair to seat her, brushing his arm across her shoulders as he said, "My son has very good taste in women. If I were younger and not married, I would take good care of you. Do you understand?"

Oh, my God. I can't believe this. She started laughing because the scene was so absurd. Here she was pregnant with Fredreich's grandchild, and he was acting like this was a seduction scene in some grade B movie. She knew he couldn't mean it, but it didn't make it any less strange.

Fredreich lit another cigarette and ordered two coffees. Danielle wished she could light one as well, but since she'd become pregnant, she'd kept her smoking to two or three cigarettes a day. She was so glad they were out of the house. One thing she had in common with her father-in-law was a love of the café life. She could sit in a café all day and watch people, read a little, or discuss anything and everything. Both she and Fredreich watched the people strolling by, and she commented that it was such a delightful pastime. Since Marvin hated it and thought it was a waste of time, this was sheer luxury.

As she sat there, content to feel the sun on her face as she sipped her coffee, she watched a little boy kick a soccer ball up the street. Fredreich must have gotten bored, because he started talking to the lady at the next table.

Danielle watched with amusement as the lady turned to him

questioningly. She must have expected him to ask her a question that she could answer by giving directions or looking at her watch. Instead, she seemed startled when he asked, "Miss, do you remember the Marlene Dietrich movie, *The Blue Angel?*"

"The one with Emil Jennings?" she asked with a low throaty laugh. Suddenly she became animated, appearing ten years younger. Her faded blue eyes even shone brighter. Danielle could tell that she must have been very attractive in her youth, and probably had been accustomed to male attention.

"Yes, that is the one," he answered. "She was a very sexy woman. Do you agree?"

The conversation continued for a while as they discussed European cities that had been destroyed during the war, and finally ended with them both singing the chorus of "Falling in Love Again." Fredreich applauded, kissed her hand, and suavely stated, "Miss, I must tell you. You are wonderful. You most certainly remind me of Miss Dietrich, a great actress as well as a great American patriot. Thank you for this pleasurable moment, but now my lovely daughter-in-law and I must bid you adieu."

"*Auf Wiedersehen,* my friend. I hope we meet again." Fredreich's new friend, Olga smiled delightedly and waved as they got up to leave.

Danielle's father-in-law took her arm as they walked back up the street, and she told him how happy he had made that woman feel.

"She even looks younger," Danielle added.

"Yes, Danielle, I know. And that is what makes me happy. Now I must tell you something that has been on my mind since Marvin brought you home to us."

"Certainly," Danielle replied, although she was a little afraid of what he had to say.

He sounded so serious. Maybe she had said something insulting or done something dumb. Or maybe, she hoped, he was going to mention Marv's drinking and offer some help.

"Danielle, now listen, I am very serious." He paused, and her worry grew. "My dear daughter-in-law, you remind me of the very sexy and beautiful Ava Gardner."

Danielle tried not to laugh. "For real?" she asked.

"Of course, for real. Why should I lie? My dear son takes after me. He has excellent taste in women."

"Okay, I believe you. So in what movie, Fredreich?" Danielle asked coquettishly.

"All of them, of course," he answered.

"Even though I'm pregnant?"

"Ava Gardner would be sexy even nine months pregnant. Remember, Frank Sinatra vas crazy over her and he had hundreds of women. For her, he almost committed suicide."

"Thanks, Fredreich," Danielle said as she kissed him on the cheek. "I never got a better compliment in my life."

Chapter 17

The next morning after Marvin had gone to work at his new business, Danielle quickly made the bed, threw in a load of laundry, and vacuumed. Although she didn't mind doing certain household tasks, she always felt guilty because she was not a good housekeeper. She was amazed at how seriously most of the Israelis took those duties.

Every day she saw housewives, including the doctor's wife, on their balconies beating their rugs after they had done *sponga*, which was the Israeli version of washing the floor. She only did what she considered necessary, as long as she had the stereo on and she could stretch and dance while she was doing her chores. That day she sang along as she shook her head and shoulders to "Good Day Sunshine," her favorite song on the Beatles' *Revolver* album. Hearing that song always made her feel good because it was so bouncy and positive. After spending the day with Tosha and Fredreich, she especially enjoyed being home. Besides, she was so relieved that the jewelry business Marv had decided to start was coming together.

Marvin had been getting depressed and worried that they'd never find a business. Although the government was providing low-cost loans, it was up to the individual to find a business to purchase or to start a new one. The Russian, Barchovsky, had finally opened the town's grocery store, and it had quickly become the town center. Everyone in town stopped in at least once a day to catch up on the latest gossip. Avi Tal, an Israeli from Tel Aviv, got the contract for garbage disposal and could be seen every day in his tractor, pulling the garbage bins to the dump outside the town limits. He always waved to the kids that he passed, and smiled or joked with the adults. Yamit was starting to feel like a real town.

When Danielle found out she was pregnant, Marv became increasingly anxious, afraid that they wouldn't find a business with potential. He knew he didn't want to work for the water company for the rest of his life, and he also knew he wanted to use his hands. When the garage he had planned with Dror fell through, he didn't take the disappointment well. He used it for an excuse to drink more.

Danielle tried not to yell and carry on, even though his drinking was becoming more and more upsetting. She still believed he would outgrow his binges. Besides, being a parent was a huge responsibility. Once the baby came, she was sure he would stop. Everyone knew that Jewish guys didn't drink. In addition to that, he was the son of survivors. If he couldn't stop for himself, then he had to stop for them. He had to. But for now, everything seemed fine, and he seemed really excited about starting this jewelry business.

It was by a stroke of luck, or perhaps *beshert*, that they found a jewelry business for sale. It turned out that Moshe Dayan's wife, Ruth, owned a company called Mazkit, which had just gone on the market. It was known for manufacturing high quality silver jewelry and had a great reputation both inside and outside of the country. When Marv had come back from meeting with Ruth Dayan and told Danielle about it, she encouraged him to take a chance. Even though he had never made jewelry, she thought he could learn easily. He was smart and had all that experience in high school. She knew he had loved going to Brooklyn Tech because he had gained proficiency on all different kinds of equipment. During their time together, she had learned that he had what she called golden hands and was very resourceful. After all, this was a man who had made a Pu Pu Platter for mice. When she told him that she had found mice droppings in the laundry room, he immediately went into battle mode. Most people would have gotten a mousetrap, stuck a piece of cheese in it, and be done. Not Marv. He carefully sliced tomatoes, cheese, and cucumbers and lay them on a bed of lettuce in a pinwheel design. Then he liberally flavored his creation with strychnine.

"Is that little fucker going to be surprised! He's going to think he and his family won the Mighty Mouse Lottery when he finds this Pu Pu platter. Instead, he's going to find himself in Mouse Heaven, dead as a doornail. That's what Darwin's about. He loses. I win."

Marv's creativity was one of the things that attracted her. So he could learn about jewelry. She had no doubt about his capability.

His partner, Gregory Braunstein, whom everyone called Yankel, had been in the retail end of the jewelry business in Philadelphia with his father-in-law. Both Danielle and Marv agreed with the philosophy of the Israeli Commerce Department: having a contact in the United States would help get a business off the ground. The plan was that Yankel would be the salesman and Marv would do the manufacturing. However, the more time Marv spent with Yankel, the faster he was coming to the conclusion that his new partner was a putz.

Right now Danielle didn't want to think about it. She gazed down at the cat's eye and silver bracelet on her wrist and smiled. It was beautiful. No one would believe it was the first piece of jewelry Marv had ever made.

Just then she heard Rachel call her name. Quickly, she shut the vacuum and left it right where it was. She opened the door and called back, "Give me five minutes." Quickly she washed her hands, ran a brush through her long black hair, and grabbed her net bag to go to the grocery store.

As Danielle carefully walked down her front steps, she looked at her best friend and thought, *That's going to be me in a few months. I can't believe it. I'm going to be a mommy.* Aloud, she said, "Hey, you look tired."

"I am. Battia was up half the night. Thank God she's sleeping now. I'm going to take her to the clinic and let the doctor check her."

"We're lucky that we have a clinic now," Danielle said as she pushed the stroller with the sleeping Battia in it down the main sidewalk. "Just think, when you were pregnant, you had to go for your monthly checkups in Beer Sheva. All I have to do is ride my bike down the block to the clinic. And the great thing is, it's never busy."

"It was yesterday," Rachel said, and her smile told Danielle that a great story was coming.

"Yesterday was Shabbat," Danielle said. "What happened? Did one of the kids get hurt?"

"No, the rabbi did," Rachel replied in a serious tone of voice.

"An accident?" Danielle asked.

"No, a fight." Rachel paused and then said, "He got his nose broken."

"Oh my God, tell me." She wondered if something had happened with the Gingy. He and the rabbi didn't get along. "Was it—"

Rachel broke in, "With a Torah."

"What happened?" Danielle asked unbelievingly.

"You know that old saying, 'If you have two Jews in a room, you'll have three arguments'?"

"Of course."

"Well, we in Yamit just started a new one. It goes like this, 'If you have more than a minyan, then you need two synagogues.'"

"Nu? Tell me already," Danielle said.

"Well, it seems that during the week some new people move in. A few of them came to synagogue yesterday morning and were very unhappy with the service. They demanded that the synagogue be a Sephardic one instead of Ashkenazi."

"I didn't even know there was a difference."

"There's enough of a difference that the rabbi of this group grabbed the Torah out of Gene's arms when he took it out of the ark. Rabbi Frankel was so angry, he tried to get it back, and the other rabbi, Shlomi Barzi, actually hit him in the face with the Torah."

Danielle started laughing, and Rachel, who had controlled herself while she was telling the story, joined her. When Danielle stopped, she wiped away a tear and asked her friend who presided over the synagogue now.

"Well, you know they say that 'might makes right.' So, today they're having a meeting with some official to get space for another synagogue."

"Oh, my God. It's too absurd. I can't get that picture out of my head." Danielle was still laughing as they reached the clinic.

While Rachel tenderly picked up the sleeping baby, Danielle

walked into the waiting room to say hello to the nurse, Naomi, who was a student in her evening conversational English class.

"Shalom, Naomi. My friend, Rachel, will be right in with her baby."

"Shalom, Danielle. What's wrong with her?" Naomi asked in heavily accented English.

"She's not sure, but she didn't sleep much last night. Hey, this is great. Rachel will be able to speak to you in English and you'll understand."

"That is why we like your class. We always practice real conversations."

"*Toda raba*, Naomi," Danielle said, thanking her. "*Lahitraot b'erev.*"

"You're welcome. I'll see you this evening," replied Naomi as Rachel came in. She took the baby from her arms. "Come, let's surprise the doctor. He's taking it easy and reading the newspaper. He thinks he's on *hofesh*. How you say in English?"

"Vacation," Rachel answered, and then turned to wave good-bye to Danielle.

Danielle said good-bye and headed over to the grocery store. As she walked down the street, she stopped to say hello to Rhoda, who had just come back from another meeting.

"I think we got it, but don't say anything yet. I'm supposed to know for sure tomorrow," Rhoda whispered excitedly.

"Got what?" Danielle asked.

"The restaurant. You know, the one on the beach. The one I've been working for since we got here. And you know that little red-haired *momzer*, Gingy, fought me tooth and nail."

"So what suddenly happened?" asked Danielle.

"He's not part of the original garin. Actually, he's a squatter. He's got nothing on paper, so the Sochnut has no obligation to him. Besides, I think my special friendship with Shlomo Avni didn't hurt."

"I'm sure it didn't," Danielle said a bit sarcastically. "What about Natan? Is he included in the deal?"

"Of course. There's no way I could do it all by myself. Besides, he's a born businessman."

"I wish Rachel's parents believed that. Their letters hurt her so much."

"Well, they're far away, so Rachel shouldn't worry so much. I have to run and get to work. I called in sick this morning because of this meeting, but I think this is finally it. See ya later."

Danielle waved as she watched Rhoda rush down the sidewalk. She sincerely hoped they got the restaurant because she knew Rachel was getting worried. Besides, it would be great having a place on the beach to get ice cream or a cup of coffee. All the months of waiting in the absorption center was receding into the past, as Yamit slowly and steadily became a real town. Now she didn't have to wait for the weekly trips to Beer Sheva. She could stop in the grocery store to get the necessities, like milk, juice, coffee, and the Israeli version of yogurt, *leban*. Some of the moshavim in the area provided the eggs and dairy products, so they were always fresh.

As she neared the grocery store, Danielle saw Myra Barker walk out of it, pulling a shopping cart full of Nesher beer.

The Barkers were not a family she would have been acquainted with in the United States. But in Israel, Danielle learned that Jews came in all shades and colors. They came from every country on earth and from very different socioeconomic backgrounds. But until she had lived in Israel, she would have never believed that Jews lived in trailer parks. Unbelievable but true, because the proof was right in front of her. Myra and her sister Ida were low class. She hated to be catty, but that was just a nice way of saying that they were trailer-park trash. Danielle had never imagined that American Jews would live that kind of life. Maybe Marv was right and she didn't watch enough television.

"Hey, how are you doing, Myra?" she asked politely.

"Sorry I almost ran ya over," Myra said. "This thing is so damn heavy. I wish Mickey would get his own fuckin' beer, especially since he's not working."

"What happened?"

"The usual ... Hey! Why don't you guys stop over tomorrow tonight. We're having a little party."

"Thanks, Myra, but we already have plans. Another time, okay?" Danielle knew she didn't mean it, but she didn't want to be rude.

"Sure. Hey, when's the baby due?"

"August. "

"You look good. A hell of a lot better than I ever looked. I just hope your kid is a lot better than my two brats."

"What's wrong? Are you having trouble with them?" Danielle asked politely.

"Shit, Sharon is running around with any soldier who points his gun at her—if you get my drift—and Scotty has more energy than a dozen boys. I'm just too old to keep up with him." Myra sighed wearily. "And now I have to put up with my biggest pain in the ass being home all day long. Thank God he's supposed to start work next week. I got to get going or he's gonna start screaming." She pushed her glasses up onto the bridge of her nose. "See ya "

"" Bye."

Danielle entered the grocery store, relieved to be rid of Myra, and waved to Barchovsky, who was stocking a shelf. She also smiled and greeted his pretty young wife, Idit, who was taking care of a customer at the register. Danielle could tell from the greasy hair that it was Myra's sister Ida. Before Danielle could hide behind a display, Ida turned and saw her.

"Danielle," she said, "I was just telling Idit that if she wanted custom closets, Pete's the man to do it. You saw his work, right?"

"Yes."

"He did almost all the houses at Modin. Don't you teach there?"

"Yes."

"Ask Dahlia if you can see what he did in the kitchen. It looks terrific."

"Okay," Danielle said as she tried escape. But Ida cornered her as Idit went back to replenishing the candy bars.

"He's so talented. I guess it's because he's so passionate. Come to think of it, he's still passionate in the bedroom." Ida spoke as proudly as a teenage girl after having her first orgasm. "After ten years of marriage and three kids, that's not something to take lightly. Really, how many women, after so many years, can say that?"

"Not many, Ida," Danielle replied blankly. So it was true. She had just heard the latest gossip at yesterday's coffee klatch. Rachel had heard that Ida was fooling around with that little nebbish, Shmulik. Danielle hadn't wanted to believe it, but this blatant declaration seemed to be an admission of guilt. She grabbed a liter of milk and a loaf of bread. "Sorry," she said as she pulled out money. "I'm in a rush, Ida, I can't talk." She paid Idit and said good-bye to both women

She walked out the door, carrying her net bag and thinking that out of the two sisters, she liked Myra better. Ida not only had that greasy hair with the bald spot, but she was so pretentious. Myra might be sad and foolish, but she didn't pretend to be other than what she was.

She and her husband were really kind of funny. What was it he said to Marvin when he got fired? "Last time I was looking for a job, I found this one. So drink up, buddy. That's the way it is." It looked like he was right. In this small town where everybody lived in each other's pockets, who would have ever thought he would get hired again? But Myra said he was going to start working. That was why Danielle knew the jewelry business would work. And if it didn't, something else would. Life was like that.

She breathed deep, loving the freshness of the air, and noticed the gardens that had been planted in front of some of the houses. The Tals had a beautiful blooming cactus near their front door.

Maybe she and Marvin should get some potted plants for the balcony, she thought. *They would look great near the hammock.* Yamit was going to be so beautiful and a great place to raise children. It was almost as if all the bad things that had happened to her before she met Marvin had never happened. They were so lucky.

She walked up the steps to her building and opened her unlocked door. She didn't think about it often, but that was really nice. She hadn't carried a house key since she'd left the United States. Much to her surprise, Marv was walking out of the kitchen.

"Hey, I wasn't expecting you for another hour," she said.

"I have some good news," he said excitedly.

"Do you want me to finish making that salami sandwich?" she asked, looking over his shoulder into the kitchen. She hoped he said no because she was too curious about his good news.

"No. Just sit down and close your eyes."

He took her hand and led her to the dining room table.

"Okay, now don't open them till I tell you."

"Nu, today's almost over."

"Don't be in such a hurry. Okay, one ... two ... three ... Open."

Danielle opened her eyes and saw the business cards. Last week Marv and Yankel had been playing with names for the business. Now it was there right in front of her eyes. *Danielle's Jewelry* was engraved in both Hebrew and English. She was so touched that Marv had named the business after her. In spite of his drinking, he loved her. That's what was important.

"Thank you," she said before she kissed him. "This is one of the nicest things you've ever done for me."

"You can thank me in bed, baby," Marv said in his bad Bogart imitation.

So she did.

Chapter 18

Danielle was absolutely delighted and amazed. The whole town was at Ari's bris. Not just the Americans, which she had expected, but the Russians and the Israelis too. She was so relieved that the Cultural Center had been completed in time for the affair, because it was the only building big enough to hold everyone. She smiled, even though she was anxious and nervous, as she looked around at all the people she knew as they chatted with one another. They were all here to welcome her Ari, the newest Jewish male, into the tribe.

Her parents were talking to Rachel and Natan, while her sister Lauren was looking for an escape route to get away from Rich, who was anxiously looking for a bride so he could get better housing. Marvin's parents had come down from Jerusalem and were chatting with his uncle Zev, who was going to be the godfather. For her in-laws it was an especially significant occasion. She knew there had been times when they both had thought they would never live to see another day, much less see their own children bearing their grandchildren. As Tosha had said, Ari's bris was "spitting in the eyes of Hitler." However, she missed seeing her sister-in-law Marilyn, who had gone back to the United States. For a while she and her husband had lived in Beer Sheva, and the two women had become close friends. The Bar Shais, Danny and Rona, had just started a small—very small—newspaper, and were busy taking photos of the historical event for the next issue.

Ari was a true Yamitnik. His was the first brit milah celebrated in the new town, and that was why everyone was here. Danielle continued to scan the room in search of Marvin. The Gingy had catered it for them with the usual Israeli spread of humus, pita, and egg salad. Of course, they also had a few different kinds of cake and cookies. As soon as the ceremony was over and everyone ate something, they would all be going back to work.

Although the affair was simple, the table looked pretty and festive, decorated with fresh flowers from the moshav where she taught, and a few bottles of Israeli wine for everyone to make a toast. Now Danielle was getting more anxious. The mohel was ready to get started, so where was Marv? She walked over to her mother, who had Ari and looked blissful as she held her first grandchild, and asked what she should do.

"Nu, so where is he?" her mother asked.

"I don't know, Mom. He said he'd be right behind us. He had to check on something at the workshop."

"So give him another five minutes and that's it. The mohel has to get back to Beer Sheva and everybody's getting restless."

"I know."

Danielle kissed her baby's sweet, soft cheek and then told the mohel they would start in five minutes whether Marv showed up or not. Then she stood outside the door, smoking a cigarette and fuming that her husband was ruining this special occasion. As soon as she finished her cigarette, she stubbed it out and went back inside. Taking Ari from her mother, she told her mother to tell the mohel they were going to start without Marvin.

Marvin's uncle Zev looked proud and happy as he sat on Elijah's chair and put the pillow on his lap. The mohel called for the godfather, and Danielle kissed her son's head and handed him to her mother. She knew she wouldn't be able to handle watching the circumcision, the ritual removal of the foreskin, which symbolized God's covenant with Abraham.

Her mother handed her grandchild to her husband, and he carried Ari to the chair where Uncle Zev, the *sandak*, sat. He placed the drowsy week-old infant on the fluffy white pillow. Ari would lie there while the mohel, with absolute precision, removed the foreskin.

Danielle closed her eyes and turned around as the mohel began the blessing: *"Baruch atta Adanoi ..."* Before she could brace herself, she heard the heart-rending wail and knew it was done. She turned around and saw the mohel blessing the wine. He placed a wine-soaked napkin in her baby's mouth as he looked around for Marvin, who was supposed to say a blessing. Danielle whispered to her father, who was right next to her, and he immediately went over to the mohel to say the blessing in Marvin's stead. The wine wasn't soothing Ari as much as Danielle had hoped, and his sobs still filled the room. The mohel gave him a drop more as he officially bestowed on him his Hebrew name, which was in honor of Danielle's grandfather, who had died a few years earlier. Everyone took a little paper cup of wine so they could all say the kiddush to sanctify the occasion.

Just as Danielle crossed the room to rescue her son and take him home, Marvin appeared at the door. She could see, even from across the room, that he was drunk. Others might not realize it, but to her there was no doubt. He walked too purposefully and rigidly as he crossed the room to where his newborn son still lay on his great uncle's lap. Before Uncle Zev could say anything, Marvin announced that he was rescuing his son from this ritual torture and picked the baby up. He placed Ari in his carriage, which stood nearby, and then nonchalantly pushed the baby out the door.

Danielle was right behind him. She was glad to see that, except for family, everyone was too busy eating and chatting to notice what was happening. When Marvin realized she was following him, he started jogging, pushing the baby carriage in front of him. She heard sounds behind her. Looking over her shoulder, she saw her mother and Tosha also following. Marvin must have heard them too, because his pace picked up.

Please, she prayed. *Just let him get Ari home safely.*

As the three women yelled, "Stop! Be Careful!" Marvin just ran faster, and Danielle's biggest fear was that he would tip over the baby carriage. The older women slowed down but continued to follow the drunk kidnapper and his precious cargo. Since they were almost home, Danielle slowed down too, even though she continued her silent prayer. Marvin looked over his shoulder and slowed his pace. When Danielle caught up with him, right at their corner, he was singing the Grateful Dead's "Truckin.'"

She first checked on her baby, who was now sleeping, no doubt exhausted from all the excitement. Then she grabbed the handle of the baby carriage and glared at Marv, spitting out the words, "How dare you!"

"How dare I? How dare you? You made a freak show of this barbaric custom by inviting everybody in town."

"What the hell are you talking about? We planned this together."

"My wife, my life, just like all the Nazis claimed in World War II"—he clicked his heels as he raised his arm in the familiar salute—"I too just take orders."

"Go fuck yourself, Marvin, because you for sure won't be fucking me."

"Well, then I guess I'll just go upstairs and take a little nap before I go back down to the workshop. Lose that lemon face and I might talk to you later." He bowed to Danielle in an exaggerated manner. "My sad-eyed lady, I am just your humble servant."

She watched as he walked upstairs. He tripped and missed one of the steps. That was all she needed, for him to fall and break his head open.

Her mother and Tosha caught up with her as she was parking the carriage under the steps. Her mother took the baby from her and whispered, "Thank God Ari's all right. Just nod and smile when his nutcase mother starts."

She carried Ari upstairs as Tosha joined Danielle.

"What did you do to my son?" Tosha asked.

"What are you talking about?"

"Why didn't you tell him what time the bris vas going to start?"

"What are you talking about? We left the house at the same time. Your son was at the workshop drinking."

"What are you saying? My son doesn't drink. Just like my father, Menachem Chaim, may he rest in peace, he is a *guten neshuma*, a good soul. Marvin has always been a good son and was raised to be a mensch."

Danielle was astounded. Was she really hearing this? Marvin's mother blamed her for his abhorrent behavior? Tosha was refusing to accept what her son had done, even though she'd seen it with her own eyes.

"Tosha, please let's drop it. I want to go up and take care of the baby."

"Drop it? Very nice. Go, I'll sit on the bench and wait for Fredreich."

Danielle climbed the stairs, exhausted, even though it was just 11:30 in the morning. All the aggravation Marv and his parents caused had drained her. How could they ignore his bad behavior? Couldn't they see what condition he was in and what he did? Then, as usual, she rationalized this latest aggravation by weighing it against the good in her life. Every time things looked bad, all she had to do was think about her past and the present didn't seem so bad.

She joined her mother, who had just finished putting an antiseptic cream on her grandson's fresh wound. Helen kissed the baby and then handed him to her daughter.

"Ma, can you believe this? Tosha just told me that Marvin didn't do anything wrong. Instead, she blamed me."

"I told you, just nod and smile. Don't start with her. She's a meshuggeneh. She's crazy. Remember, my mother always said you get more with honey than vinegar."

"So, I'm just supposed to pretend the morning didn't happen? How can I do that?"

"Sometimes you just have to do things you don't want to do for peace in the family.

I'm going to go find your father and then we'll be over later. By the way, the arrangements you made were excellent."

"Since Hannah and Dror are visiting family in the States, she said you could use her house. I figured that would be perfect."

"Forget your crazy mother-in-law and go feed the baby. By the way, I wish you would use a bottle. I don't know why you want to nurse. It's so old-fashioned. Breastfeeding reminds me of a cow. "

Danielle ignored her mother's remark, "And Marv ..."

"So he was a little anxious. Try and forget about it. Everything ended up okay."

Her mother left, and Danielle sat in her rocking chair, rocking her precious son back and forth as he nursed. This was her favorite time. She examined his tiny face and hands and heard his utter pleasure as he sighed in comfort. Suddenly a flashbulb popped in the doorway. She looked up to see Marv standing there with his camera.

"My honey, my wife, my life," he said, "I'm sorry. I love you." Then he grinned. "By the way, I think I got a great picture of you feeding Winston Churchill."

Danielle smiled wearily because she had noticed the similarity too. "Marv, you have to start acting like a grown-up. You're a father now. Come hold the baby. He just finished drinking."

"Nah, I might drop him. Besides, I have nothing in common with him yet. When he can hold a conversation, I'll talk to him. I really am sorry. Having the parents here and all those people ..."

"Yeah, yeah, yeah. I understand it, but I don't like it."

"You have my promise. I won't drink anymore. Okay?"

Danielle had been waiting for that. This was the first time he'd acknowledged his drinking at all. She put the now sleeping baby in his crib and hugged her husband. She looked in his startlingly clear blue eyes and could see he was truly sorry. The question was, did he have the resolve?

"Okay," she said. "I believe you. I love you. Now we have a beautiful baby son. We're parents, Marv. We live in the most beautiful spot on earth, and our business is getting off the ground. Please don't ruin everything."

He kissed her. "Don't worry. It will be fine. By the way, I fired that guy Uri. You know, the one who taught me how to use the kiln. I'm ready to do it myself. It will save us a lot of money."

Now Danielle understood the morning's shenanigans even better.

"I'm working on a special piece," he went on. "I'll see you later. Okay?"

"Okay. Make sure you're back by three to take your parents to the bus."

They heard a knock at the door before it opened, and Marvin's parents and uncle entered the living room. Marv brusquely told everyone he'd be back soon, but Danielle knew she wouldn't see him again until three o'clock. Tosha acted as if nothing had happened at the bris, so Danielle offered to make coffee for everyone. As she went into the kitchen , she heard Tosha whispering loudly to her brother and Fredreich in Yiddish. She heard her name mentioned a few times and froze. Tosha said that it was a shame Danielle wasn't a good girl like her daughter Marilyn. It was too bad little Ari would have to deal with such a bitch for a mother. Her poor Marvin.

At first, Danielle told herself she was imagining what she was hearing, but as her blood started to boil, she knew she couldn't ignore this. She walked out of the kitchen, saying, "I heard that, Tosha. I understand Yiddish. And you know I do."

"What did you hear? You heard nothing. I said how lucky Marvin was to have a girl like you."

"You're a liar, Tosha. Don't tell me what I heard. But you're right on one count. I'm not a doormat like your daughter."

"Danielle, you must be so tired from all the excitement," Fredreich said calmly as he lit a cigarette. "Why don't you go take a nap while the baby's sleeping? You'll feel so much better."

Danielle took a deep breath and stared at them both. She couldn't believe that they would look her straight in the eye and lie. Getting away from them was an excellent idea. She walked into her bedroom and collapsed on the bed. She didn't move until her baby's cries woke her up. By then everyone was gone.

Chapter 19

The day started out like any other. Ari opened his eyes at about six a.m., and Danielle lay listening to him gurgling until she got up to make Marv his breakfast—a couple of scrambled eggs in a pita sandwich—and a cup of coffee for herself. Everyone said that she was lucky Ari already slept through the night and didn't start to fuss until about seven. Marv left for work soon after the baby awoke. Before he left, he always patted him on the head and said "good boy." Danielle had never seen anything so ludicrous. He treated the baby the same way he would treat a dog. Actually, he would probably treat a dog better. How could he rationalize that? How could he not pay their son any attention?

She carried the baby to his bedroom and laid him on his bassinet so that she could diaper him. As his chubby little legs kicked and pumped the air, mother and son smiled and stared into each other's eyes. Suddenly Danielle had an amazing epiphany. At that moment she realized that by being a parent, a human being had a brief glimpse of God.

To Ari, I am God, she thought. When he looked into her eyes, he saw nothing else. She was the one who gave him nourishment, kept him warm and dry, and held him when he cried. She fulfilled all his needs.

Lost in this realization, she was startled when she heard that voice. The same voice that had told her to follow the rules and that had said she was going to marry Marv. She had thought she would never hear it again. As she finished diapering her son, the voice said,

"This marriage won't last." She wanted to shrug the message off, because even though Marv could be an annoying drunk, she had faith that eventually he would stop. Besides, he didn't drink every day. He binged. More importantly, she loved her life in Yamit and was proud of the business they were building. Luckily, before she could give the words any more thought, she heard a knock on the door and then someone walked in.

Rachel called to her, and with what sounded like panic in her voice told her to turn the radio on. "Hostages have been taken to the airport in Uganda."

"You turn it on, Rachel. I'll be right out."

Danielle came out of the bedroom with Ari on her hip. Battia was sitting on the floor, and Danielle put Ari on his tummy in the playpen while Rachel fiddled with the radio dial.

"When did it happen?" Danielle asked.

"Yesterday but we're just finding out now. Okay, I got it." She stopped when she got the news station. They both sat silently, looking at each other while their babies explored their new worlds, and listened intently to the announcer. Although neither could speak Hebrew well, they both understood the language well enough to follow the news. According to the announcer, two members of the Popular Front for the Liberation of Palestine and two German terrorists had hijacked a plane and forced it to land at the airport in Uganda. In exchange for the more than two hundred hostages on the plane, they demanded the release of fifty-three convicted terrorists held in various countries, including, of course, Israel.

"Rachel, did I hear right? Children were taken too?"

"Yes," Rachel said grimly.

"The scariest thing," Danielle said softly, "is that they separated the Israelis and other Jews from the rest of the hostages."

"Why don't they ever leave us alone?" Rachel asked rhetorically.

They looked at each other in horror, repeating "oy vey," their heads nodding back and forth. Then both of their bodies sagged, and they keened and wailed in empathy for the victims, as millions had done over the centuries. Danielle and were no longer themselves. Instead, their souls were marching to their deaths in concentration camps, along with unknown uncles, aunts, and cousins. They were the *bubbes* and *zaydes* in the shtetls hiding their grandchildren from murderous Cossacks. They were the ancient Marranos, tied to the stake, hot oil dripped on their bellies, forming the words Jesus is Lord.

Danielle rose like a sleepwalker and shut off the radio after she heard that the Israeli government was entering negotiations with the terrorists. "Rachel, do you think they'll get out alive? What a nightmare! Those poor people. They must be terrified."

The phone rang, and she jumped. She answered it, hearing Marv's voice on the other end.

"My wife, my life, we just got a great order."

"No kidding? From who?"

"Georg Jensen."

"That's great. Mazel tov! I told you we were producing first-rate quality. But Marv, did you hear about the hijacking?"

"Sure I did. The big problem, as I see it, is if that cannibal, Idi Amin, likes kosher meat, then they'll never negotiate."

Danielle rolled her eyes at her husband's sense of humor. Still, he had made her feel better. "Thanks, Marv. A little levity was just what I needed."

"Who's joking?"

After she had hung up, Danielle told Rachel the good news about selling to Georg Jensen. Then she told her what Marv had said about Idi Amin, and they both laughed. Rachel said she had to go back home and clean up before her sister-in-law and her husband came for Shabbat.

"You know, Danielle, I know I'm not the best housekeeper, but Amira, Natan's sister, makes me feel like I'm a slob. I know she looks down on me because I'm not Orthodox. Then, in case I don't get the message, she also insults me as a wife and mother. When she comes over, I always catch her looking in my refrigerator or opening up a closet, and then giving me that 'tsk, tsk, my poor brother lives in filth and eats tref' look. I get so nervous when she's around. And now it looks like I'll have to put up with it even more."

"Why?" Danielle asked as she walked Rachel, who was carrying Battia, to the door.

"Don't tell anyone, because this is a real embarrassment to Natan's family, but Amira and her husband Yeshua may be moving here."

"Why here? There are no religious people here."

Rachel rolled her eyes and let out a deep breath. "Yeshua was arrested for embezzling from the bank where he works."

Danielle was flabbergasted. "What?" she asked incredulously. Then she started laughing because it was so absurd. After a moment, Rachel laughed too. The two friends hugged, and Danielle said, "This is great. Every time Amira makes you feel bad, just remember that Mr. I Pray Three Times a Day is a thief."

"You're right, Danielle," Rachel said. She added shyly, "That's why I love you. You just make life a lot easier."

As the two friends hugged again, Danielle looked over Rachel's shoulder and saw that Ari was asleep.

"Hey, I just thought of something else."

"What?"

"I bet those terrorists don't give a damn if any of those Jews they've taken hostage eat unkosher food or go to synagogue. Neither did Hitler. To the outside world we're all the same—just Jews." Danielle said as they walked down the steps.

"Unfortunately, you're right," Rachel said. "God, I hope those people will be okay."

As the two friends were parting, Arianna Elimelich, Danielle's new downstairs neighbor, opened her door to shake out her rug.

"Shalom, Arianna," the two women called in unison.

"Boker tov," Arianna said in return, and bustled out to ask them if they had heard about the hostage crisis. Arianna spoke to them in Hebrew, and Danielle was proud that she could understand what her neighbor said. After Arianna, in her typical supercilious and condescending manner, told the women her husband had been involved with building the Entebbe airport in Uganda, the three women parted ways. Danielle returned halfheartedly to her son and chores, still thinking of their compatriots whose fate was yet to be decided.

Back upstairs, Danielle mopped the floor while Ari slept. As she worked, she thought that when she wrote to her family, she would mention her new neighbors, the Elimelichs, who had moved in downstairs a few weeks earlier. They were originally from Egypt, and her new next door neighbors were from Russia.

Adella, Arianna's mother, lived with her daughter and son-in-law. If she caught Danielle on her way out, she would always corner her and complain about how fat and lazy her daughter was. Other days she would tell romantic stories that Danielle loved to hear, about sailing up the Nile from Alexandria, and traveling to Beirut. She said that when she was a young girl, not only was Beirut the banking capital of the region, it was also considered the Paris of the Middle East. Adella would smile as she reminisced about her mother taking her on extravagant shopping trips, while her father did business with other Jewish merchants in Lebanon's capital city. Then she would return to the present and spit, and then complain about what Islamic terrorists groups, led by that murderer Arafat, were doing to the beautiful city she remembered with love.

Danielle still marveled at the diversity of Israeli society. Living in Yamit she had learned that being Jewish had nothing to do with skin color or nationality. Jews lived in Morocco, Iraq, Tunisia, and even Ethiopia. Ashkenazi Jews from Europe and Sephardic Jews from North Africa had come together to build a country of their own. They no longer would be second-class citizens in somebody else's country, or depend on the mercy of alien governments to save them when it was fashionable to hate and persecute Jews. Still, the world wouldn't leave them alone. *Just look at this Entebbe incident,* Danielle thought. Why couldn't more people appreciate Jews? She was thinking specifically about Meili, a beautiful Eurasian woman who had married Moti, a Sephardic Israeli. They had recently moved into town, and Danielle and Meili had started talking to each other at a Friday night gathering. Speaking softly in her French-accented voice, Meili had told Danielle that she had met her future husband in Jerusalem while on a pilgrimage with the Catholic Church.

Meili had been born in Vietnam to a Vietnamese mother and a French father. She told Danielle that in Vietnamese society, she had always been an outcast because of her mixed blood. Her family moved to Paris when she was eleven years old, and with a child's hope and innocence she had assumed her life would become easier. While they lived in Saigon, she had listened to her father reminisce about the grand boulevards and culture of Paris, and so she expected its citizens to be more civilized. Instead, it was almost worse. She was continuously made to feel she was not *right*. Even in her church school, the nuns labeled her "the little yellow girl." Danielle had almost cried with compassion when Meili said, with tears in her eyes, that living in Israel was the first time in her life she'd been treated with dignity. As Meili said she was so grateful for being in Israel, Danielle squeezed her hand and felt a surge of pride in her religion and her adopted country.

Since it was another sunny day, she thought she would hang the diapers before she sat down to type her weekly letter to her family. To Danielle, the climate was perfect. Even though they were in the desert, the sea breeze modulated the dry heat so that it was always comfortable. Danielle was glad she hadn't listened to her mother when she had scolded her for not buying a dryer to go with their washing machine. So far, she had not regretted the decision.

Whenever a load of wash was done, she hung the clothes on a line Marvin had rigged on the side of the balcony. Actually, the whole routine was rather soothing, so she didn't see the point in wasting money on a dryer. Besides, she wanted to fit into Israeli society.

When Ari woke up, she changed and fed him and then put him in his carriage to take a walk to the jewelry workshop. To Danielle, one of the benefits of living in Yamit was that their business was only a five-minute walk from the house. She could stop in to bring Marv his lunch and still have time to go to the beach.

On her way there, she smiled and called "Shalom" to everyone she passed along the central walkway. Flowers were blooming, and she noticed a bright new yellow slide had been installed in the playground.

Although the commercial center had been completed, most of the spaces were still vacant. The only exceptions were the supermarket, which had the biggest allocated space, and their jewelry workshop, which was the only tenant downstairs.

The original makeshift grocery store was now a full-fledged supermarket. The Barchovskys had asked Hannah and Dror to be their partners, and they had enthusiastically agreed. At that time, Hannah had been concerned about their livelihood, because they hadn't found the right business and were slowly going through their savings. She had told Danielle she was also tired of monitoring Dror's moods, afraid that he was slipping into depression. Dror had been extremely disappointed that the military garage had fallen through, and his original enthusiasm for the new city was eroding. So when this opportunity fell into their laps, they grabbed it. They knew being partners in the town's only supermarket would be a lot of work, but the tradeoff was that it would be highly lucrative. So since the supermarket's grand opening, Danielle had seen less and less of Hannah. But now, as she passed the store to go downstairs, Hannah came outside to say hello and ask if she had heard about the hostage crisis.

After the two women had debated the pros and cons of negotiating with the terrorists, Danielle parked the carriage against the wall and walked down the stairs to the workshop with Ari peeking over her shoulder. She went over to Marv, who was sitting on his stool, smoking a cigarette while waiting for the buzzer on the kiln to sound so he could take the latest batch of jewelry out. She still couldn't believe this all belonged to them. It gave her so much satisfaction to look around and see what they had already accomplished. Two long worktables held the tools of the trade, while the kiln stood in a corner. In a separate room Marv did electroplating. There was an office as well, and some extra space where she hoped to eventually run a little retail store.

When Danielle kissed him hello, she noticed he had been working on a design. As usual, he patted his son on the head and roared. Danielle rolled her eyes. She knew why he did it. Ari meant lion in Hebrew. This was Marv's odd way of communicating. She hoped Ari liked it better than she did. At least it made her son smile.

"So what are you working on?" she asked.

"That order that Yankel finally got from his father-in-law."

"No, silly. What's that on the table?"

"I'm playing with some ideas for a town symbol."

"Oh? How come?"

"Izzy Bar Shai wants one for his newspaper."

"That's great," Danielle said enthusiastically. "He is going to pay you, right?" She added, "I can't believe we have a town newspaper already. I sent my family that first issue with the photo of Ari. They loved it. Now all of a sudden my mother thinks we made the 'best decision' to move here."

"The thing is," Marv said, obviously thinking out loud, "we can make jewelry with the Yamit symbol on it. Rhoda and Natan can sell T-shirts and key chains at their restaurant on the beach. Tourists are starting to come. I think they'd sell."

"Wow, you're right. It's a very good idea. Let's see what you got."

Marv turned the paper over before she could grab it. "Not yet. So, do you think the government will negotiate with the terrorists?"

"I sure hope so. It's sickening to have to deal with them, but I don't want to see any lives lost. Here." She changed the subject by handing him his lunch. "I brought some hard-boiled eggs and herring for lunch."

"Is the pita fresh?"

"I just baked it over the camel dung," Danielle said sarcastically. "Seriously, it's yesterday's, so it won't kill you."

"What I would do for a piece of fresh rye bread," Marv said dreamily.

"What would you do?" Danielle asked.

He thought a second, smiled, and said, "I'd kiss my mother."

"Would you kiss my mother?" Danielle teased coquettishly.

"Yup, I'd kiss your mother."

"Well," she said, moving Ari to a more comfortable position on her hip, "would you kiss me?"

"You? No way, my wife, my life. I'd never be able to finish this drawing."

"Okay, then, I'm going down to the beach. I know Rhoda won't reject me." She kissed him on the cheek and waved Ari's little hand at his father. After putting Ari back in his carriage, she strolled down to the beach and spent the rest of the afternoon with her friends Rhoda and Rachel. Battia was so excited when she saw them, she toddled over to Ari and kissed his hand. She looked at him with her big brown eyes and said, very seriously, "I wuv you." *Dreams do come true*, Danielle thought, *It can't get any better than this.*

Chapter 20

Rhoda was lying in bed on the morning of July 4 when Danielle dropped in to return a book that she had borrowed. Although she had the radio on, neither of them was listening to the broadcast because Rhoda was avidly discussing the merits of her latest young lover. He came from Kazakhstan and was about fifteen years younger than she. To top it off, he spoke no English and liked to sleep with his army-issued Kalashnikov.

Danielle couldn't understand why her friend kept going out with guys who just wanted sex. Suddenly, in the middle of Rhoda's ravings about her three continuous orgasms, a special news bulletin caught their attention. Rhoda sat up as the newscaster, with unsuppressed excitement in his voice, announced that the hostages had been rescued from Entebbe and were on their way home to Israel.

Both Danielle and Rhoda started screaming and hugging each other. Rhoda's boys came rushing in from the backyard to see what had happened. Happy to see that their mother was okay, they all huddled on the bed to listen to the rest of the story. The coverage turned to an interview with a government official, who announced that all but three of the hostages were returning unharmed, and at that moment were landing at Ben Gurion airport. He added that, tragically, the heroic leader of the rescue mission, Lt. Col. Yonatan Netanyahu, had been killed in the line of duty.

The cameras rolled as the TV coverage turned to Ben Gurion Airport. Many other people joined friends and family at the airport to greet the survivors. The rescued hostages gingerly stepped off the plane, obviously still in a state of shock, stunned by the flashing cameras and cheering crowd. Reporters did their jobs by shouting inane questions like, "How did you feel during the ordeal?" and "What did they feed you?" One reporter indelicately stuck a microphone in a survivor's face and asked, "What did you do while you were sitting in that hangar suspended between life and death?" The young woman, holding a small child, stared straight at him and said simply, "We sang and we prayed. Then we sang some more. What the hell do you think we did?"

Before Danielle could tell Rhoda how much she liked that woman's attitude,

Rhoda's sons started singing, "The hostages are back, the hostages are back, hi ho the IDF, the hostages are back," to the tune of the "The Farmer in the Dell" and ran out the door to see if their friend Riva had heard the good news. Before Rhoda could finish saying, "Don't slam the door," the door slammed. Danielle and Rhoda laughed giddily and decided that it was the best Fourth of July ever.

———

Over the next few days information about the miraculous rescue was released. Israelis once again felt that same pride in their country that they had felt after winning the Six Day War. Danielle and her friends eagerly read about the brilliant planning and execution of the rescue. They were astounded to learn that the whole operation had only lasted fifty-eight minutes. The soldiers had killed all eight hijackers, and thankfully only three hostages had been killed in the crossfire, as well as the leader of the mission.

One afternoon after returning from Rachel's house, while Danielle parked Ari's carriage under the stairs, Arianna came flying out of her apartment like a fat Greek fury to complain that her toilet had overflowed again.

"I'm so sorry, Arianna. What do you want me to do?" Danielle asked, intimidated by the force of her neighbor's anger.

"Tell me what you do with your toilet paper!" Arianna demanded.

"Before or after I use it?" Danielle asked, truly puzzled.

"After, of course, you *tembel*." Arianna glared at her.

"I flush it," Danielle answered hesitantly.

"That's what I thought. So it's your fault. Don't you know you're not supposed to put toilet paper in the toilet? That's what caused this."

"What!" Danielle couldn't believe what she was hearing. "That's ridiculous. I've never heard of such a thing."

"Just because you never heard of it doesn't make you right. Believe me, here you can't flush. You must put toilet paper in the trash can." Arianna calmed down and started explaining the intricacies of the plumbing system to Danielle, as if she were talking to a mentally handicapped child. "These pipes are very thin. Not like in the United States."

"Oh." Danielle was starting to believe that she was singlehandedly ruining the plumbing system of Yamit.

"Nobody explained to you?" Arianna asked. "So, now you know. My husband Miki, he worked on the construction on the airport in Uganda. I told you already? Believe me, he knows what he's talking about. Just think if his company didn't do that work, Israel wouldn't have had the blueprints and the hostages would be dead."

"He's a hero, Arianna, a real hero. Maybe the Bar Shais will do a piece about him in the newspaper."

Feeling like she had been hit in the stomach, Danielle carried her precious Ari upstairs. She was especially careful because she felt weak and was afraid they'd go rolling down the steps. Luckily it was time for Ari's nap, so she quickly fed him and put him down. All she could think about was that now they would have to leave Israel. There was no way she was going to put dirty toilet paper in the trash can. That was too gross for words.

She crawled into bed and pulled the blanket over her head, too depressed to start supper. The idea of leaving her beloved Yamit made her sick, but she knew there was no way she could live so primitively. She must have dozed off because the next thing she knew, Marvin was waking her up.

"Hey, are you okay?" he asked gruffly, almost as if he was embarrassed to show concern.

"Marv, I think we have to go back home," Danielle answered

groggily. She looked around, dazed from coming out of such a deep sleep. "Is Ari up yet?"

"I don't know," Marv answered. "He's quiet. So tell me what the hell you're talking about."

"Okay," she said, and proceeded to tell him about her conversation with Arianna.

"You are a sucker, Danielle. That's bullshit."

"But Arianna said—"

"I don't give a shit what that fat fuck said. The pipes are fine. Remember, I dug the holes for them. They're the right size. Those primitive bastards downstairs don't know how to use a toilet. They're probably washing their vegetables in it. Now get up and forget about it. We're not leaving."

"Okay." Danielle immediately brightened and kissed her husband. "So what do you want for supper?"

Chapter 21

It was hard to believe that they had been in Yamit for more than two years. The original settlers had been joined by others who were like them and following their dreams, or were like Mickey Barker, escaping nightmares and creating new ones. The town was growing quickly and steadily. The empty stores in the commercial center were now occupied, and the growing population insured the new businesses with customers. Across the way from the supermarket, Rabbi Izzy Frankel had opened a general store that stocked everything from nuts and bolts to pots and pans. Another American couple, the Goldsteins, ran a children's clothing store. There was even a small nut stand to satisfy the Israeli craving for sunflower seeds.

Even better and more surprising, tourists had started to visit. About once a week an Egged tourist bus delivered a group of Americans who would freely spend money at Rhoda and Natan's beachfront restaurant and then visit the commercial center. The tour guides earned 10 percent of whatever was spent, the tourists were able to see how their contributions to the Jewish National Fund were being spent, and the business people heard the cash registers ringing as they watched their gambles paying off. It was an arrangement that made everyone happy.

Ari spent part of the day at a *gan*, a daycare center run by Naamat, a professional women's group. Danielle believed it was an ideal situation for a working mother. While she was working, her son was being taken care of by other Jewish mothers. What could be better? The women who worked there seemed to love their jobs, treating the toddlers in their care as their own. That meant that the children were hugged and kissed and generally were treated like royalty. The center was situated in its own building with a volunteer guard sitting outside its gate, and was only a five minute walk for Danielle from both home and work.

She and Marv had opened their jewelry shop, and to Danielle's delight she discovered she was a born saleswoman. She gained skill and confidence by managing the retail operation and being responsible for its growth. The shop was located behind the heavy steel doors that opened to the front of the workshop. Although it wasn't too large, it could hold about eight customers comfortably and it utilized space that had been empty. Since she and Marv wanted to minimize costs, they had bought second-hand display cases and a used cash register. They decorated in typical outlet style, which meant no frills or decorations. They slowly began to see busloads of tourists, and Danielle slowly learned how to assess her customers. She found that Israelis didn't buy much, because they would rather just argue about the price. The easiest money came from the American tourists. They liked the fact that they were getting a bargain by buying straight from the jeweler, and were doing a mitzvah at the same time.

Marv's partner Yankel had a different philosophy of business and argued that they should put more money into the way the store looked. Marv got frustrated with him since Yankel didn't seem to understand that customers didn't need an elegant retail space. They knew they were buying direct. Also, Yankel had never brought the business that he promised he would from his father-in-law, who owned three jewelry stores in Maryland. Marv always threw that in his face, reminding him that his father-in-law's business was the reason they became partners in the first place. After about a year of Marv yelling at Yankel, they got one small order from the father-in-law. That was it. Even though Marv ranted and raved to Danielle about how stupid Yankel was, Danielle knew Marv actually felt sorry for him because he was such a putz and his wife was a spoiled bitch who hated being in Israel.

"I keep telling him," Marv would say to her, "to forget his father-in-law and make new contacts. I told him that I think her father figures if he doesn't give us business, then we'll all starve and his precious daughter and retarded grandson will come home."

Danielle was proud that Marvin had designed the Yamit logo. He had used the motif of a date palm tree, and it was on the masthead of the Bar Shais' newspaper, as well as silk-screened onto T-shirts sold at Rhoda and Natan's restaurant. At their jewelry store, small pendants and sterling silver key chains that sported the logo had turned out to be popular souvenir items. Besides selling to Georg Jensen and a number of other European jewelry venues, Danielle's mother was getting enough orders from synagogue gift shops that Marvin had to hire three employees.

Danielle was also thrilled when ground was broken for the community swimming pool and tennis courts. That was when she and Marvin realized just how dumb Yankel was. He told Marv that he'd been taking a walk around the cordoned- off area and spotted something sticking up in the overturned earth. Since he was curious, he ducked underneath the rope, grabbed it, and ran to the police station with it. Marv said he wished he'd been there when Yankel came running in, because sure enough, it was a land mine. Marv said he was lucky it was dead and that he couldn't believe Yankel didn't understand how dangerous it was.

"That stupid schmendrick. Doesn't he understand that you're not supposed to pick up land mines?"

Of course Marv continually joked and teased him about the incident. Then one day he turned serious and asked Yankel what was in the boxes that were delivered regularly from the States. Marv was flabbergasted when Yankel admitted it was prescription medications. Yankel had lesions on his cranium. Once Marv learned that, all the joking and teasing was over. The drinking wasn't, though.

Danielle was worried, because she had expected the drinking would stop once he became a father. Like most Jewish girls, she had grown up with the myth that Jewish guys didn't drink. It was the goyim—the Irish especially—who drank, not Jewish boys from New York. Especially one who was the only son of survivors. Right now Ari was too young to know what was going on, but many nights they would fight over Marv's drunken behavior, and Danielle would pray they wouldn't wake Ari up. One night, after Marvin ruined their beautiful Oriental rug by accidentally spilling a liquid cleanser on it, he started blaming her, calling her a ball buster. She got so upset that she ended up sleeping in the car. Then she felt guilty because she had left Ari in the house alone with Marv. Then she felt even guiltier about the way she felt about her husband because she loved him. It wasn't like he drank every night. And when he did drink, it wasn't like he was a violent drunk. Just the opposite.

When he went on a binge, she knew what to expect. The routine had an established pattern. First, he would be happy and quite loveable, and then he would talk nonsense. Finally he would follow her around, telling her how much he loved her and trying to get her in bed. After she had run away from him or played possum under the sheets, she would eventually find him passed out on the floor. Sometimes she'd have to step over his unconscious body to get around the apartment. It was so undignified. Actually, it was just plain disgusting. Especially since he had no reason to do this. They had everything a young couple could want—a beautiful home, business, and child, and now she thought she might be pregnant again. She could never leave Marv. Not after he had saved her from all those terrible things that happened when she was single.

Still, she was embarrassed even people outside their intimate circle knew that Marv drank. When they had the big Purim party, he got so loaded that on the way home, he carried her up the stairs and into the living room of the wrong house! Thank God that couple wasn't doing anything intimate or embarrassing! They were just sitting with another couple, having some coffee and cake, when Marv barged in carrying her like a sack of flour. The other two couples were so astounded, all they did was stare. No one made a sound, and then Danielle, regaining a semblance of civility, managed a very embarrassed, "Sorry!" Marv quickly put her down, and they ran out the door. She hoped it all had happened so fast, no one would recall their faces. The worst thing was that her dear husband didn't even remember the incident and accused her of making it up. She couldn't help being ashamed, but it wasn't like everyone else in Yamit was an angel. No, she knew that the couple Udi and Lili were playing around with was, of all people, Jeannie and her husband Tsvi! Who would have ever thought Jeannie would do that? She had seemed like such a prude when they shared that apartment in Beer Sheva. She had even complained to Danielle that she was embarrassed because she could hear Marv and her when they made love. The funny thing was, she and Marv never heard Jeannie and her husband making love.

Every time Danielle remembered the time they had Udi and Lili over for dinner, she cringed. Soon after had they first moved to Yamit, both she and Marv had been glad that another young American couple had bought a home down the block. Lili had been born and raised in the United States, while Udi's parents had made aliyah after his bar mitzvah. He was tall and good looking with curly brown hair, and had the cockiness of a sabra. She dressed in the new bohemian look, had gone to the University of California in Berkeley, and moved with the grace of a dancer. Both of them enjoyed a good laugh and were good natured enough not to embarrass Danielle after she accidentally used laundry detergent instead of salt when cooking their Shabbat dinner. Even now, more than a year later, she couldn't believe she was so dumb that she'd put them in identical plastic containers and didn't label them.

The week after that Shabbat dinner, either Udi or Lili would stop over to say hello every afternoon. She and Lili played Scrabble while they waited for their husbands to come home from work. Eventually the games felt endless. Or Udi would come over to borrow a tool. She was so naïve that she never realized that there wasn't anything to fix. She hadn't figured that since the houses were brand new and made out of concrete three feet thick, they wouldn't need repairs for a while. She didn't mind at the beginning, and neither did Marv, but pretty soon they just rolled their eyes at each other when they heard one of them at the door. By the end of the week neither one of them would take the subtle suggestion to go home. Finally, one night out of sheer frustration, Marv turned out all the lights and said, "Good night. We're going to sleep now."

Now, according to town gossip, they were wife swapping with Jeannie and Tsvi. Should she worry about them and what they had thought of her and Marvin?

Or maybe she should be concerned about what Mickey Barker thought. He went from one construction job to another, when he could remain sober for a couple of weeks. Even if Myra was trailer-park trash, Danielle felt sorry for his wife having to schlep that cart filled with empty beer bottles every morning. Myra's sister-in-law, though, made her absolutely nauseous. Her hair was so thin and greasy, it would have been a good idea for her to become religious just so she would be forced to cover her head. It was unbelievable, but she did have a lover, just as Danielle had suspected. Her boyfriend was that short fat nebbish guy Shlomo, nee Steven, who was in so much debt to his bookie he'd had to get the hell out of the United States. Between the two of them, they had two spouses and six children!

And to top it off, the whole town was talking about Hannah and her girlfriend Dalit. Danielle had thought Marv was just being cynical when he had called her a dyke, but it looked like he was right. Dalit had made aliyah from South Africa, like a lot of Jews who were afraid of the changes going on in that country. She was very pretty, a great tennis player, and spoke with that beautiful cultured accent. Her husband Isaac was not only the new town doctor, but was so handsome, all the young mothers ran to the clinic the minute their children had a runny nose just to flirt with him. Dalit, like Hannah, had two beautiful children who were about the same age as Hannah's. Danielle would see Hannah and Dalit riding bikes together with their kids. They would always wave and smile, but she noticed that they didn't stop to chat. Danielle hated to believe it, but too many people said they had seen them down at the beach early in the morning with their arms around each other. One woman even reported that she had seen them kissing!

Or maybe she should worry about what Shoshi, Izzy Frankel's wife, thought of Marv? According to the grapevine she was fooling around with Adi, the lifeguard.

Danielle wondered if Shoshi provided him with challah for the Sabbath as an added benefit, since Shoshi was known for her delicious cooking. Until recently she had seemed to spend most of her time in the kitchen, but the word around the city was that she and Izzy had an open marriage. If that was true, then the rabbi was fooling around too. Danielle occasionally wondered with whom, but she didn't really care.

And of course there were Rachel's in-laws, the Shabtais, the first religious family to move in. Because of the trouble Rueven got into embezzling funds from the bank he worked at, the orthodox community of Haifa thought it was best he move to Yamit while he was waiting to go to trial. Whatever the outcome of the trial, he and his family could be far away from all the talk.

Danielle and Marv were sitting on their balcony right before sundown a few days earlier, and Rueven was on his way to synagogue looking like a pompous king penguin. He was dressed all in black except for a white shirt that was pulled tight over his round stomach. His short arms seemed to propel him as he walked with a purposeful stride. His prayer book was tucked under his arm, and he held his head high, as if he were sniffing the purity of the higher realms of the universe. He didn't look right or left but kept his eyes straight ahead, so no one would mistake this for a walk of pleasure.

"What a fucking hypocrite," Marv said, and spat sunflower seeds into an empty ashtray.

"How does he rationalize being a thief?" Danielle wondered aloud as she automatically pushed Ari in his baby swing.

"Easy. He obeys all the rules like wearing his tzitzit and going to synagogue on Shabbat, so in his eyes that makes him a better Jew than the rest of us."

"Yeah, but wrong is wrong. It's like that girl my old college roommate Sarah told me about. Sarah was the kind of girl that everyone talked to, so this girl Chaya came to her one day and told her she was being sexually molested by her uncle. Sarah told her that she had to tell her mother. The mother sent her daughter to study in Jerusalem, I think. Meanwhile, the uncle was still lurking around, probably looking for another victim. Nothing happened to him, and I'm sure he's still davening every day because it's the law. The religious ones are the worst when they're hypocrites. What I don't understand is if they're so afraid of God, why would they do anything that hurts other people?"

"My wife, my life, don't you get it? Their heads are so far up God's ass, they don't even see the connection."

She laughed, once again astounded at his audacity, and then kissed his cheek. "What can I add to that? You just say things so succinctly. I think I'll just go in and make dinner."

Chapter 22

It felt a bit strange to stand on the balcony on Saturday mornings and see tourist buses driving down the road to the beach. Danielle was a little jealous, because the beach was steadily being taken away from her. It was so crowded on Shabbat, she couldn't go down there. Families from Tel Aviv and Jerusalem would come for the day, bringing hampers with enough food to sustain them for a year. Rhoda would complain that the town should pass a law to prohibit food on the beach, because it took money from her coffers. Danielle would sympathize, but she knew Rhoda and Natan were making a good living just selling just ice cream and drinks. After all, they marked up the ice cream more than 100 percent.

Although the beach wasn't as crowded as Danielle knew the Jersey shore got in the summer, it was fast becoming a favorite place for Israelis to visit. Just like explorers marking their territory with their country's flag, each family would plant their umbrellas in their chosen spot. The umbrella served a dual purpose. It not only warded off the unrelenting sun's rays, but it let everyone know that this was their private area. Now that they had found their Eden, they would do their best to protect their sliver of paradise. Rhoda told her that a fight had broken out the previous week, when a guy started yelling at a stranger who stepped over his blanket. The two shouted insults and shook fists at each other. Of course a huge crowd formed, with people taking sides, yelling, and goading the antagonists in the hopes that someone would throw a punch. Eventually, the police intervened, calming the men down before blood was drawn. The disappointed crowd dispersed and went back to lounging and relaxing in the sun. Considering that the beach had been empty just two years ago, the scene was amazing.

The last time Danielle had been on the beach on Shabbat, she could see that many of the tourists were from Sephardic backgrounds, Jews that had fled Arab countries in North Africa and the Middle East, countries like Morocco and Tunisia, Iran and Iraq. Although many came from families that were wealthy and well established in their native countries, when they immigrated to Israel, they were forced by their countries' governments to leave everything behind so many came to Israel poor and, by European standards, uneducated. So in Israel, the homeland of their prayers, their Ashkenazi brethren looked down on them. It reminded Danielle of the waves of immigration in the United States, when the German Jews looked down on the Russians.

Many of the toddlers ran around the beach stark naked. They looked ecstatic in their freedom, reveling in the sensual pleasure of the sea, sun, and sand. She thought that their mothers had the right idea. Maybe she would let Ari go naked too. It made a lot of sense and would save a lot of work. No, on second thought, she couldn't do that. She could hear her mother's voice saying how disgusting and primitive that was.

The changes on the beach weren't the only ones that Danielle noticed as Yamit grew. Even the Bedouin family that lived outside the gates of the city appeared to be prospering. The family still lived in the hut made of mud and sticks, but the old rusted truck had disappeared and a new diesel-fueled Mercedes was parked outside the family compound. If she wasn't mistaken, they had another goat tethered outside too. Apparently they made a good living selling their pita and some fruits and vegetables from their roadside stand.

The previous day the whole town had turned out for a combined Simchat Torah celebration and a reception for a government official who had come to break ground for a memorial to Israel's fallen soldiers. She had actually gotten teary, seeing all the children dressed in blue and white and waving flags as they waited for the first strains of "Hatikva," Israel's national anthem. Then they stood still as they sang the bittersweet lyrics. *Soon*, she had thought, *Ari was going to be one of those children.* She was so glad he was a sabra, a person born in Israel. It was easier to raise children as Jews here than in the United States. Now she was starting to understand why she always felt different. She was.

She was surprised that when she looked around, she only knew a handful of people. When had that happened? Many of the people must live in the apartments that had been completed during the past year.

Shaking off her reverie, Danielle walked back inside. She better stop daydreaming and get busy if she was going to be ready for Ari's birthday party. Marvin was down at the workshop and had said he would be home when he finished the last batch of silver key chains. Since they had got word a tour bus was coming on Monday, he wanted them ready.

As she set the table, she prayed that Mickey Barker didn't stop by to visit Marvin, as he had done the previous week. They must have sat there all afternoon bullshitting and drinking, otherwise the accident wouldn't have happened. She literally got nauseated when she thought about finding Marvin after he fell down the stairs.

He had been so unsteady on his feet that when he tripped near the top step, he hit the railing and cut his head. She heard the thud and came running out just as he was trying to get up. He was unaware of the stream of blood running down his face. She screamed so loud when she saw the blood that Arianna heard her and came out to see what was wrong. She called the doctor and then ran to get towels. In the end he needed six stitches and a tetanus shot. Just thinking about it made her sick and angry, and she didn't want her mood to ruin Ari's second birthday.

She had set up the table on the balcony because she was having their whole little American group, and of course their children, over for cake and ice cream. Yankel's wife, Patti, would be over with little Yossi who, everyone was starting to realize, was a little slow. Sarah, who had moved in with her schlub of a husband about six months ago, was sweet and good natured. She had been a registered nurse in the States and was planning to teach a Lamaze childbirth course. It would be just in time for Danielle's second birth. Danielle liked her a lot, but her two-year-old daughter Ruti was obnoxious and wild. It was hard to be around her, so Danielle didn't see as much of Sarah as she would have liked Of course Rachel would be over with Battia, and their little group would schmooze, laugh, and good naturedly complain about their husbands while keeping an eye on their children. She felt sorry for women in the United States, like her old friend Karen, who was stuck out in the suburbs with two little boys under five years old. Her letters were always so bitter because she felt isolated.

Suddenly Danielle felt cramps in her uterus. More curious than concerned, she went into the bathroom. When she pulled her pants down she saw a dark stain on her underpants. The blood drained from her face.

"God, please," she whispered. "Please don't let me lose this baby. Please, please, God."

She was too afraid to get off the seat, fearful any movement would jar the fragile life within her, and she could hear Ari waking up from his nap.

Trying to be logical instead of giving in to panic, she realized there was no actual blood flow. Okay, that was good. She wiped herself, pulled up her pants, and while she was washing her hands realized that she shouldn't pick up Ari. He would just have to wait. Although it felt like hours, just a few minutes later Sarah rapped lightly at the door. Danielle let her in and almost fell into her arms.

"Oh, Sarah, just the person I need."

"What's wrong, Danielle? You look terrified." Sarah quickly put the wrapped present she had brought on the nearest chair.

"I had what felt like a contraction and found blood on my underpants."

"How much?" Sarah asked professionally.

"Not a lot. Kind of like the last day of a period. Tell me the truth, Sarah. Am I going to lose this baby?"

"To be honest, I don't know. First, lie down. Come, let me make you comfortable on the couch." She lifted her daughter Ruti into Ari's playpen. "I'll call the doctor and see what he says. Do you want me to call Marv? "

Danielle hesitated. "Let's see what the doctor says," she finally said.

Sarah was already dialing Isaac, the South African doctor, and Danielle listened as she described the situation and answered his questions. Lying there on the couch, she felt relieved knowing she was in capable hands. Sarah hung up the phone and said that he would be over in a couple of minutes.

Danielle shook her head. "What a birthday party. Oy, I hear Rachel and Battia coming up the stairs."

She automatically started to get up, but Sarah told her to stay.

Little Battia walked in with Rachel right behind her. She was dressed like a little doll in a pink and white dotted Swiss dress that her grandmother had sent from the States. She ran over to Danielle to excitedly show her the "big girl" pink nail polish her mommy had brushed on to match her dress. Rachel didn't say anything, but questioned Danielle with her eyes. Danielle hugged Battia and told her how beautiful she looked, and then said that she should go into Ari's room. He had just woken up and was still in his crib.

"I'm going in to Ari to sing 'Yom Huledet Same'ach,' Ima," Battia proudly informed her mother.

"Okay, Bebe, he'll love that," Rachel replied offhandedly, her attention on Danielle.

Danielle smiled weakly. "I'm sure she'll put on some show."

As soon as Battia was out of the room, Rachel demanded to know what was wrong.

"Actually, we don't know," Danielle said. "I stained a little, so Sarah called the doctor, who's on his way over. That's the story."

Rachel turned to Sarah. "Nu, is she going to miscarry?"

"I don't know. Let's wait for the doctor."

When Patti showed up, she immediately offered to take the kids over to her house across the way.

"That's a good idea," Rachel said. "I'll get Ari up and ready and then come over with him and Battia." She turned to Danielle. "We'll come back over later and see what's what."

Danielle was so grateful for all the help, she didn't know what to say except thanks.

Once the tumult of the kids leaving was over and they couldn't hear their voices anymore, Sarah offered to make tea. Danielle declined, saying she didn't want to put her friend to anymore trouble.

"What are you talking about? It's just hot water and a tea bag. It's not even mine. It's yours, so what's the big deal? Isaac should be here any minute," she called over her shoulder as she started for the tiny kitchen.

"The tea bags are in the cabinet next to the refrigerator. God, Sarah, if I wasn't so worried I could enjoy this pampering."

A heavy knock at the door announced the doctor. When he stuck his head inside and called "Shalom," Danielle felt her body heat up. He sure was good looking.

"Nu, what happened Dani?" he asked in his intriguing South African accent. "Sarah said there was some spotting."

"*Nachon*, I felt a cramp or a contraction, and when I went to the bathroom there was a little blood on my underpants." As Danielle answered, a little abashedly, she noticed that he had a small scar near his right eye and wondered how that happened.

"When was your last period?" he continued professionally.

"I guess about ten weeks ago."

"Okay, all I need to do is an internal exam to see what's going on. Do you want to go to the office or should we just go into the bedroom?"

"Oh, doctor," Danielle said flirtatiously, "you mean now I can tell all the girls that we went into the bedroom together?"

He grinned. "You hear that, Sarah? Suddenly Dani is thinking how to make babies, not about saving this one."

Danielle was so surprised, she couldn't come back with anything witty. She just hoped he didn't know how close to the mark he hit. Although she found herself almost hypnotized by his accent and lanky frame, she mentally scanned the bedroom and was relieved that she had made the bed that morning. She wondered if Isaac's wife was a good housekeeper, since she had heard knew that in South Africa every white family had maids and houseboys.

"I'm going to wash out this cup," Sarah called from the kitchen, "so Isaac can have tea with us when you're done, and then I'll be right in. So no hanky panky, you guys."

Trying to keep her eyes off him, Danielle focused on a small crack in the wall that she had just noticed.

Isaac picked up his black bag and said, "Come, Dani. Let's see what mischief we can do before Sarah gets done."

Danielle pretended she didn't hear his comment and followed him into the bedroom, pausing to grab a towel from the linen closet.

Isaac saw the towel and nodded his approval. "Hopefully though, there won't be any more blood. Nu, I know this must feel awkward for you, so we'll wait for Sarah."

"Did I just hear my name?" Sarah asked as she bustled in. "Dani, I think the best way to do this is to take off your bottoms and cover yourself with the throw. Then Isaac can examine you and you'll feel comfortable. With luck, everything will be fine. Come, Isaac, let's give Dani some privacy."

Danielle nodded, relieved that she didn't have to get undressed in front of the doctor. "It will take two seconds."

Sarah signaled for Isaac to come with her and then shut the door behind them. "Just call when you're done. We're right here."

Dani was already out of her cutoffs and panties, but decided to switch the cotton ones she was wearing with the new lace bikini ones she had never worn because they had to be hand washed. She quickly threw the stained ones in the hamper and ripped the tag off the sexy new ones. After laying the new panties on top of her cutoffs, she covered herself with the EL AL throw her mother had taken from the airline as a souvenir and presented to Danielle the last time she had visited.

"Okay, guys, you can come in now," she called.

"All right, Dani, just lie back on the pillow and put your knees up." The teasing tone disappeared as the doctor took control. "The speculum may be a little cold because I just swabbed it with alcohol."

Danielle tensed in reaction to the shock of cold metal sliding into her vagina.

"Just try and relax," Isaac said as his hand investigated her womb.

Danielle tried to read the verdict by watching his body language. Judging from his distant, professional expression, bad news was all she could expect. She closed her eyes and waited for the verdict, promising herself that she wouldn't cry. *Having a miscarriage wasn't the worst thing in the world,* she thought. *It would be much worse to have an abnormal baby. Not just worse—unbearable.* Her mother said that a miscarriage was a blessing in disguise, because it meant something was wrong with the fetus.

"Okay," Isaac said. *"Beseder,* Dani. It's okay."

His words were so unexpected, she immediately sat up. "Do you mean okay, as in 'okay the examination's over,' or okay as in 'the baby looks okay'?"

"Both, Dani."

Without thinking Danielle hugged him because she was so happy, and was surprised that he hugged her back.

"You mean that?" she asked, looking directly into his eyes and thinking she had never seen such green eyes before.

"Yes, I do. But that doesn't mean I want you picking up Ari or riding your bike. As a matter of fact, just to err on the side of caution, I want you to stay off your feet for a week. "

"How am I going to do that? I have to take care of Ari. I have the store too."

"You have Marvin," he said.

Danielle didn't even hear as she continued her frantic litany. "And the cooking, and the laundry, and ..." Isaac's comment registered. "Oh, God, you don't know him, Isaac. I don't know how willing he'll be."

"He's your husband. And Ari's father."

Thankfully Sarah spoke up, assuring Danielle that she and the other women would help with anything she needed.

"Starting now," she added. "I saw you were defrosting a chicken. I'll put that in the oven with some potatoes. You have some, yes?"

"Yes. Yes, of course, and there're carrots in the bin. How can I thank you for all the help, Sarah?"

"Nonsense. Just a thank you is fine. You would do the same for me. I know that. Besides, someday you'll do a good deed for someone who needs it. That's the payback. Now get comfortable. Why don't I call Marvin and tell him to come home? That way Isaac can talk to him face to face."

"That sounds fine, Sarah. Do you have the time to wait until he gets here, Isaac?" Danielle asked, relieved that Sarah was so competent.

"Sure, no problem. I'll finally get to have that cup of tea Sarah promised."

Now that the crisis was over, Danielle felt even more awkward with Isaac. What could she possibly say to this very sexy and very married man who just had his hand up her vagina? Apparently nothing, because at that moment she heard the front door open. When she turned her head, Marvin was standing in the bedroom doorway, Sarah right behind him. He looked disheveled, and she prayed that it was from working all morning in the electroplating room and not from nipping at the bottle that she was now sure he kept down there.

"What's going on?" he asked belligerently. Danielle recognized that tone of fear in his voice, even though he tried to cover it up.

"Nothing really, Marv. Come sit down," she said as she patted the edge of the bed next to her.

"Standing is good," he said as he stared at Isaac. "I can tell the news isn't, though. So just tell me quick and fast."

"No, Marv," Isaac said, walking over to Marv. "Everything is okay. Much better than Danielle imagined when Sarah called me."

Danielle was amazed how professional Isaac had become. In that instant, she could feel Marv's defensiveness disappear. It was like Isaac had just soothed a wild beast.

"Okay," Marvin said. "So why did she call you?"

"Well, Danielle found some blood and asked Sarah to call me. She was afraid that it was a miscarriage, but if Danielle takes precautions, everything should be fine. I recommend that she not overexert herself, and that she rests in bed for the next week."

Danielle thought that now would be a good time to ask. "What about Ari, doctor?"

"I'm sure Marvin will help in every way possible," he said, looking pointedly at Marv.

"Of course," Marv said gruffly. "What do I owe you?"

Danielle felt guilty comparing Marvin to Isaac as the two men stood side by side, but she couldn't help it. Isaac seemed so cultured and gentlemanly. Marv just seemed so … boorish.

"You owe me nothing," Isaac answered. "Believe me, I'm just glad I could help. Besides, did you forget that this is a socialist country? I'm just another government worker."

"Thank you both so much for all your time and concern," Danielle interrupted. "Now that Marv is here, he'll be able to get Ari. Isaac, Sarah, both of you go and enjoy the rest of the day."

"I'll stop in tomorrow to see how you are," Sarah said.

"That will be great."

Isaac picked up his black bag . "Remember, don't get out of bed unless you're going to the bathroom."

"Then I guess I can't walk you to the door," Danielle joked. "Sarah, tell Rachel Marv will come get Ari in a moment."

The other two left. The moment the door shut Marv shook his head and declared, "What a faggot. No wonder his wife is licking Hannah's pussy." Then, almost as an afterthought, he asked, "So, does anything hurt?"

"Not now. I had a little cramping and spotting, so Sarah decided to call Isaac. But how can you call him a faggot? He just happens to be nice and polite. Classy. Remember, he's from South Africa, not New York City, New York. We were lucky that he was nice enough to come over. And he didn't even want to be paid."

"He got paid, all right."

"Marv, what are you talking about?"

"By diddling your pussy."

"What? You just called him a faggot. You can't have it both ways. Now, hopefully everything will be okay. So do me a favor, go get Ari so Rachel isn't stuck with him while she's trying to prepare supper."

"Your wish is my command, madam." He bowed playfully, and she figured it was his way of apologizing. "I'll be back with him in a minute. Don't go away."

"I thought I'd go for a run," she said, throwing the pillow at him as he left. Once he was gone, she mentally crossed her fingers that he really would help her and that he would not guess that Isaac was very, very heterosexual.

Chapter 23

Two more days and this long week would be over. Danielle couldn't wait to be up and about again, especially since it was pretty damn embarrassing how Marv got everyone to watch the baby. He had even gotten Arianna, that big, fat blob downstairs, to make two or three meals. That meant Danielle would have to help her with her kids when she was on her feet again.

Already bored even though the day had just begun, she picked up the *Time* magazine that lay beside her. It had the new president, Jimmy Carter, on its cover. She turned to the article about him again. Just looking at his picture gave her the creeps. She couldn't stand his phony smile and holier-than-thou attitude. She certainly could see why a lot of Israelis didn't trust him. How the hell did he get to be president? He was just a peanut farmer from some backwater in Georgia, for God's sake.

According to the article he was pushing hard for a peace plan in the Middle East, and the buzz was that Sadat would make a trip to Jerusalem to demonstrate his goodwill. How was that going to affect them here in Yamit? Danielle didn't want to think about it, but she'd heard rumors that the Israeli government was going to give this land back to Egypt. Better not to think about it.

Another couple of hours and Minna would be bringing Ari back from the *gan*. Danielle didn't know how he did it, but Marv managed to get every one of their friends to help with Ari so he didn't have to. Thank God Rifka's daughter Minna loved Ari like her own little brother and was delighted that she could babysit for him every day.

Danielle sighed and admonished herself for complaining. She should look at the positive. At least Marvin did something. It could be worse. At least he took Ari to the gan every morning after she fed and diapered him.

Within twenty-four hours of the beginning of her mandatory bed rest, the bedroom became the center of operations. Since Marvin complained about feeding Ari, Danielle told him to set the high chair next to the bed. That way she could feed Ari his breakfast and dinner just by swinging her legs over the side of the bed. Dirty diapers posed a different problem. After she nagged him for most of the first evening, Marvin finally put into the washer the load of dirty diapers that had been soaking. Minna could hang them up in the morning.

She had gotten halfway through the article when she heard a knock at the door. Grateful that a visitor would break up the monotony of the day, Danielle cheerfully called, "Come in." Even though it was still early, she expected to see Rachel, who stopped in every afternoon.

"Hey, Dani."

Danielle felt her stomach tighten when she saw who it was, and prayed she looked composed and nonchalant.

"Well, Dr. Rosenberg, what a nice surprise." She smiled and batted her lashes in a well-practiced manner. "I do believe this is twice that I've rated a home visit."

"And why not?" Isaac replied, just the trace of a smile on his face. "You're my prettiest patient."

"Well, thank you kindly, sir," she said in a Southern accent. "Ah do believe you are a flatterer." She extended her arm in a welcoming gesture. "Welcome to my humble, and very messy, center of operations."

To Danielle's surprise and delight, Isaac played along, bowing deeply before kissing her hand in imitation of a courtly Southern gentleman. Then the two of them looked at each other and started laughing.

"I guess Jimmy Carter was stuck in my head," Danielle said as she held up the magazine cover to show him. "What do you think this Bible Belt farmer is going to do?"

"I don't know, but I'm sure Prime Minister Begin will never give an inch."

"What makes you so sure about that?" Danielle asked, although that it was difficult to act like an intelligent human being while looking at Isaac's green eyes. Actually, when she looked again, she thought she might have caught some flecks of amber. And if his looks and charm weren't enough, she also had to pretend that he wasn't sitting on the edge of her bed. Wrong, it wasn't her bed. It belonged to her and Marvin—her husband and Ari's father.

"He's not only prime minister and the head of Likud," Isaac answered, "but when he was young he was one of the Stern gang. You know, the group that blew up the King David Hotel."

"Oh, right. Weren't they considered terrorists?"

"*Nachon.* David Ben-Gurion and his boys disagreed with the strategy and felt negotiating would work better. Big difference philosophically. Ben-Gurion got out of Europe before the war, while Begin was a survivor and came to Israel with another perspective entirely. But the truth is, a phone call was placed to the hotel before it was bombed in order to give the Brits a chance to get away before it went off."

"Nu, how do you know so much Israeli history?" Danielle asked.

Isaac picked up the pack of cigarettes lying on the blanket and asked if he could take one. Danielle automatically said yes. As he lit it, she thought, *Uh-oh, it looks like he's staying for a while. This could get dangerous.* She adjusted her pillows to get more comfortable while he started telling her the story of how his parents made it to Cape Town from Kobe, Japan, during World War II.

"Did you say from Japan?"

"That's right. Not too many Jews know the story of Mr. Sugihara."

"I'm one of them."

Isaac smiled, and Danielle noticed that he only had one dimple.

"He was just a civil servant who turned out to be a very brave and compassionate man. He was a Japanese consul general who disregarded his governmental orders and saved thousands of Jews."

"How?" Danielle asked.

"By stamping their visas for entry into Japan. Of course, the Japanese government wasn't happy about that arrangement. So, once the Jews started to arrive, they were asked to leave as soon as possible. The Japanese government shipped them out to new unknown shores. That's how many Jews emigrated to South Africa, including my parents."

"I never heard that story. That's astounding."

"Yes, he and his wife risked their lives to help us. Eventually, his government stripped him of his post and livelihood. And the irony is, he had never even met a Jew until he was dispatched there."

"Thank God there are people like him." *Otherwise*, she added silently, *there wouldn't be people like you.*

"My father's visa was one of the last ones he stamped. The rest of his family never made it out." Isaac took another drag on his cigarette and watched the smoke disappear into the air before he looked at Danielle.

As usual, anytime she heard wartime stories her throat would tighten and her eyes get teary, but she tried to stay calm by asking, "So, both your parents came from Latvia originally?"

"No, my mom was saved in one of those kiddie transports sent from Germany, and then a British family adopted her and brought her to Cape Town. The South African Jewish community is made up of many survivors. That's why it's so Zionistic."

"That makes sense, but it seems like a lot of your generation are making aliyah. At WOJS I knew a couple of students from South Africa as well as Rhodesia, and then of course there's that *moshav* that grows the hydroponic tomatoes."

"Excuse me, but you must mean tomahtos," Isaac said with a twinkle in his eye.

"No, I meant exactly what I said," Danielle retorted. "Tomatoes. And since I am a Jersey tomato, as Marv likes to say, then I must know how to pronounce it."

"Aha! But since the *moshav* is a South African entity, then they must be pronounced tomahtos."

Danielle was glad to see that Isaac had a quick wit, but what was she thinking? Quickly she started a silent mantra: *I am married.*

I have been married for three years to Marvin Steinberg and we are the parents of Ari, who has two sets of grandparents—

"Dani, I just asked you how you were feeling. You must not have heard me."

"You're right, Isaac, I didn't." And she could die of embarrassment that she had been so lost in her lascivious thoughts that she hadn't even heard the object of her lust.

"What were you thinking?" he asked softly, slipping his hand over hers.

Danielle looked straight into those spectacular green eyes and lied so perfectly, she almost believed herself. "I was thinking about whether Minna will have to do a load of clothes as well as hang Ari's diapers when she comes over."

"And what was your conclusion?" he asked, grinning as she slid her hand away and started fiddling with the blanket.

"That it was very nice that you stopped by to check on me, doctor."

"Any more bleeding?" he asked, apparently reading her cue and turning serious,

"No, thank God."

"Okay, Dani. Finish out the week of bed rest just to make sure."

"You're the boss, doctor," she said, trying for a light tone.

"Oh, and one more thing," he said over his shoulder as he walked to the bedroom door.

"Yes, Detective Columbo?"

"I'll stop by tomorrow."

Danielle was so happy, her heart felt like it would burst with joy. Still, she managed to answer nonchalantly, "Sure. I'll be here."

"Good. I'll see myself out."

Oh my God, Danielle thought once he was gone. *What the hell am I doing?*

Chapter 24

"Minna, I don't know how I could have gotten through this without you," Danielle said, folding the clothes as Rivka's daughter took them off the clothesline. She breathed deeply and turned her face to the sun. Sitting on the balcony was a treat she would no longer take for granted after the frustration of staying in bed for a week.

"And I don't know if I ever would have learned how to play Scrabble if I wasn't over here every day," Minna said. "Besides, I love Ari. He's the cutest baby in Yamit."

"What are you going to say when the new one is born?" Danielle teased.

"I'm going to say that they are the two cutest babies in Yamit."

"Ari's going to be a big boy already. Thank God he's potty trained. I don't think I could have handled diapers for two."

"Look at him, Danielle. He is so proud of that tricycle."

Both peered over the railing to watch Ari straining to peddle the bright yellow tricycle his paternal grandpa had sent to him from Germany, where he had gone for business recently. The moment Marvin had put it together, Ari climbed on the seat and worked very hard to reach the pedals. As they watched, Minna suggested that they add blocks to the pedals. That way he could really get somewhere and she wouldn't have to worry about him standing up and falling.

"That's a terrific idea," Danielle said. "Maybe Marv can use a couple of blocks from that building set Ari got for his birthday. Did you want to eat supper with us, Minna? It won't be much more than scrambled eggs and cantaloupe, but I can promise you there's still enough chocolate cake left from yesterday."

"That was so nice of the doctor to bring that! Yummy too."

"Mmm." Danielle's body tensed just at the thought of Isaac, but she continued to make small talk. "I didn't know his brother-in-law owned that bakery on Hayarkon Street."

"Me neither, but my mom goes in there all the time while she's waiting for the bus. That's why she's so fat."

"Minna, that's not nice."

"Well, it's true." She added petulantly, "Maybe if my mom didn't get fat then my dad wouldn't have left her for Janice."

Danielle shook her head. "Not true. Your mom is one of the nicest people I have ever met. Talented too."

"If she's so nice, why did he leave her ... and ... and us?"

"I don't know, *chamudi*. Sometimes love just isn't enough. One decision can change your life. Nobody's perfect and we all make mistakes."

"I'm not getting married." Minna shook her head, sending her cherubic curls dancing. "No way, no how, nowhere. 'Cause no one around here is happy. Except maybe Rachel and Natan. And of course, you and Marv."

"Hmm." Danielle nodded in agreement, but she thought of Rivka arriving at her home almost in a state of panic after Ari was born, bringing a dire warning.

"Make sure you give Marv attention. Go out for a walk together. Do something," she advised. "Men need attention." Then she added softly, "That was my mistake."

Danielle didn't want to make a mistake. She would not be one of those sad marital statistics that seemed to be a staple of newspapers and magazines. Society was changing. Divorce was no longer an embarrassment. In some cases it seemed to be de rigueur. She saw it differently though. At the wedding, the two of them had stood under the chuppah and vowed "till death do us part." That meant something. It had to, or else why get married? Marv was just a little immature still. At least that was what she kept telling herself. Things were going to get better. Besides, she had a new baby coming. She had everything she wanted. She loved being a mother. She loved

Marv, her home, her friends, and especially Yamit. Then why did she look for Isaac everywhere she went? Even when she knew he was at the hospital and there was no chance she would catch a glimpse of him.

Danielle was excited that she would be back at work the next day, just in time for a big tourist group from the United States. The Hadassah women could always be counted on to spend a lot of money. All the groups that came, from national groups like Hadassah to small local organizations like the Peoria Men's Club, wanted to do their share to help Israel. Spending a lot of money was a mitzvah that all American tourists believed in. It didn't matter if they were religious or not, prayed at every minyan or hadn't set foot in a synagogue since the last Rosh Hashanah and Yom Kippur. Since it was a win-win situation, everyone was happy. Retailers made money and paid their bills, and the customers got quality product for their money. The best part was that they could go home and show off the beautiful Israeli mezuzah or bracelet they had bought and brag about the big bargain they got. Besides, it assuaged the guilt that was unconsciously part of their psyche. Didn't every Jew say those words, "Next year in Jerusalem" at every seder, in every country, every year since time immemorial, and then sit at that same table the very next year and recite those very same words?

Danielle felt guilty herself when she thought about all the support the American synagogues had given them. As a matter of fact, their business wouldn't even survive without support from the Jews in America. Her mother, accustomed to Danielle's decision to live in Israel, had become their top promoter and sales manager in America. Thanks to her mother, many New Jersey synagogue gift shops carried their silver jewelry. It bothered Danielle that her mother didn't even take ten dollars for herself. Izzy's father-in law, the big jewelry distributor, had refused to help them at all. He just wanted his daughter home.

Maybe in a couple of weeks, Danielle mused, she'd be able to take a tour group around the city the way she had done before she ended up in bed. The last time she'd been able to walk as far as the pool, it was still being built. Rachel said that the Misrad Ha Pinui, the Office of the Interior, had finished all of the landscaping and people were starting to use the tennis courts. She couldn't wait to see it, because she was starting to think that this was all just a dream.

Didn't her grandma used to say, *"Life is a dream. It passes by in front of your eyes"*? She was afraid she was starting to see what her grandma meant. Just as her life was starting to get normal again, she was hearing about returning the Sinai to Egypt. Some people said that this new president, Jimmy Carter, wanted a Nobel Peace Prize and was looking at the Middle East to help him. The day before Rachel had told her it looked like Sadat was going to come to Jerusalem. Danielle didn't like that at all. It was just a show to make himself look good in the eyes of the world and put the onus on Begin. He would have to do something in return, otherwise he would look horrible. The whole world was watching.

"Minna, while you're here I'm going to go down to the grocery store and get a couple of things. I'll be back in about a half hour."

"Sure. I'll sit down at the sandbox so I can keep a closer eye on Ari."

"Sure you don't mind?"

"No, Danielle, I'm just glad you can be on your feet."

"I think you're glad that the sandbox is right outside Shaul's house too," Danielle said with a laugh, but stopped when she saw Minna's face turn red.

She gave Minna a quick hug and then walked over to the kitchen door to grab the net bag to carry groceries.

"I'll be back in a little while," she called.

She carefully held onto the railing, afraid she'd fall down the steps. Her family had always called her klutzy, and for a good reason. So she didn't want to take a chance, not when she was almost safe. She pretended that she didn't see Marjorie Ben-David hanging up her laundry while she screamed at her two little boys, who were running through the jungle of drying sheets and pillowcases. *Wouldn't that be the ultimate cosmic joke if the messiah came through the Ben-David clan,* she thought. God should forgive her, but she had never known that a woman could be that ugly. Not only did she have pock mocks and hair growing on her chin, but massive layers of fat hung from her upper arms, and her breasts drooped down to her stomach. Everyone said her family had money. Why else would Shlomo have married her, except for the benefits of marrying a wealthy American, even a fat and ugly one?

And Marvin called her fat! So she had gained weight lying in bed all day. It hadn't been funny when he'd covered his eyes with his pillow the night before as she got ready for bed.

"Look at you," a man said from behind her. "A real *balabusta* doing your own shopping."

Danielle flushed when she heard Isaac's voice, but she managed to act light and playful as she turned to him.

"Ye s, it's time. Inertia was setting in. I think my legs forgot how to walk. I've been so spoiled by Minna and my other friends, it's going to be difficult to get back to normal."

"Personally I liked spoiling you."

"Who included you, doctor?" Danielle raised her eyebrow and smiled the half smile that her father said reminded him of the look on the Mona Lisa. Her mother called it stupid.

"Then I guess tomorrow," he said, "when I go to Tel Aviv, I won't have to bring back that cheesecake from the bakery. I don't want to start spoiling you now."

"Well, now that you mention it, that cheesecake is pretty tempting."

"So tomorrow we'll celebrate that you're on your feet."

"Since I start work tomorrow, that would be lovely. How about three o'clock before I have to get Ari?"

"Certainly, I'm always at your service." Isaac bowed gallantly and then excused himself, saying he had someone waiting for him in his office. "Until tomorrow, Dani."

Oh my God, she thought. *There wasn't even a pretense of a doctor-patient relationship any longer. What the hell had she done?*

Chapter 25

With the Grateful Dead's "Sugar Magnolia" playing on the stereo, Danielle unpacked the items in her blue string bag and daydreamed about seeing Isaac. She still felt guilty about being so excited to see him. Somehow she knew this was different from all the times he had come over to "check" on her. Maybe because this time he wasn't using the excuse that she was bedridden and could have a miscarriage.

She heard Minna and Ari coming up the stairs, chattering and singing.

"Let's count the stairs, Ari 'One, two …'"

"'Bugga my shoe,'" Ari said.

"'Three, four …'"

Danielle could hear Ari stomping on each stair. "'Tree, four, shut the door.'"

"Be careful so you don't fall."

Danielle opened the door, smiling as she watched Ari finish climbing the stairs.

"Imala!" he said when he saw her.

"Watch. Hold onto the railing."

"Imala, Battia play too!"

"They started throwing sand at each other," Minna said, "so I figured that was enough. That's why he's got sand in his hair."

"No problem, I'm going to give him a shower now anyway."

"You sure you can do it all by yourself?"

"Absolutely. It's time that everything got back to normal. Let me give you this." She pulled a fifty lirot note from her pocket. "Thanks, Minna. Thanks for taking such good care of Ari."

"I love him, Danielle, and I love you too. Thanks." Minna handed her charge over and glanced at the crumpled note. "Hey, you don't owe me this much."

"I know, but I wanted you to know how much I appreciate you."

"Thanks. I'm going to put it toward a set of pastels. We started working with them at school and I really like using them."

"*Ima.*"

They both turned toward the voice and started laughing when they saw a naked Ari standing there looking impatient.

"Okay," Danielle said, "it looks like someone's ready for his shower. Lahit, Minna."

Danielle took her son into the bathroom and washed him while she listened to his babble and chatter about the day. Kris Kristofferson had replaced the Dead on the stereo, and as she listened to him sing about "Sunday Morning Coming Down," she thought about how Isaac kind of resembled him, except for having green eyes instead of blue, and she wondered what was going to happen tomorrow and if she was going to wake up the next day hating herself.

"Come on, Arilah," she said to her son. "Let me dry you off, then we'll go in the kitchen and you'll have a nosh before Abba comes home."

Wrapping him in the bath towel, Danielle patted him dry and breathed in the wondrous fragrance of her son as she rubbed baby lotion into his skin. She made a raspberry into his tummy, and Ari laughed in delight.

After he was dry, she told him to go into the kitchen and climb into his high chair. She watched him, holding her breath as he scrambled like a little monkey onto the closest chair and then hopped into his high chair, grinning with satisfaction. Joining him, she placed sliced cucumbers and carrots on his plate. As he ate, she looked at her kitchen and wondered why anyone would design a home with a kitchen so tiny. It was so small and cramped, she could stand in the center of the room and open the refrigerator door on one side, or grab silverware from a drawer on the other side. And as she gazed at her son, who was singing joyfully about a little clown instead of eating his cucumbers, she suddenly got an overwhelming sense of homesickness for her parents and the rest of her family.

What a difference! Her mother's kitchen, which some people considered small, was big enough for a family of six. Certainly all of them could comfortably sit around the Formica-topped table, play games of Scrabble and Chinese checkers while their indecently loud conversations were occasionally punctuated with yelling and tears, but mostly with lots of teasing and laughter. She couldn't imagine what Marvin's family did in the evenings. Did they all sit in the living room vigilantly listening for the dreaded sound of pounding knocks on the door? Or were they just incredulous when another day passed and they awoke safely in their beds instead of in a cattle car?

As she started preparing Marvin's favorite dinner of schnitzel—a thin breaded chicken fillet—mashed potatoes, and salad, she glanced at the clock and realized it was getting late. Any minute she'd hear his booming voice doing a bad imitation of Desi Arnez. Instead of bellowing, "Lucy, I'm home," it would be, "Danielle, I'm here." She hoped he would be sober.

Just as she was growing perturbed, because everything was getting cold, she heard his loud, "Shalom, *habibi*," to their downstairs neighbor as he passed by.

"Here's Abba," Danielle announced to Ari, who was playing with a toy.

"Abba!" Ari shrieked in delight as the door opened and he recognized his father's voice.

"Stay in your seat," Danielle warned, knowing her son would use this as an excuse to jump out of his high chair.

Marvin walked over to Ari and patted him on his head. To Danielle, he said, "What's for supper?" He sat on a chair and pulled her onto his lap.

Checking his eyes and smelling his breath were the first things Danielle did every time he returned from anywhere, and she concluded he was close to sober. That didn't mean he would be there later, but for now he was okay.

"Your favorite - schnitzel. I just need to put it back in the oven for a few minutes to warm up."

"Stop for a minute, babe, and let's have a drink. I've got good news."

"No. You know I don't drink when I'm pregnant. Besides, dinner's ready and I'm starved."

"Come on. I'm not telling you what happened until you get the bottle down."

"How about we eat dinner first and then you have a drink afterward?"

"How about you stop acting like my mother and start acting like my wife?" Marvin retorted.

Danielle knew it was futile. Resignedly, she took the bottle down and watched him break the seal.

"What are you waiting for?" he said. "Glasses! We need two glasses."

"One glass is fine, Marv. I told you, I can't drink."

"Enough with that lemon face. What kind of celebration is this?"

"You tell me."

"We got that airport account."

"What?" she exclaimed.

"You heard me. My wife, my life, we're going to supply the jewelry store at the airport."

"Oh, my God, Marvin. That's wonderful! And if my mother hadn't stopped in and talked to them, it wouldn't have happened."

His festive spirits disappeared like a picnic lunch during a sudden downpour.

"Who cares if your mother helped?" he said.

"Marvin, I didn't mean anything. Nothing. You're right. Who cares?"

Her whole body had tensed, because she knew she was already at the point of no return.

"It sounded to me like it did matter," he said. "Like, without your parents, where would we be?"

"Really, I didn't mean it that way. All I meant was that it was nice that my mother helped us. Nothing more, nothing less."

"And if I didn't work like a dog while you stayed home getting personal doctor visits …"

"I know, Marv, I know. I've told you. I'm going to come down to the store tomorrow. What did you want me to do? Lose the baby?"

"You don't miss what you never had," he snapped.

Danielle stared at him, realizing that he meant it. He didn't want another baby. How could that be? Without saying a word to him, she turned and walked out of the room. Tears already blinding her, she stumbled into their bedroom. Lying on the bed, she took deep breaths through her tears and tried to make sense of the muddle in her brain.

What the hell could she do? She'd had no idea he didn't want this baby. This couldn't be true. How could he not want their baby? He never said anything until now. Had he meant it?

She heard him rolling around on the floor with Ari like nothing had happened. Maybe he didn't mean it. Just like he hadn't meant it when he called her fat. What a dummy she was. She opened her eyes, and he was standing in the door holding their son.

"Sorry," he said.

"What do you mean by 'sorry,' Marv? Sorry that you hurt me, sorry that you don't want this baby, or sorry that you're turning into a drunk?"

She had to give him credit. He didn't even blink an eye. "Now, now, my wife, my life, you're scaring our son. This is supposed to be a happy occasion. Calm yourself down my honey, my bunny. You're making a big deal out of nothing."

"Calm down?" she shouted. "You don't want this baby. And that's nothing in your book? What the hell is wrong with you ? Do you think your mother crawled out of Auschwitz for this, to live to see a drunken son that doesn't want any more children? Guess what, Marv? Hitler is sitting on his throne in hell having the last laugh!"

Instead of yelling back, he just looked at her quizzically and said, "Hey, do you think he makes all the little demons still salute and say, 'Heil Hitler'?"

"What?"

"Yeah, I was wondering how that works. Does Stalin have a throne too? And since Torquemada wasn't the ruler of a country, does he get a throne or does he have to share a couch with Hamen or something?"

"I don't know, Marv." She could feel a smile starting, despite her best effort not to give him the satisfaction. "But I do know you don't want this baby."

"I never said that."

"Well, you said I was fat and that you wouldn't miss the baby."

"But did I ever say I didn't want another kid?"

"Not really. No, I guess not."

"So, my wife, my life, forget about it. Let's celebrate the good news after you put the kiddo to bed."

So Danielle, who was exhausted from fighting, picked up Ari and started counting the hours until Isaac would come to visit.

Chapter 26

Nobody drove their cars inside the perimeter of Yamit. That was one of the unique features of the design. It was small enough to walk or ride bicycles throughout the whole town, but every group of houses and apartments had its own parking lot located behind it. The road went all around the perimeter, starting at the entrance where one entered the secure community. Danielle hated to leave and would get a headache every time they had to make a trip outside. She tried to concentrate on what Isaac was saying instead of the angles of his cheekbones, as he explained his plan in his mellifluous South African accent.

"Look, my dear, we'll go on a picnic at the end of that new road where they're building the new yeshiva."

"I don't know …"

"Why are you so worried?"

"All the yentas will be working overtime."

"You're not giving me enough credit. Look, I'll drive out of here like I'm going to the hospital while you leave on your bicycle a little while later. We'll meet up at the yeshiva and have afternoon tea together."

How could she say no? They weren't doing anything except having tea and the cake he had brought from his brother-in-law's bakery. No big deal. She would pick up Ari on her way back. And after last night she didn't even want to think about it. She ended up falling asleep in the rocking chair in Ari's room after locking the door behind her. She didn't have to think about it much longer …

"Okay, Isaac. I give up."

"Danielle, look at me." He lifted her chin so she could look into his eyes. "We're not doing anything wrong. We're just two friends setting out to have a picnic."

"Okay, okay," she said. "See you in a little while."

She didn't walk him to the door. Instead she went back to the bedroom to comb her long hair one more time and look at herself in the mirror. She doubted she'd ever be able to look at herself again.

When she'd given Isaac enough time, she got on her bike and rode down the sidewalk. She automatically glanced up at Rachel's window, even though she knew the blinds would be down. Rachel was working on a paper to complete her PhD in genetics, and she said the hardest part was sitting down every day and writing. Suddenly she had become so busy, working a few days a week at Ben Gurion University and using the DNA research project her department was working on to finish her dissertation. Danielle missed the daily visits with her friend, but even though they were closer than sisters, she could never tell her what she was doing today.

Danielle loved the freedom of riding her old Schwinn, and as she pedaled down the new road, she breathed in the fresh air and gave silent thanks for living in such a perfect place. Even though she was riding farther into the desert, the gentle breeze from the Mediterranean Sea would still help disguise the actual temperature, which was close to one hundred degrees Fahrenheit. She didn't bother to do the math anymore, converting centigrade to Fahrenheit. She just knew that forty degrees centigrade was hot. Just like she knew that a quarter of a kilo was enough cheese to buy for the three of them.

Avi, the garbage man, beeped his horn as he went by. He always had a big smile for everyone and always seemed to know what was going on. Danielle wondered what made him so happy all the time. Maybe he just liked collecting garbage. She waved and kept traveling down the road to the new one-story yeshiva.

It really was astounding, she thought, *what we we've created in a short time.*

As she neared the school, she saw Isaac's car. Since the school wouldn't open until next week, it was the only one in the parking lot.

On the ride over she had forced herself to stop thinking about her picnic and who she was meeting. Suddenly she felt a little nauseated and for an instant thought about turning around.

Since this area was so new, no landscaping had been done. A spray of sand and pebbles flew under her tires as she continued riding through the parking area to find a bit of shade to park her bicycle. When she saw that the entrance had an awning, she decided she could leave her bicycle right there. No one would steal it. Besides, there was no one here, including Isaac.

She parked the bicycle and walked around the side of the yeshiva. Like all the buildings in Yamit, it was made of reinforced concrete that had been brought in pieces from Tel Aviv. There were no aesthetic touches and wouldn't be. Flowers and shrubs would be planted to create a garden, but the building itself was utilitarian. She decided to continue around to the back. Maybe Isaac was there. If not, then she was going straight home.

She'd be able to forget this whole unsavory rendezvous.

Just as she turned the corner, lost in her righteous fantasy that she was going to turn around, she felt him behind her.

She turned around, smiling. "How did I miss you?"

"You missed me? It's only been a half hour, my dear," he teased.

Danielle knew that if she had a lighter complexion, her face would have turned red. "You know that's not what I meant. Missed *seeing* you. It's not like there's a big crowd gathered here."

"Come." He took her hand. "I found a little patio with an awning that we'll be able to sit under."

"Isaac ..."

"Don't say another word. Just come with me."

Danielle noticed that he didn't let go of her hand, but she rationalized that this was not exactly cheating. She was allowed to have some fun too. Marv had his bottle and she had Isaac.

She noted how comfortably her small hand fit into his. His hand reminded her of a pianist's, long fingers, strong and capable. They walked together naturally, and to Danielle he certainly appeared more comfortable than Marv in showing everyday affection.

They rounded the corner to the back, and Danielle was surprised to see not only a blanket laid out, but a thermos, two paper cups, a white cake box, and a small plastic vase filled with three different kinds of flowers.

"Isaac, how nice!"

"It's just my way of welcoming you back to the world of the living."

"But where did you get the bouquet? There's no flower shop nearby, and I can't believe you ransacked anyone's garden."

"Why not? Didn't you see me creeping beneath Rhoda's kitchen window with a pair of shears?"

"Now that you mention it, I do remember seeing you hide behind the rose bush. But I thought you were just an ordinary Peeping Tom."

"Believe me, if I wanted to enjoy voyeurism, I would choose someone with a bit more sex appeal."

"Like who, for instance?" she teased.

"Like the someone I stole the bloody bouquet for so that our picnic would be perfect."

"Please, don't be insulted. I'm just playing. In all seriousness, I'm very flattered."

She couldn't help adding, "I just don't remember seeing flowers like these in anyone's garden."

He shook his head. "I give up. You are incorrigible, my dear girl. Actually, they were a gift. Doctors have some very grateful patients."

"Oh, well, thank you for all your trouble, doctor. This is very ro— beautiful."

"A beautiful woman like you deserves to have beautiful things in her life."

"You're making me blush. For that compliment, the least I can do is pour your tea."

"No, Danielle, the least you can do is kiss me."

He pulled her down next to him before she could do anything but acquiesce. It was the perfect kiss. It was the kiss Danielle had dreamed about and never received until that moment. When it finally ended and every cell in her body tingled for more, Isaac looked in her eyes and said, "I've wanted to do that for a long time."

"Oh God, Isaac. What about your wife, Marvin, the children? I have to go." She got up and started to walk away.

"Danielle."

She kept walking and commanded herself not to turn around as she rounded the corner to where her bicycle was parked.

I'm going home and taking a shower, she told herself. *Then I'm going to pick up Ari, return home, make dinner.* A tear trickled down her cheek and she quickly wiped it away.

She heard his footsteps as he called to her again. She kept walking, pretending that she didn't know he was there.

But he grabbed her arm, and she turned to look at him.

"I can't do this, Isaac."

"Why, Danielle? I know you enjoy being with me as much as I like being with you."

"You're right, I do, but this is all wrong."

"I don't want to hear that. Aren't we both entitled to some happiness?"

"I don't know about being entitled to happiness," she said softly. "My mother always said that only retards are happy."

"I don't believe that. We have one life, and it's up to us to make the most of it."

"Yeah well, Isaac, I wish it were different, but this happens to be one of the big ten."

"What are you talking about?"

"Ever hear of the Ten Commandments, Isaac?"

"Bloody hell, Danielle, and what about honoring Shabbat? I know you don't do that."

"I may not sit in synagogue or light candles , but I don't work and we spend the day as a family."

"Don't rationalize, Danielle. I've seen you hanging the laundry and riding your bicycle. Why one commandment and not the others? Maybe it's just that you don't like me the way that I like you."

"It's not true. Of course I like you." Looking down at the ground she added, "Very much."

"Well, you should. I spent a lot of time with you when I didn't have to."

Her head snapped up. "What? What's that supposed to mean? Oh, now I get it. Now you want your payment."

"That's life."

"I thought you were a mensch."

"Of course I am. I gave you my time because I like you, sure, but I thought you liked me too."

"I do and you know it. But what you seem to forget is that we're both married."

"And when two people meet who belong together yet who happen to be married to others, do they just let that chance pass them by?"

She shook her head. "Don't do this to me, Isaac. I need to think."

"Danielle, just remember, if you didn't want to, you didn't have to come."

"I know, Isaac. It's going to be hard enough to look in Marvin's eyes knowing what I did today. Please, give me time to think."

"Danielle, I'm not going to force you to do anything you don't want to do. That's not my modus operandi."

"I appreciate that, Isaac. And I appreciate all the care you gave me. I know that you probably saved this baby."

"And that's all you care about in the end, isn't it?"

"No, Isaac. But I have to live with myself. So, if you'll excuse me, I have to go. *Now.*"

She quickly mounted her bicycle and pedaled home as fast as she could, all the while praying that no one would notice her tears.

She decided that before she went to pick up Ari she needed to go home, in order to give herself time to calm down. She rode her bike back the same way she'd come, but it appeared unfamiliar. She didn't remember the road being this bumpy and dusty. Before, her anticipation had been like fuel that coursed through her veins. She had never even felt her legs pedaling. Now she struggled the last mile anticipating what her reality now held. How was she going to live? Isaac was like a magnet pulling her closer, and she was starting to feel like she had no control. It had taken all her strength not to give in to him that day, and she was afraid. Marvin was her husband and Ari's father. She kept reminding herself that she would never betray him and that today's little adventure was the end of the story.

As she rode into the gate, lost in her thoughts and feeling completely depleted, the Gingy waved and shouted to her, "*Boi,* Danielle. Come here."

Oh, no, she thought. Her stomach felt like it was in a thousand knots. This little red-haired munchkin not only had his finger in every pie, he also was the town's biggest gossip.

"*Shamat ha chadashote?*" he asked.

"English, *bevakasha,* Gingy, I want to be sure I understand the news."

"Sadat is coming to Jerusalem!" he shouted, even though he was no more than three inched from her face.

Danielle was so shocked that for once she was able to ignore his bad manners, even though his proximity guaranteed an accidental spray of his spittle.

"They just announced it," he added.

"What?" Danielle just stood there, stunned. "I need to sit down. I feel like I'm going to faint."

Suddenly, the picture changed. No more personal soap opera. This was definitely more important than her petty emotional turmoil.

"Gingy, tell me what's going to happen now," She wiped her face as nonchalantly as possible, using a napkin she taken off the counter.

"Sadat will speak to the Knesset—"

"No, no, I mean to us. What's going to happen to us? "

"*Pitzuim,* Danielle, *pitzuim.* We're going to be rich."

"Compensation?" she retorted. "You think that's going to make up for our losses? Throw money at us in return for our lives. No, Gingy, I don't think so."

"That's why a lot of us came here."

"Really? Not me. I came here to make a life. The government promised us that they would never give Yamit back. Besides, I really don't get it. I thought Sadat was a Nazi who swore that Israel was his lifelong enemy. Something must have happened to change his mind."

Gingy tried to smile but it looked more like a grimace. "Actually, something did happen. Listen, you're not going to hear this on the news, but I heard that the Mossad alerted Sadat to an assassination attempt by Mu'ammar Gadhafi. "

"Shit, Gingy, we should have let him die. I have to go get Ari. See you later."

Danielle knew that if Gingy had told her about that Mossad warning, it must already be common knowledge. Nothing could stay secret for long in such a small town, but as an American, an immigrant, she was virtually the last to know or hear anything, unless the gossip was about one of the Americans. Since she was extremely ignorant about the government and its machinations, she had to rely on the information buzzing around her and what other people said. She couldn't read or understand Hebrew well enough. Slowly, she returned to her bicycle, confused and feeling as if the wind had just been knocked out of her. She had no control of what the government could and couldn't do. They were pawns. Nothing more. She always knew that the government was not concerned about individuals, and ironically, that made the whole ordeal easier to accept.

Chapter 27

Rachel and Danielle were sitting beside the round concrete sandbox that was situated in the small common area right outside their homes.

"So tell me again," Rachel demanded. "And don't leave out one tiny detail."

"Come on, Rach. It's embarrassing. Like anybody's going to care what Marvin or I think."

"You never know. Stranger things have happened."

"Like what?"

"Like Area 51 in Roswell. New Mexico," Rachel said in a bad imitation of a German accent.

The both laughed at Rachel's nonsense, and then Danielle finally told Rachel again how a reporter from the daily newspaper *Maariv* had been strolling around with his photographer in the commercial center. Danielle had bumped into him when she was coming up the stairs from the workshop.

"I was so embarrassed, because I actually ran straight into him with Ari's stroller. You know how I get totally oblivious. Luckily, he was very nice about it. Very un-Israeli."

"Be specific, Danielle. Remember, I'm a mathematician. I have no imagination."

"Well, when I ran the wheel right over his foot, instead of screaming, 'Idiot, what are you doing?' he said, 'Hey, it looks like you're in a rush.'"

"You're right, that's very civilized."

"So, then he asked me where I was off to in such a hurry, and I said to get my son—"

"Was this all in English?"

"This was in Hebrew, but the actual interview was in English and Hebrew."

"Okay. You know me. Details, details, details."

"He asked if he could come along and talk to me because *Maariv* wanted to get an article about the peace accord from the settlers' point of view, and he wanted to get an American reaction. His English was very good. He said he had traveled to the US and bummed around after serving in the army.

"So as we walked and talked on the way to the gan he asked me questions about my background and why we decided to settle here. Then he came home with me, and I made coffee. I was so Israeli, I even set out a tray and offered cake to him and his photographer, Benny. He asked me to call Marv. So Marv came home and he interviewed him too. And you know Marv, he had everyone laughing, and Benny took quite a few photos of all of us."

"This photo is great! You look like a movie star!" Rachel flipped the pages to the article again.

"Thanks. The photo is really good, but—"

"No buts. You not only have a full page article written about you, you also have your picture in the paper. Did you ever think you'd be famous? This is really exciting!"

"I hate to admit it, but you're right, Rachel. As a matter of fact, I already put the article in an envelope to send to my parents. Even though they can't read it, my mother can show the photos to her mah-jongg group and *kvell* a little. But to tell you the truth, that reporter was kind of ... slimy."

"Why?"

"He acted like he was a friend so we would open up to him. But then he printed things I asked him not to print, and there were even quotation marks around it."

"Like where?"

Rachel scanned the article while Danielle told her which paragraph to look at.

"See? About how we came here to make a life as a couple of

young pioneers. He made us sound like stupid idealists. And this?" She pointed to the middle of the page. "This was supposed to be 'off the record.' Thank God he didn't print Gingy's name, because I used him for an example of how some people came here figuring that the government would go back on its word and they'd be able to make a lot of money. And then when we told him how we started the business, with the government grants, it makes us look like freeloaders. Even the headline, 'First to Settle … First to Leave.' I don't know, Rachel. It's like he really wasn't listening or else he didn't care what I actually said."

"I think you should just enjoy your moment and don't take it too seriously. Danny Barel is one of the top reporters in the country and your photo is terrific. You look like a movie star. The reality is, Yamit is news and now you're part of it."

"I guess one has to be happy for small favors. At least the photo was just a close-up of my face and not my whole body."

"Before you know it the baby will be here and you'll have that sexy, svelte figure back again."

"Yeah, well, Rach, I have to tell you, I have this feeling that I never had with Ari. "

"What are you talking about?"

"I'm just so afraid that there's something wrong with this baby."

"That's because it hasn't been an easy pregnancy, Danielle, but don't start scaring yourself."

"Not an easy pregnancy? Are you kidding? It's been difficult and scary. I'm amazed that she's going to be brought to term."

"She?"

"I'm positive. Only a daughter can make a mother this miserable. Believe me, I feel so much different than with Ari. I just hope she's normal."

"Be positive. If Dr. Isaac was concerned, don't you think he would have said something?"

Danielle felt her face flush at the mention of his name and hoped she didn't give herself away. She adeptly changed the subject.

"Rachel, you have to admit that maternity care here is very basic. I think it's a holdover from the kibbutz mentality. The five-minute visit consists of, How do you feel? Any spotting or pain? Let me check your ankles for swelling. Beseder. See you next month."

"I think that's good. So if he was concerned, you'd know it."

Danielle changed the topic again, afraid that she would tell Rachel what was really bothering her.

"I got a call from someone from *US* magazine when I was at the store today. They're sending a crew next week."

"*US*? That new, glossy American magazine?" Rachel exclaimed. "This is getting weird. We're really going to be front page news."

"I'd rather be the centerfold in *Playboy*." Danielle stood up and posed, her fingers running through her hair and her chest thrust out above her distended belly.

The two friends laughed, and then Rachel said, "Actually, you know Anat Levin, the one that wrote that book, *The Many Faces of Moshe Dayan*?"

"Of course," Danielle answered in mock seriousness, imitating the radio ads she'd heard. "'Soldier, archeologist, and patriot.'"

"Not to mention womanizer," Rachel added. "Well, she was at the restaurant with Dr. Isaac this morning."

Danielle felt her body freeze and hoped she sounded nonchalant as she said, "I guess he was being interviewed for a new book she's working on."

"Well, I don't know. Not if what Rhoda told me is true."

"What are you saying?"

"She said that they were very cozy and that she overheard snippets of conversation."

"Like?"

"She was thanking him for the flowers he brought her ... even though they were a little wilted."

"What? No, if they were having an affair, why would they be in the open so everybody could see?"

"It's a good strategy, if you ask me. People will buy 'we're only friends.'"

Danielle felt that her best friend was looking at her a little too pointedly. Did she know? But they had never done anything, so it didn't matter. Or was she just fooling herself?

"When did she get here?" she asked casually, although it was get harder to breathe.

"A few days ago. Apparently she stayed in that extra apartment Gingy bought."

"So she's been here for about three days?"

"Yeah, why?"

"I'm just surprised that no one has been talking about seeing her. It should be the big buzz."

"Maybe no one's seen her. They're probably busy feathering their love nest. Now that his wife is visiting family, maybe they decided to be bolder."

"Has he been seeing her for a while?"

"That's what Rhoda says, but you know Rhoda. According to her, when he goes up to the hospital in Tel Aviv, he sees her too."

"I'm such an ass!" Danielle blurted out.

"What are you talking about?"

"Everybody knows this stuff but me!"

"Not really, I just found out yesterday. Danielle, why are you so upset?"

"I don't feel well, Rachel. It's all is too much. First the government tells us to build towns and moshavim in this area, and then it decides we're expendable. Then the media rushes down here like vultures. We become their carrion. And now I find out someone who I respected has been cheating on his wife."

"Yeah, well give him a little *rachmunis*."

"He doesn't deserve pity, Rachel. Wrong is wrong."

"His wife and Hannah are definitely a couple. Rhoda sees them rolling around behind a sand dune some mornings when she's opening the restaurant."

"I don't know. It's really hard for me to believe something like that. Probably even if I saw it with my own eyes, I would rationalize it. But you're probably right. Let's take the kids in. It's an awful lot to think about."

"Before I forget, and since we were speaking of journalistic vultures, someone from Sally O' Brien's staff called Rhoda to make reservations at the restaurant for tomorrow morning."

"Sally O' Brien?" Danielle repeated, her voice rising. "Sally O' Brien from the *Washington Post*?"

"Uh-huh, that Sally O' Brien. So meet me at the restaurant as soon as you bring Ari to the gan."

"In the morning, Rachel? Isn't that going to screw up your studying schedule?"

"Who cares? It's Sally O'Brien!"

Chapter 28

Both Danielle and Rachel pretended they were oblivious to the celebrity journalist, but they were covertly watching Sally O'Brien. They observed every tiny detail, from the way she held her coffee cup to the way she tossed her blonde hair and then twisted the ends with her fingers. They were seated at their usual table, where they could either gaze hypnotically at the undulating Mediterranean or scan the customers to find something humorous to laugh at. Today, though, their sole preoccupation was Sally O'Brien, who wrote a popular lifestyle column for the *Washington Post*. What had really made her a household name was that the rich and debonair editor of the newspaper, Guy Hardin, had left his wife for her. As part of the settlement, he had surrendered millions of his inherited fortune to his ex-wife. Between sips of their coffee, Rachel and Danielle avidly dissected her.

"It must be true love because she's got those awful horsey teeth."

"And she's so tall …"

"Guys just like those long legs."

"To tell you the truth, Rachel, I'm surprised. I expected drop dead gorgeous."

"It's her breeding, dahling. And don't forget all her riding practice."

They both giggled at the double entendre, and then Danielle sighed. "She's got to be something special in bed, because I don't think she's that great looking. Do you ever read her column?"

"No."

"Me neither," Danielle exclaimed. "The media make it sound like everybody in America reads it. I only heard of her because of the big divorce scandal that made the front page of every major newspaper. I guess the key to being taken seriously is to have an affair with the right person."

"That leaves me out," they both said simultaneously, and then burst out laughing. As their laughter died down, Danielle realized they were getting nasty looks from the celebrity's table.

"Let them look," Rachel said, "because the joke's on them. They must feel like the biggest fools. Remember, they actually called for reservations. They must have thought they were still in DC and probably congratulated themselves that they had the foresight to call ahead."

Danielle was laughing so hard at Rachel's sarcastic remark as she looked around the nearly empty restaurant, she wasn't sure when she felt the first contraction. Then another came about fifteen minutes later, and she was positive. It was time to get to the hospital.

"Rachel, I just had a couple of contractions. We need to go." She hoped she appeared calmer than she felt.

"Okay, stay calm. I'll have Natan call Marv and I'll pick up Ari later. He can stay with us until Marv comes back or your in-laws get here. Do you have anything packed?"

"Not really. It's a couple of weeks early."

"Don't worry, it's going to be fine. Look, stay here. Walk around a little if the contractions start coming closer. I'll go up to the house and pack a few things for you. Natan's here so you won't be alone. I'll send the bag down with Marvin and you'll be on your way."

"What would I do without you, Rachel?"

"Live, of course. Don't be silly. Just relax, You should be out of here in less than an hour. Natan," she called loudly to her husband, who was in the kitchen. "Call Marv now. Immediately. Danielle has to go to the hospital."

A minute later Natan walked out of the kitchen to ask Danielle if she needed anything else.

"So far, I'm in no discomfort, Natan. Thanks."

"I called Marv. He said he'll be here in ten minutes. Don't worry."

Danielle looked at her best friend's husband and was once again amazed at how handsome he was. Handsome but almost pathologically quiet. Getting a complete sentence out of him was like getting a two-year-old to share a favorite toy. Maybe that was why their marriage worked. Rachel talked and Natan listened.

Rachel waved good-bye to them, and Natan asked Danielle if she wanted one more cup of coffee.

"Why not?" she said. "This will take a while, so it can't hurt. It will have to be the last thing that I put in my stomach."

"Mahmud," he called to his lone employee, who was chopping vegetables for salad. "We need some more coffee here."

"Excuse me," a woman said, "but I couldn't help hearing your conversation."

Danielle couldn't believe it, but the tall blonde shiksa goddess, Sally O'Brien, was standing right behind Mahmud as he put the coffee down on her table.

"I don't want to be rude or presumptuous," the journalist went on, "but it sounds like you're going into labor."

"No. no you're not being rude at all," Danielle said. "I'm sure we've been so loud, my husband probably heard us all the way at the workshop."

"Would you mind if I joined you?" Sally O'Brien asked, smiling with what appeared to be real warmth.

"Sure. Why not? "

Natan asked Sally if she wanted anything besides coffee, and Danielle chuckled to herself when the famous columnist made a definite faux pas by asking for a couple of scrambled eggs with bacon on the side.

"No bacon here," Natan said gruffly. "This is Israel. Have some fresh tomatoes and cucumbers. It's healthier anyway."

"Oh, excuse me for my ignorance! I certainly wasn't thinking, That sounds great." She turned to Danielle. "Are you sure you're okay? You seem so calm."

"'Seem' is the key word. I have a long way to go until pain actually kicks in."

"So, you sound like an American."

"I am, but I've been living here for a while."

"Oh, an expatriate. This could be my lucky day."

"Why's that ?" Danielle asked .

"You see, I'm with one of the American newspapers. They sent me here looking for a story. And now I think I've found one." She paused dramatically. "How would you like to be it?"

"Well, it depends. What newspaper do you work for?" Danielle asked with feigned ignorance.

"How rude of me. I was so excited that I found a story, I forgot to introduce myself. I'm Sally O'Brien and I'm with the *Washington Post.*"

"Well, Sally, I'm flattered to be your interest, although I don't know how long we could do this interview. As you must have heard, my husband should be coming to get me in a few minutes."

"No problem. So where is the nearest hospital?"

"Beer Sheva."

"How far away is that?"

"About an hour."

"So we can follow you there. Is that okay?"

Danielle shrugged. "If that's what you want to do."

"Now let's finish our introductions. You got my name, but I never got yours and where you're originally from."

After a few minutes of Danielle answering similar questions, they heard a loud, boisterous "Danielle!" It was Marv. Of course he had to let everyone know he had arrived by reciting a litany of complaints, starting with, "I can't believe I had to drive down here to get you. You know I hate the damned sand. Why didn't you just walk up to the city with Rachel?"

Danielle acknowledged him by replying, "Don't be silly, Marv. And by the way, I'd like you to meet Sally O'Brien." She purposefully added, "She's a reporter for the *Washington Post.*" Daniellle tried to signal him with her eyes, but it was already too late.

"Big deal! And I'm the owner of a jewelry factory."

Sally O'Brien, former debutante and present Washington celebrity, was so taken aback by his rejoinder, she started laughing.

Danielle had noticed this weird phenomenon. Most people

were so surprised by Marvin's rude comments that instead of being insulted, they laughed.

"Okay, ya allah," Marvin said gruffly. "Let's hit the road." He called good-bye to Natan, and then turned to Mahmud, who was standing at the kitchen door smoking a cigarette. "Mahmud, I hear you're getting married. See what you're in for."

Mahmud nodded seriously and waved.

"Marv, how about my things?"

"Don't worry. Rachel packed a bag for you. It's in the car."

"Did you call your parents?"

"Yeah. My mother was making gefilte fish. She sounded like I was bothering her. So she said to call her when you give birth. Let's hit the road."

He drove their little Passat out of Yamit. After he drove carefully over the old railroad tracks to the main road, he turned left and headed north to Beer Sheva. Suddenly, she felt another stronger contraction.

"Whew, that one was kind of rough."

Marvin patted her shoulder. "Rough? My wife, my life, rough is going to be when my parents stay with us."

She laughed and had to give him credit. At least he was trying to take her mind off the coming ordeal.

"So, Marv, let's go over this one more time. Who are we naming the baby after?"

"My father's brother Iggy, who was killed by the Nazis, after he beat one of the Aryan scum in the ring."

"Well, I'm sure your father will be very happy that we name the baby after his brother. Although I have to tell you, I'm glad we decided on Ilana. I think the name Irving is a little outdated. And Ilana ..."

"I have to stop and get cigarettes at that stand."

Danielle took a deep breath and counted to four in her head. She thought that latest contraction had come a little faster than the last. When he stopped, she saw Sally's car pull in right behind them. She got out to say hello and to move around a little while she waited for Marv.

"I don't know what's taking him so long," she finally said to Sally. "Let me check."

Inside her husband was sitting at one of the small tables. "Marv, what the hell are you doing?"

"I figured I'd get something to eat. I'm starved. This is going to be a long hell of a day."

"What about me, Marvin?" she asked, trying to stay as calm as possible. She knew if she turned around she would see Sally right behind her.

"Have some," he said. "I ordered humus and eggplant 'cause I know you like it."

Danielle was so shocked, she wanted to scream at him for being so selfish, but she knew that every nuance would be recorded and interpreted by this albatross that she had invited to join them.

"Marv, I know you must have forgotten, but I can't eat anything," she said through clenched teeth, "Once a woman goes into labor, she can't put anything in her stomach."

"Oh, well, it's too late now. Come sit."

"What do you say, Sally? Are you up for some Israeli cuisine?" Danielle smiled at her audience while trying to ignore the bile that was building in her throat, especially when she saw the Nesher beer that the waiter had brought with the food.

"Sure, why not?" Sally said. "But what about you?"

"I'll just sit and hope that we make it to the hospital in time," Danielle answered resignedly. She started to pray, *God, just let this baby be all right. Please. Nothing else matters.*

Meanwhile she listened to Marvin start a conversation with Sally. "So, Blondie."

Sally laughed. "My name is Sally O' Brien. You have so much to deal with now, I'm sure my name is the least of your concerns."

Marvin nodded. "*Sally.* That's such an all American name. I remember those reading books Dick and Jane and their little sister Sally, with the fluffy blonde hair."

"I do too!" the journalist replied. "As a matter of fact, I used to hate those books so much because the other kids would tease me."

"Tease? Please. My name is Marvin, and I was a short, skinny

Jewish kid who grew up in New York with immigrant parents who spoke Yiddish. I really don't think the teasing was comparable. "

He got a chuckle as a reply, and then he added, "This child is going to be named after my dead uncle who was killed by the Nazis because he was Jewish, and who didn't have fluffy blonde hair."

Danielle saw Sally O'Brien almost imperceptibly catch her breath and decided that it was time to go.

"Marv, come on, we still have a ways to go and I just had another contraction."

"You'll be fine. I just have to ask Miss Fluffy Blonde Sally O'Brien, what she plans to write about."

"That's fair enough, Marvin," Sally replied in a professional tone of voice. "I just want to get your reaction to this peace process."

"Reaction?" He banged the beer bottle on the table. "This is my reaction. It sucks. Now I dare you to write that."

Sally replied that she would, and Danielle noticed that her smile disappeared.

"Do you realize what you're doing?" Marv went on. "You're following us to Beer Sheva where my wife is giving birth today. How do you rationalize that fitting in with 'our reaction to the peace process'?"

"Good question," the reporter answered. "I thought it would be interesting to our readers to glimpse a real couple's life, so they could understand the human element of this historic accord."

"Well, our life is not for you to scrutinize, probe, and then evaluate according to your own skewed values."

"Marvin, I want to portray you guys sympathetically—"

"Do me a favor, lady. Get the hell out of here."

"Well, if that's the way you feel, I'll leave now." She rose from the table and said good-bye to Danielle in a courteous but cold manner.

"You're a parasite, lady," Marv called to her back as she walked out the door. "You make a living out of other people's misery."

As the door slammed, he added for good measure, "And you have no tits!"

Chapter 29

Thank God the baby was all right. That was the most important thing. Ilana Sophia Steinberg was alive and well. She was tiny but otherwise perfect. The nurses called her Honey because the little fuzz on top of her head was that same warm golden color. Danielle already felt motherly pride that Ilana was a nursery favorite.

Giving birth had ended up close to being a nightmare. To make matters worse, the maternity ward was so crowded, at least a dozen women were on beds in the hallway. Danielle would need to thank Isaac, because it was only through his intervention that she had got a bed in a room. The morning after her emergency caesarean section, when she slowly shuffled down the hall attached to an IV, she saw two women in labor on beds in the hallway, moaning and writhing in pain. She felt bad for them, because they didn't even have the simple luxury of a screen, which would have provided some privacy. Instead, they had to deal with a constant barrage of hospital noise and traffic.

The five women who shared the one room in the ward were a diverse mix. One was a very young Bedouin girl. Danielle felt sorry for her because she couldn't be more than fourteen. She didn't talk to anyone, so she probably didn't know Hebrew. Danielle had noticed that the last two mornings, two older men came into see her about four a.m. One looked like he could have been her grandfather and the other could have been her father. Or maybe he was her husband. It was a bit unnerving because they were as quiet as two cats. Even though she was in the bed next to the girl, she didn't hear a sound while they crept to her bed and brought her food. They fed her fruit and pita and then left as silently as they had arrived. Every time Danielle looked at her, she appeared dazed, as if she didn't know what had happened to her. One of the other women, the one nearest the window, had had a caesarean section. The previous day her sister-in-law, who was dressed in a beautiful sari, visited. On the way out, she imperiously requested that all the women on the ward to try and talk to her sister-in-law because she was very depressed. Danielle wasn't surprised to hear that. The poor woman would stare out the window all day and then at night, when she thought everyone was asleep, she cried.

Today was the first day that Danielle had enough strength to walk farther than the chair in the corner of the room. The nurse's aide who was helping her kept telling in Hebrew to move a little faster. "You're not the only patient I have."

"Beseder," Danielle answered brusquely. "We're almost there. Leave me here at this bench and then you can come back in a little while."

Danielle was thrilled that she could finally walk to the main hallway where smoking was allowed. She pulled the package of cigarettes from her bathrobe pocket and relished the comfort of inhaling. She sorely needed the nicotine to soothe and calm her jangled nerves. Finally her head was clear enough for her to think about what had happened.

When she and Marvin had finally arrived at the hospital and the nurse did an initial exam, she couldn't hear the baby's heartbeat. She told them Danielle would need a caesarean section. Then she found the heartbeat and told her not to worry the baby was just sitting especially low. When Danielle had dilated enough to be wheeled into the labor room, the medical team hooked her up to a fetal monitoring machine and discovered that the baby wasn't getting enough oxygen. To Danielle's horror, instead of immediately doing a caesarean section, the midwife and the intern started debating the pros and cons of a vaginal delivery versus a caesarean section.

Danielle screamed in Hebrew and in English that they should shut the fuck up and open her up immediately in order to save the baby. Thank God Isaac walked in when he did and ordered that she be immediately wheeled into the operating room.

Totally oblivious to what was happening, Marvin went back home to pick up Ari. Or at least, that was what he said he did. When Rachel had come to visit the previous day, Danielle got the actual story.

Marvin's his parents had gone straight to Yamit when they got the news from Marvin that Danielle had gone into labor. Since no one was home, Arianna directed them to Rachel's house to pick him up. She gave them the extra key so they could get into Marvin and Danielle's home, and then Marvin arrived. He had bought a bottle of Dewar's from the Gingy to celebrate the baby's arrival and, Danielle guessed, to take the edge off his parents' visit. At that point, Danielle didn't want to hear any more, because she knew it was going to be bad. She grimaced when Rachel reported that he rode his bicycle up and down the main walkway, yelling that he had his baby girl. He was so drunk that he ended up sleeping in the car.

That son of a bitch, thought Danielle. *After all I went through. That selfish son of a bitch.*

She was preparing herself for the torturous walk back to her room, when she felt a familiar touch on her shoulder.

"Danielle, how do you feel?"

She looked up and smiled. "Better today, Isaac."

"Let me help you back to your room."

He gently grabbed her under the elbows and helped her up. "You have to be very careful until the stitches come out, you know."

"I know," she replied. *And I know,* she added silently, *that I could listen to your refined and gentle voice forever.* "I'll never be able to wear a bikini again, Isaac."

"Do you really care?" he answered.

"Yes," she said emphatically, and they both laughed.

As Isaac guided her back to her room, he mentioned that because of his dad's poor health, he would have to go back to South Africa for a while.

Danielle thought her heart would stop but continued to make small talk, pretending she hadn't just discovered a giant crack in her fragile world. When Isaac gently helped her into her bed, he said, "Danielle, I was afraid that I would lose you."

She fell asleep with a smile on her face.

Chapter 30

All the women were given candles and matches when the overcooked chicken dinner was distributed that evening. The week had been a blur, and Danielle hadn't even realized it was Friday. The highlight of the day was nursing her little Lani and kissing each of the tiny fingers that wrapped tightly around hers. That day, after Lani was taken back to the nursery, Ruti, the woman in the bed across from her who had almost died from toxemia, announced in Hebrew to everyone that they would light their candles in exactly eleven minutes. She looked straight at Danielle and added, "I know you won't light because you're an American."

Danielle was so taken aback she decided to pretend she didn't understand.

Lighting the Shabbat candles was one of those things that proclaimed that this was a Jewish country, and yet not one of her friends regularly performed that obligation. Danielle hated to admit it, but Ruti was right.

She decided that when the other women did it, she would do it too. Even if she felt dumb and awkward, she was so thankful that her baby had turned out healthy, it was the least she could do.

So when she saw Sarah, the beautiful Indian women at the end of the row, put the napkin on her head she, did the same thing. And when Ruti started the prayer, *"Baruch atta Adanoi ..."* she followed her lead, welcoming the Sabbath queen into their midst. Memories of her childhood suddenly replaced the awkwardness, and the image of her grandmother benching lecht soothed her and changed the mood of the room. After everyone wished each other Shabbat Shalom and good Shabbas, they started talking to each other for the first time. Ruti apologized for her comment, and Danielle said she was right. American girls didn't perform the mitzvah.

Then Sarah, the Indian woman who was so depressed, started talking. It was the first words she had spoken, so they all listened intently.

"All you girls are lucky. I am from India. I know you are surprised to know that Jews live in India, but we do. And like Jews all over the world, we assimilated with the country that we live in.

"In India we are called Benai Israel, the children of Israel. This, my third child, is another little girl. They were all delivered by caesarean section. Every time it takes me longer to recover. I can't go through another birth. The doctor already warned my husband that the next time I could die. But he told me that he doesn't care. A man must have a son. He told me I must bear him a son and that he didn't care what the doctor said. It is my duty."

The other women were appalled and made comforting sounds, but they felt helpless against this archaic cultural belief. Ruti started singing the melody, *"Bim, bam, bim, bim, bam ..."* One at a time, each woman joined in, and the ward was filled with the plaintive Shabbat melody. For a moment they were one.

Marvin's voice abruptly broke the mood. "Move that fucking cart out of the way."

Usually her stomach would have been tightening in embarrassment. That evening Danielle just smiled and continued singing.

"What the hell," Marv said as he entered the room. "I thought this was a hospital, not a shul."

As usual, he had everyone laughing. Danielle saw that even Sarah smiled.

"It's Shabbat, Marvin."

"As if I didn't know."

To Danielle's surprise the sullen nurse's aide, who was standing directly behind Marv, actually smiled and placed a vase of flowers on the small table next to Danielle's bed.

"Shabbat Shalom, my wife, my life," he said before he kissed her on her forehead.

Surprised at his unusual display of tenderness Danielle, wrapped her arms around him and stroked his cheek.

"They're beautiful, Marvin."

She saw him blush as he pulled away, and he made a show of pulling up a chair.

"So, how's my big boy?" she asked.

"I can't take it anymore, Danielle."

"Silly, I'm not talking about you. I'm talking about Ari."

"Oh, yeah. He's fine, but my parents are going to kill me. No doubt in my mind."

"Why? What's going on?"

But Danielle knew. It was the same old story. Every time she and Marv visited her in-laws, her stomach would cramp into knots and an overwhelming lethargy would invade her body. She used to think she was imagining it, but then she realized Marv threw up every night before a visit. First she blamed his drinking, but it happened even when he didn't drink. It was just the idea of seeing his mother.

Danielle hoped she wouldn't regret it, but she said it anyway. "Marvin, it's almost like your mother is an energy vampire."

He looked at her with an expression look of profound gratefulness. "Thanks," he said, and kissed her.

"For what?"

"For giving it a name."

"It wasn't me. I borrowed it from some Colin Wilson science fiction book."

"No, no, I don't care where you got it from. That's the best description I've ever heard. Energy vampire. Did I ever tell you that I lived on blackbirds my whole junior year of school?"

"Blackbirds? As in 'Four and twenty blackbirds baked in a pie'?" She knew what he was saying but she wanted to keep the tone light.

"No, I mean amphetamines," he answered seriously. "Not only would my mother noodge me every second that I was in that house, telling me how much I was like her father, Menachem Chaim, 'of blessed memory.' Then I wouldn't be able to sleep. I'd have these nightmares every night. All the stories would swirl around my head. It was so realistic that I would swear the SS were there in my room.

Some nights I could feel the bed spinning around and the next thing I knew I was in the camp barracks lying on a bed of plywood with a dead body next to me. Then I'd have to get up and ride the subway to Brooklyn for school. After nights like that, she'd be up smiling that fake smile of hers and asking me if I wanted cereal or eggs. But it was like she knew. I can't explain it, but it's like she sent me her demons."

Danielle didn't know what to say. She was angry that he didn't even ask about the baby or how she was feeling. She wanted to tell him how happy she was that she had been able to walk down the hall that day, but she knew he wasn't interested. He would sit there and rant and rave until the venom was disgorged. So she let him talk and pretended to listen, until his eyes closed and she realized he had fallen asleep.

Chapter 31

The article by Sally O' Brien portrayed Danielle and Marv as lunatics. Danielle read it when Rachel brought it over for their afternoon coffee date. "I knew you were in no shape to read it before," she said.

Danielle read the article carefully. "It looks like she left us and then went back to the restaurant and interviewed Mahmud."

"You mean the Mahmud who no longer works for us," Rachel said.

"I can't believe this shit," Danielle said. She read out loud, "'Once Yamit is returned to us, the Palestinians who are the true inheritors of this historical and beloved land will finally have peace and security from the Israeli oppressors. After my marriage I will be able to take my bride to a real home and not to a camp where we are kept like dogs.'

Of course he doesn't mention that he didn't have enough money to get married before he worked for you, and that his money isn't taxed. Not to mention that Natan gave him a car."

"And that the son of a bitch was treated like family. We just gave him and his fiancée $100 for an engagement present. Do you know how many times he's been at the house? I can't even count. He's probably been over more than Marv. "

"And didn't you get his fiancée work with the Gingy?"

"You're right. I almost forgot."

"Who knew that he was in that PLO group with Arafat?"

"We're lucky he didn't kill us in our beds."

"Meanwhile, Marv looks like a rotten son of a bitch, I look like an abused wife, and Mahmud looks like a poor victim of Israeli hate and oppression. The only good thing is that she stuck it in the middle of the article, so maybe nobody will read this far."

Danielle shook the newspaper at Rachel. "All the hard work we put in to developing this wasteland becomes, according to Sally O'Brien, 'Bending the land to our iron will.' No other country gives back land that it gained in war without a full surrender. Especially the Arabs. Only we're supposed to. By the way, who is in charge of the refugee camp in Rafiah?"

"UNRWA."

"That's what I thought, but of course it doesn't mention that here." Danielle shook her head. "I can't read another word of this," she said as she threw down the paper. "It's sickening."

"Well, that's the end of reporters. Natan is so angry at Mahmud for making him a *friar*—in case you forgot, that's Hebrew for big-time sucker—and that bitch for making Mahmud a downtrodden martyr that he won't even allow anybody he even thinks might be a reporter in the restaurant."

"Who knew that meeting Sally O'Brien would turn into such a disaster?"

"We have to look on the positive side. At least she said you were beautiful."

"Yeah, it was a real compliment being called 'a beautiful innocent taking orders from a willful, self-serving husband.' This is one article I can't send my parents. My mother would have a conniption fit and be on the next plane to get me out of here. Not to change the subject, but what are Natan and Rhoda going to do for help at the restaurant now?"

"Rhoda's kids will help on a more regular basis, and Natan's sister Amira is going to pitch in until they find someone full-time."

"It's lucky she came down here."

"Well, then, I guess it's lucky her husband's in jail."

"You know, religious people believe that everything is God's will. If you look at it that way , this whole incident was supposed to happen."

"I don't know about that, but did you notice that some religious families moved into that last apartment building?"

"Yes, and I thought it was strange. Now that everyone is thinking about leaving, a new family comes. Well, that's good for Amira, so that she has another religious family down here. Rachel, I just heard the baby, so I'm going to get her in a few minutes. It's amazing how different she is from Ari. She's so quiet and content, sometimes I go in just to make sure she's breathing."

"I was just going anyway. I'll pick up Battia and Ari and be back in about a half an hour."

"Thanks, Rachel. You know how much I appreciate your help. I'll walk downstairs with you and get the mail."

"So did you hear," Rachel asked on the way down the front steps, "that they're starting to hammer out the terms of the compensation package?" .

"I did. But to tell you the truth, I can't really deal with this. I can't imagine leaving here, even though I know it's going to happen. I just don't like to think about it. You, Rhoda, and the rest of the Yamitniks have become my new family. I can't imagine my life without you."

Danielle opened the mailbox, distracting herself so she wouldn't cry. She quickly sorted through the mail, looking for a letter from her family, and saw an official-looking envelope addressed to Marvin with the state of Israel logo in the corner.

"I'll see you in a little while, Rach," she said. "Lahit."

Danielle quickly turned and went back up the stairs, throwing the mail on the table before picking up Lani. She cupped her daughter's delicate head and made herself comfortable in the rocking chair so the baby could nurse. Lani looked up at her with the clearest blue eyes while her mouth latched on to Danielle's nipple. Within a few minutes her eyes closed as the baby was satiated and gratified.

A little while later, Danielle heard the door open and Rachel call, "Ari's here. See you later." Battia added like a miniature woman, "Lahit, Ari."

Ari called "la-hi" over his shoulder as he ran into the bedroom. Danielle kissed his head, told him to be quiet so that he didn't wake his sister, and then put the baby back in her crib.

"Come, show me what you made in gan today."

"*Keshet,* Ima."

"A rainbow? Did you learn the story of Noah today?"

Ari smiled and nodded.

Danielle started singing, "'Rise and shine and give God the glory, glory …'" Ari clapped and danced until there was a knock on the door. Danielle opened it. Surprised to see who was standing there, she smiled and motioned to Isaac to come sit down. She hugged Ari and told him he could go down to the sandbox for a little while and play with Ruti while she was there with her mom. She got him his pail and shovel and reminded him to hold onto the railing on his way down the steps. When the boy was gone, she smiled at Isaac.

"Whew, that was exhausting," she said.

"You still have to take it easy. Remember, you went through a major operation."

"Believe me, I know. All I have to do is look at my ugly scar and fat stomach."

"It will take a while to get back into shape, but I have no doubt that next summer you'll be in that sexy black bathing suit again."

"Hey, doctor, you're supposed to tell me I look beautiful as I am. But to tell you the truth, the most important thing is that Lani is alive and healthy."

"And God willing, she'll stay that way. You're a good mother, Danielle."

"Ooh, another compliment from the doctor."

"Stop playing with me, Danielle. I came to tell you something serious."

"Serious? Do you want something cold to drink first?"

"No." He took her hand and led her to the couch, urging her to sit down with him. "There's no easy way to say this, so I shall just state it bluntly." He paused and took a deep breath. "Remember I told you after Lani was born that I would have to go to South Africa for a while. I still need to go, but now I don't know how long it's going to be."

"Oh." Feeling like she had been punched in the stomach, she turned away from him.

"Don't," he said. "Please look at me."

"What do you want, Isaac?" she asked as she controlled a sob from escaping.

"I'm not sure. But I do know I think about you almost constantly."

Danielle was stunned.

"Look," he went on, "I have to go back to complete some business arrangements and help my parents."

"Didn't you say that your father was ill?"

"Yes, but thank God he's fine. Still, they need help getting their finances in order and selling their property."

"Why? What happened?"

"South Africa is facing some serious problems and my parents aren't taking any chances. So, they're planning to make aliyah as soon as possible."

"Oh." Danielle didn't know what else to say. She was bereft. Isaac had become an important part of her life. He had even saved Ilana from possible death.

He spoke again, his words coming out in a rush. "My marriage isn't what a marriage is supposed to be." He looked at the floor. "It's a marriage in name only. When I come back I want to talk about us, Danielle."

"Us, Isaac?" She knew she shouldn't ask, but the question came out, like it had been waiting to be spit it out like poison. "What about Anat?"

"Anat?" he asked, appearing puzzled.

"Anat Levin, the famous author and hidden paramour."

Isaac laughed. "Famous author, yes, hidden paramour, no."

"What?"

"That's right, my love."

"But ..."

"But nothing," Isaac was still laughing. "You know that cheesecake you like so much?"

She nodded.

"It comes from the Levin family bakery. Anat is my cousin. Her dad is my mother's older brother. He made it here to Ha'aretz before the war."

"Oh, Isaac."

Danielle was so happy, she wrapped herself in Isaac's arms and kissed him. The kiss was so long and deep, they were both startled when the door opened.

"Ima, look!" Ari exclaimed, holding up his pail. He was so intent on whatever treasure he had found, Danielle was sure he didn't notice how she and Isaac jumped apart.

"So, Danielle," Isaac said as he stood up, "I leave tomorrow."

"What?" she said.

"Did you forget? That's why I stopped over. To say good-bye."

She looked over at her son. He had poured colorful stones out of his pail onto the floor and was busily sorting them, paying no attention to her and Isaac. "So soon?" she whispered. "No, you can't!"

"Look, I'm going to take care of everything as soon as I can."

"Okay, Isaac. I believe you. We'll take it from there when you get back."

"I love you, Danielle. I want this to be right. But you must be patient. I might be gone for a month or more."

"It's okay, Isaac. This is moving much too fast for me anyway. I need time to think."

He tilted her chin upward to look in her eyes and brushed her lips with his finger. Ari pulled on her leg to come look at his stones. Danielle turned to him, and Isaac was gone.

Chapter 32

Danielle was numb. She was still in shock from Isaac's announcement that he loved her and the imminent reality of his absence, but willed herself to go about her routine as if nothing had happened. Luckily, Marvin was a totally self-absorbed husband. He was, as usual, completely oblivious to her state of mind. Normally, Danielle would be furious. Now, she was grateful.

That whole night she lay awake imagining how empty her life was going to be with Isaac gone. She had grown so accustomed to the addictive charge of anticipating seeing him that she dreaded the next minute, the next hour, because she knew she couldn't see him. When she woke up that morning, she faced that Isaac was gone. Natan was taking him to the airport, and they were probably on the road to Lod right now.

"Hey, bring me a glass of apple juice," Marvin yelled from the balcony. "I need to fix the wheel on this piece of shit scooter."

"Okay, I'll be there in a second," Danielle called. She took a couple of deep breaths and reminded herself that Isaac was just an amusement. Marvin was her husband. Marvin was the father of both her children. Marvin and the children were her life.

"What are you doing?" she asked as she placed the apple juice on the small child's table that Marv had built for Ari.

"This wheel is just about ready to fall off, so I'm replacing the bolts. As my father would say, *Das es Scheisse*. Definitely not German made.".

"We're lucky that you're so good with your hands. I don't know anyone else that could have done what you've done with so little experience."

"You don't know anyone else? Whaddya mean? Gingy did, Natan did, Rhoda. Everyone here did. We all took a big chance."

"Of course. But this is different. You started a silver jewelry factory."

"So?"

"Our silver jewelry isn't just sold here. We have clients in Europe and the US. It's not like you came from a jewelry background or family business."

"Yeah, but I went to Brooklyn Tech."

"Oh, you ..."

"It's the truth. I learned about lathes, welding, and mechanical engineering. I wasn't lying when I said that I learned more in high school than I did in college."

"But it's amazing that you were able to apply everything to a brand new field."

"And while you're bragging about me, don't forget that I got rid of Uri as soon as I could."

"It's true. You learned extraordinarily fast, but I still don't know if getting rid of him was the right thing."

"Who knows? Now it doesn't matter. Maybe he's the one better off. He's back in Tel Aviv, working for another jewelry manufacturer while we're sitting here waiting for Godot. Anyway, the deal was that he was only going to stay until I got the hang of the kiln. I guess he didn't figure I would learn it so fast."

"We're going to have to start all over again if they give Yamit back."

"Look, nothing's signed yet. It's bullshit. All of a sudden, after all these wars and Egypt happily ass fucking the Nazis since before World War II, we give them this piece of land and they're going to be good neighbors?"

"You think there's hope then? You think maybe the whole thing will fall through and we'll be able to raise the kids here?"

"Who knows? Right now, all we can do is wait. These political fuckers have our lives in their hands."

"I wonder what happened to Begin? I can't believe his back wasn't up against the wall."

"I think you're right, my wife, my life. But he's dealing with that Southern anti-Semite Jimmy Carter. First of all, he probably never even met a Jew in that butt hole he calls a town, Plains, Georgia. Then of course, what are plains full of?"

"I don' t know. Anti-Semites?"

"No, bull shit Lots of it."

Danielle smiled. "Cute, very cute."

"Abba, done?" Ari asked.

"Patience," Marv said to his son. "I want to tighten this bolt too. I don't want you falling on your head. Hurting yourself and scrambling your brains would upset your mother."

"You're so right, Marv. It would. As a matter of fact, my mother said all little boys should wear helmets so they don't get hurt when they fall."

"Yeah, great. And they'll also grow up to be pussies. Here buddy." He pushed the scooter toward his son and patted him on the head.

Ari quickly put his cup down and dragged his scooter to the door.

"Ima, down."

"Okay, I'll bring it down. Just be careful."

She carried his toy down the stairs and then watched him scramble down the walkway as fast as his chubby little legs would take him. He careened down the middle of the sidewalk, quickly veering to the right to avoid a couple who were strolling in the opposite direction. Then she quickly went back up the stairs, knowing Lani would be up any minute.

As she walked back into the apartment, she asked Marvin if he wanted a salami sandwich for lunch.

"Sounds good. Then maybe we can play a little Hide the Salami before I go to work."

"Classy, very classy. Let's see how long our golden girl sleeps. Put some music on while I make your lunch."

"You're the boss," he said, playfully clicking his heels.

Danielle shook her head as he put on her favorite Grateful Dead album, and soon the catchy "Sugar Magnolia" was playing. Marvin sang with Jerry and the boys as he put his tools away, and Danielle bounced to the beat as she sliced bread and salami. At that moment she could almost forget her longing for Isaac.

"Hey," Marvin called. "I just heard a knock at the door. Get it, will ya?"

"Sure." She wiped her hands on the dish towel before she walked to the door. "I'm coming."

She expected to see Rachel or another familiar face when she opened the door. Instead she was surprised to see an odd-looking couple. Not only were they strangers, but the woman had her head covered with a scarf and the man was dressed in gray slacks and a white button down shirt.

"Yes. Can I help you?"

"I am Hassan and this is my wife Farida."

"Yes?"

"Who the hell is it?" Marvin called.

"I think you better come here, Marvin," Danielle replied. "How can we help you?" she asked the couple.

"We are from Gaza and friends of Abu Amman."

"Who?"

"Abu Amman. You must know him as Mahmud. He is correct. Yamit is a very beautiful town."

"Thank you," Danielle replied cautiously.

Hassan continued speaking pleasantly in a mixture of Hebrew and English. "Abu Amman says that now that we will have our land back, we will be living here. Abu—"

"What!" Danielle body had gone taut, and the tightness in her windpipe made it hard to breathe.

Marvin came up behind her and said in clear English, "Get the fuck out of here now."

"Mister, I will get out of here now, but you and all of your neighbors will be gone soon. Abu Amman told us that when the infidels flee, we will return to our rightful place. I just wanted to show my wife how nice it will be."

His wife, standing about an arm's length behind him, nodded.

"Your rightful place," Marvin said, "is that pile of dirt and shit that you call home. Get the hell out of here." And he slammed the door.

"You believe that shit?" he said to Danielle.

"The chutzpah, to come to our home like that."

"I'm going down to the workshop for a little while."

"You're going to leave me alone after what just happened?" Danielle said frantically.

"You'll be fine. I have work to do," Marvin answered gruffly, not looking at her.

"Okay, yeah," Danielle answered dully. "Here, take the sandwich and the letter on the table."

"What letter?"

"I don't know who it's from, but it looks like it's from the government. It came yesterday and I forgot about it."

"So give it to me. Maybe they changed their minds. It will read, 'Concerning the Accord to return the Sinai which includes our model city Yamit, sorry, we made a boo-boo. You're going to stay right where you are.'"

Danielle smiled nervously, scrutinizing her husband's face as he read the letter. Then he just stood there staring at it.

"Nu?" she said.

"It's a double fuck," he said, calmly nodding his head. "This is a mother fucking nightmare." Like a sleepwalker with a direction and purpose known only to himself, he just turned and walked out the door.

Danielle followed him, asking, "What is it? What did the letter say?"

Marvin looked back at her and said, "I've been drafted."

Chapter 33

Anger permeated the air as Marvin slammed around the bedroom, throwing clothes into his backpack. The last two weeks had been unbearable for Danielle. Most nights he didn't bother coming home, just collapsed drunk on the cot he kept at the workshop. Danielle exulted in those nights, because when he did come home, he was worse than scary. He was disgusting.

One night she even slept scrunched up in the backseat of the car, preferring that to his alcohol-fueled rants against the government and the way life treated him in general. Another night she hid under a pile of laundry to escape his slobbering pseudo-affection, which masqueraded as a sheepish apology after his nonstop cursing of God and Israel. The worst part was that she didn't know what to do. During those agonizing nights she would silently repeat Isaac's name like a mantra, praying that somehow he would hear her.

In the last two weeks she had acquiesced to lovemaking only once, and she had felt nothing but Marvin's desperation. Afterward her told her that the evacuation process had already started.

"What are you talking about?" she asked him. "There's nothing in the newspaper yet."

Since she didn't want to believe him, she assumed that it was his alcoholic despair and justifiable paranoia speaking.

Unfortunately she was wrong. A lawyer from Jerusalem had already contacted Marv and other Yamit businessmen. Secret meetings that weren't reported to the newspapers had been held, meeting that were filled with blistering shouting matches as the settlers argued the terms of the compensation packages they were willing to accept from the government.

Now, as he threw his toothbrush into his bag, Marvin said in a monotone, "All the old jewelry orders are ready to go. The ones to Jensen and Stern are all new orders, so I'll take care of them when I come back from basic training."

"Don't worry, Marv. I have the store covered, and new business will just have to wait." Looking at him, she said, "Put the bag down, Marv."

She was surprised that he listened to her. She looked into his bloodshot eyes and caressed his cheek. "We can get through this. Please, I love you. Just stop drinking. The drinking makes everything worse."

"Now I'll have to."

She smiled. "See, something good will come from this yet."

They hugged, and Danielle prayed that her strength would seep into her husband's blood.

Marv took one more look around and said uncharacteristically. "I love this place, Danielle."

"I know Marv"

"How can I fight for a country that is taking my home away? It's not just a home, but a home that the government begged us to come to. I still have the blueprints! They promised us that they'll never give it back. Moshe Dayan swore to all of us. Remember, Danielle?"

"How can I forget? You're probably the only person, beside his doctors, who saw the secret behind the patch!"

Marv ignored her comment. "It makes no sense. Now I'm supposed to just go march in formation and take orders like a sheep dressed in an Israeli uniform?"

"I don't have any answers, Marv, but we have to believe that we'll get through this."

He took a deep breath. "Okay. I'm ready. Let's go."

Ari ran down the stairs ahead of them. He was excited because he knew they were going to Jerusalem to see his grandparents. Danielle carried Ilana in a baby carrier close to her chest. The family filled the little Passat and they headed out to the main road that went straight through the Gaza Strip.

Danielle loved the road that wound through Gaza and the town of Khan Yunis. After driving through the perpetual arid scenery of rocks, tells, and scrubby vegetation beaten down and dried by the relentless sun, to Danielle the town resembled an oasis. Graceful trees lined the road, providing luxurious shade and an arched canopy of natural beauty. The crumbling stone and mud wall surrounding the ancient town had been eroding for centuries. It was just tall enough to allow only seductive peeks of fields and houses in the distance, and between the chinks and bullet holes that memorialized every past battle, Danielle glimpsed fecund orange groves.

Marvin, who was normally garrulous, appeared to be locked in his own hell of thought. She was grateful that his slow driving provided added protection from him hitting any of the children who appeared to be everywhere along the road. She wondered why they weren't in school, and then realized it probably wasn't mandatory. Why would it be? The girls would grow up to be living, breathing incubators swathed in black chadors, chattel belonging to their husbands. The boys? They probably had to help their parents in the fields. Or, she corrected herself, they were taking lessons on how to play shesh besh and drink tea. She was appalled as she watched one little girl, about six years old, hold the reins as she led the donkey that her father was riding like a prince. Such dissonance between the two worlds that lived side by side. Hers was in the twentieth century. This one was living in an ancient time warp.

Engrossed by her contemplation of the surreal quality of the scene around her, Danielle was startled by Marvin's voice. "So, look, why don't you call your father and see if there's a business or something that we can buy when we go back to the United States."

"What?" she said.

"Yeah, I've come to a decision. The best thing is just to take the money and run."

"What are you talking about? You're going in the army. This is our country now."

"Oh, yeah," he said derisively.

"Marvin my— our children were born here. This is their country. Our country. I'll start looking and researching, so that when you come home we'll have a couple of choices to look at—"

"I'm not living here," her husband said. "Call your dad. He knows people. Maybe someone is selling a business."

Danielle knew she couldn't dissuade him, now that his mind was made up. She also knew that with this pronouncement, the marriage would end in divorce. Ominous chills ran up and down her skin. She knew their decisions had been made, but now was not the time to discuss the future. Now was the time to come together and try to bear up under this crisis. Now was also the time to have coffee with her father-in-law and make him smile as they sat together at a coffee shop and he relived his cosmopolitan youth by flirting with haggard, older women, who blossomed into the girls they had once been. Now was the time to bring the grandchildren, who were a breath of life to her mother-in-law, a woman who had forgotten what life could be after the flames of the Nazi ovens and the face of relentless evil had sucked it out of her. Now was the time to pretend everything was all right. Later, there would be Isaac.

Chapter 34

Marvin parked the car on the street, and the family trekked up the hill to his parents' apartment in the Rehavia section of Jerusalem. Marvin was once again lost in his own thoughts while Danielle was hoping they would manage to get out of the house to take the kids to the park, not to mention get a decent cup of coffee. Otherwise, they'd be stuck in the house like hostages, caught in her mother-in-law's intricately woven net of tears, guilt, and tortured memories.

When they knocked on the door, Tosha swooped down and grabbed Ari before anyone could even say "Shalom."

"Come in, come in. Oy, my *neshuma*. Just seeing my Arila makes my heart feel better." Her arms enclosed him like a vise. "Look at his precious face. His smile is like a sweet balm. The heaviness on my heart lifts just to see him. Come, you must be hungry."

Marvin looked at Danielle, shaking his head and rolling his eyes. Then he patted his father on the shoulder. "Hey, Pop, you're looking good."

"Thank you, my dear son. Your mother takes good care of me. As a matter of fact, I am feeling so well that I shall go to Frankfurt next week for the furrier show that Mr. Schneiderman would like me to attend."

"That's great, Pop. Make a toast to old Willy Brandt for me."

"Yes, son. I will enjoy myself in a beer garden and be thankful that I am once again in my homeland."

Danielle wondered how he could even visit the country that was the place of such horror, and then she watched Marvin awkwardly kiss his mother, and felt bad for them both.

Tosha brushed Danielle's cheek with her dry lips and announced that she made a delicious sponge cake to go with the instant coffee, and Danielle knew it was the time to speak up.

"Let me first nurse the baby and then I'll just have a small piece of cake. We can have coffee later. It's such a beautiful day. I thought it would be nice to go for a walk."

"That is an excellent idea, Danielle," Fredreich said. "You are not only beautiful but clever. Yes, my son is a very lucky man." He lit a cigarette and exhaled a thin plume of smoke. "It is important," he added pointedly as his gaze followed the smoke, "for a woman to not only be beautiful, but to have joie de vivre."

Danielle smiled and nodded in agreement.

"Even in Siberia," Fredreich went on, "I found this to be true."

"Fredreich, enough with this *narishkeit*," his wife scolded. "The children didn't come here to listen to your stories. Tomorrow, God willing, our son is going in the army."

"God willing?" Marvin said. "Sure. And I'm sure God willed that the government take our home and business too." He picked his backpack up off the couch and headed toward the bedroom. "I'm taking a nap. Call me for dinner."

"I said something?" his mother asked, looking at Danielle.

"No, Tosha, it's not you. He's just very upset and nervous about tomorrow."

"He was always such a good boy. All the time so good to his sister."

Ari was occupied, happily sitting on his grandfather's lap playing a game with him that had Ari giggling. Although she had thought Lani would want to nurse, the baby had fallen asleep. Danielle knew it had started. They were stuck in Tosha's nightmare labyrinth, and they'd never get out of the house.

"I think only from when he got married," Marvin's mother went on. "That's when he started behaving like this."

"Tosha, stop," Danielle said. "He's going in the army and the government is taking our home and business. It's hard for him. Our government lied to us."

"Governments lie. But this, *kinahura*, is Jewish government. This is our government."

"Of course, but—"

"It is a wife's job to keep shalom beit. She must keep a husband happy. In my home there was never any fighting. You heard Fredreich. My husband says I take good care of him."

Danielle turned to look at Fredreich for help, but he just smiled and shrugged as if to say, "What can I do?"

Tosha continued, "The children had everything they needed. They were such good children. I told you? Marvin was named after my father Menachem Chaim of blessed memory. He was so learned, like a rabbi. The people in our village called him Rav."

"I know, Tosha. I'm sure that's why your children are both so intelligent."

The tears welled up in Tosha's eyes as she whispered, "People say it never happened. They say, the Jews, they lie. What's going to happen when we're gone?"

"Tosha, your children and others ..."

"*Safta*, don't cry." Ari had left his grandfather's lap and wandered over to the kitchen table where the two women were sitting.

"*Tatala*, come sit on your grandma's lap. Just to have him here makes my heart lighter. Here, drink a little tea with the cake."

"*Safta*, look." Danielle's stomach lurched as Ari innocently pointed to the blue tattooed numbers on the inner part of his grandmother's arm. "I can say these numbers." He traced them with his chubby index finger. "See? Three, six, nine—"

"Ari," Danielle interrupted sharply. "Leave Grandma alone. Come here."

But he was so entranced with the small blue numbers that he didn't appear to hear her. "Safta," he asked " write these numbers?"

"Ari," Danielle said before her mother-in-law could answer, "let's go for a walk. Go use the bathroom."

" Don't have to. Grandma, why?" he asked again.

"*Tatala*, I didn't."

"Who? Safta, why don't you wash them ?"

"I can't," she replied softly as new tears formed.

"Why not? Ima won't let me write on myself It's bad."

Tosha nodded and replied that his mother was right.

"So who put those numbers there, Safta?"

"Bad people, Arila. Bad people who killed lots and lots of our people. Jewish people."

"People like us, Safta?"

"Yes, people like us. My family, Arila, my whole family. My father, my mother, my sisters and their husbands and children."

While Ari wiped a tear from his grandmother's eye, Marvin bellowed from the bedroom, "Don't start!"

"Tosha, Marvin is right," Fredreich said. "Listen to him. I am getting my hat, Danielle. Come. Let us enjoy this exhilarating weather with a stroll to our favorite café."

Suddenly the bedroom door opened with a loud slam against the wall.

"Take the kids and go with my father," Marvin said to Danielle. "Now. Don't start with this, Mom. This kid will soon enough have to deal with his own problems ... like losing his home for some bullshit political scheme."

Danielle took one look at her husband and realized he must have smuggled a bottle of vodka into his backpack. His enunciation was just a little too controlled and his posture just a little too taut. Of course, his parents were oblivious to his condition. She anxiously watched her mother-in-law dab at her eyes with a tissue, and then willed herself to keep moving as Tosha wailed, "To be treated like this from my only son? For this God saved me?"

Danielle hesitated.

"Just leave her and go," Marvin insisted.

"That was exactly what I told your beautiful wife, son. We shall be back in time for Tosha's delicious gefilte fish and brisket. Come, my dear, let's get the stroller from the car."

"Ari, go with your mother and grandpa," Marvin bellowed at his son, who had wandered into the bedroom to hide from the cacophony of noise and emotions.

"Sha, the neighbors will hear," Tosha said, her eyes still filled with tears.

"Can we go to swings?" Ari asked.

"Absolutely," Danielle replied, relieved that they were getting out of the house. "Why don't I just carry the baby," she said to Fredreich, "and then we can put her in the stroller when we get to the car, instead of schlepping it up here?"

"That is a very practical idea, my lovely daughter-in-law. As I have always told Tosha, Marvin is a lucky man to have a wife who is not only beautiful but smart."

Danielle just smiled at the flattery. She was so grateful to be out of the house, she thought the best thing was to just change the subject altogether. "So, Fredreich, I'm so glad that we were able to name Ilana after your brother."

Her father-in-law, who had just opened the outside door for her, looked surprised. "What brother?"

"Your brother, the one who was a famous boxer? Iggy?"

"Ach! You mean Sigmund. Yes, yes, he was so agile and strong. In the Jewish newspapers he was called Kid Samson. He was a contender for the lightweight division for boxing in the 1936 Olympics. We were all so proud of him. My parents, they named him Sigmund, but we called him Siggy." He paused before adding somberly, "The Nazis, they called him Kike Samson."

"Oh, no, Fredreich," Danielle exclaimed in embarrassment, "we made a terrible mistake. We wanted to name the baby in honor of him, your brother. Marvin told me his name was Iggy."

Her father-in-law lit a cigarette. After pensively exhaling, he shrugged and smiled wryly. "Siggy, Iggy, what does it matter? They murdered him. Just so that a Jew couldn't win, That, my beautiful daughter-in-law, is what matters."

Chapter 35

The next few weeks flew by as Danielle had to oversee the business and ensure that the final shipment of dainty filigree rings and hamsas—Middle Eastern good luck charms— went to the correct New Jersey gift shops. As Danielle rolled the shopping cart around the supermarket one day, she had to admit to a chaotic mix of ambivalence about Marvin coming home for Shabbat. The everyday routine of caring for the children and managing the retail store exhausted her, but at least the routine wasn't punctuated by his bouts of drinking and her retaliatory histrionics. Their macabre dance scared Ari and left Danielle both weak and depleted. She was still hoping to keep her family intact. Since she had received only one letter from Isaac, her relationship with him had slipped into a dreamlike fantasy that she would take out and examine like a piece of precious jewelry, locked away for safekeeping.

She absentmindedly reviewed her purchases as she stood in the checkout line, making sure she had all the ingredients to bake the chocolate cake that both Marvin and Ari liked so much. She vowed that his time home would be pleasant; anything negative was off limits. Ari was thrilled that his "Soldier Abba" was coming home, and Minna had helped him make a welcome-home card. Danielle was concerned that he didn't fully understand that his father would only be home for a few days.

When Marvin walked in, the first thing Danielle noticed was how scruffy he looked. He hadn't shaved in a while, and although his camouflage uniform almost hid the dirt, it smelled acrid and pungent. She could see she'd have a lot of washing to do. Then she saw his eyes. They were so sad and puzzled, she knew she would be as accommodating and sweet to him as possible.

After the hugging and kissing, a shower and change of clothes from the green military fatigues to his worn, comfortable jeans and a T-shirt, Ari crawled onto his father's lap and said, "Abba I'm glad you home."

Marvin ruffled his son's hair and said, "Me too, buddy. But it won't be for long."

"Come, Abba, I want to show you something."

"Not now, buddy."

Danielle saw Ari's stricken face, and with a forced smile told him to get it and bring it to his father.

"Okay, Ima." He immediately jumped off his father's lap and ran to his bedroom before Danielle could remind him to be quiet and not wake up his sister.

Running back, he handed the card to Marvin. "Minna and me made it for you." Welcome Home was printed in Hebrew and English across the blue and white Israeli flag. His eyes bright and eager, he waited for his father's approval.

Marvin took the card, opened it, and then just crumpled it up.

"Hey, Marv," Danielle said. "Ari worked hard on that all afternoon."

"Thanks," Marvin replied gruffly.

Seeing the disappointment in the slump of Ari's body and the way he closed his fists into tight balls, she knew he was on the verge of heart-wrenching sobbing.

"Hey! Why don't you guys go for a bike ride together?" she suggested with counterfeit cheerfulness. "When you get back we'll eat something. Okay?" She looked at her husband meaningfully.

"Good idea, Danielle," Marvin said as if nothing had just occurred. "You want to ride on the back of my bicycle or ride your own, buddy?"

"With you, Abba, with you," Ari said, once again happy to be with his father.

"Okay, let's go. Mommy and sister can cook and do girl stuff. We'll go down to the workshop."

"Be back by six so we can eat," Danielle said. "And Marvin, please be careful. You have your son with you."

"Don't worry," he said angrily.

They clattered down the stairs together, and she was relieved when she heard Ari laughing.

After she was sure they were gone, she started making the chocolate cake. While she sifted the flour and added the eggs, she prayed for her husband and children. She continued while she added the melted chocolate and tears streamed down her face.

Later that evening, when the children were finally asleep and Marvin was still able to pretend he was sober, Rachel and Natan stopped over. While Rachel helped Danielle bring the coffee and cake into the dining room, the two men started talking about the army. Natan mentioned that he heard about Marvin's sharp-shooting skills all the way here in the Sinai.

"You're kidding, man," Marvin said.

"No, honestly. You know my brother Rami? He was up there bringing some supplies and your sergeant ... What's his name? Moki? He asked him about you. He said they were thinking of putting you with the snipers. That's a big deal for a new immigrant."

"Deal, schmeal," Marv replied. Danielle could tell he was surprised by the compliment, but was trying to make light of it. "I'm in with these guys that never saw a toilet before. Dima, some Russian guy from the Georgian mountains, was actually washing his potatoes in one."

"What?" Danielle and Rachel asked at the same time.

"Yeah, you heard me. In the toilet."

Marv continued with a colorful description of how he had found his bunkmate squatting on the toilet, flushing madly in order to clean his five pounds of potatoes. As usual, he had his audience howling as he proceeded to tell his tale. "I hear all this flushing, so I knock. You okay? I say."

"'Da, my friend. It just doesn't work so good,' this idiot tells me. I tell him it sounds okay from here and ask what's wrong? So he says, 'The potatoes just don't get clean!'

"I open the fucking door and this inbred Georgian Neanderthal is squatting on the toilet seat dipping his potatoes in the water and flushing to give them a good scrubbing! You believe this shit? So when a guy is used to taking a crap in a hole in the ground, what's my big competition?"

The two women laughed so hard, they had tears in their eyes. While Danielle went to the kitchen to bring in more coffee and the rest of the chocolate cake, Marv started a diatribe about the Afghani in his unit.

"The guy is like a monkey. He's got these long skinny brown arms and he's the size I was when I was a bar mitzvah boy."

"That's the size of a peanut, Marv," Danielle said, smiling as she set the tray down.

"That's right. He's so primitive, he makes Dima look like Herr Doctor Kissinger."

"I didn't even know there were Jews in Afghanistan," Danielle said.

"Come on, *chaver*," Natan said, playing straight man, "how can he be more primitive than a guy washing potatoes in toilets?"

Marvin immediately took the bait. "This guy can climb anything. You'd look up on the ceiling and there he was grinning like a lunatic with a mouth full of rotten teeth, hanging by his feet, totally oblivious that the rest of the world was walking on the ground. Remember that scene in *Yankee Doodle Dandy* when Jimmy Cagney dances up the wall?"

"Of course," both women said in unison, while Natan scratched his head and muttered, "Yenkee Doodle Dendy?"

"I watched that movie every day for a week on Million Dollar movie," Danielle said . "Seeing Jimmy Cagney dance up the wall was—"

Marvin interrupted, "Well, this little Afghani puts on a better show. He'd climb up the wall using nothing but his hands and these unbelievably long, skinny feet. There was nothing to grasp onto. And then when he got to the ceiling, he'd give one of those loud Middle Eastern war whoops that they do."

"Oh, yeah, that ululating tongue thing," Rachel said. Of course, after he finished his description of his Afghani bunkmate, the conversation, like almost every conversation in Yamit, turned to the promised compensation.

Natan said that he just hoped the money would cover all the debt he owed on the loans the government had granted him for moving there in the first place.

"Frankel said that we would be compensated by the number of children we have, the size of the apartment, and how long we've been here," Rachel said.

"But that has nothing to do with the businesses and the debts we all face," Natan said.

Marvin took a deep drag on his cigarette and said, "Fuck them. They're a bunch of liars. Someone was telling me about this group called Gush Emunim."

"Yeah, yeah," Natan said. "They're religious. My sister said a couple of families moved into that last group of apartments that were built. They're using the empty apartment on the bottom floor for a Bet Knesset."

"How come people are still moving in when we know we have to leave?" Danielle asked. "It's just a matter of time now."

"Maybe because they're religious and they think God will intervene?" Rachel suggested.

"Yeah, sure," Marv said. "Like He intervened in the camps when Jewish bodies went up in smoke or Jewish babies were ripped out of their mother's pregnant bellies." He took a deep drag on his cigarette.

"What the hell are we going to do?" Danielle asked Rachel sadly. "Yamit is like the Garden of Eden. We all get along, there's no crime, and the town is beautiful. The pool and tennis courts were just finished this year. As a matter of fact, they just started putting in that other playground by the apartment buildings."

"It's only starting to hit me now. The thought of leaving makes me ill. It's getting harder and harder to study for my final. You know, the one I've been studying for this last month? When I stop to think about what we're losing ..." She smiled sadly at Danielle. "We've been closer than some families."

"You have been like a sister. Actually, better than my own sister," Danielle said with tears in her eyes.

"Okay, ladies," Marv said. "That's enough of the crying festival.

Put on the Grateful Dead and let's start 'Truckin'.' We'll do just what the government wants us to do."

The two women swallowed their tears, had a shot of arak, and pretended for the next few hours that Yamit would still be their home and everything would be all right.

Chapter 36

Danielle had taken both children to the gan and was luxuriating in having time to herself when she heard a knock the door;

"Just a minute," Danielle called as she finished toweling off. She threw on her raggedy terry cloth robe and wrapped a towel around her hair before she went to the door. To her surprise, a strange man in an Israeli army uniform was standing there.

"Yes?" she asked caught by surprise.

"*Geveret*, I can come in?"

"What? For what?" Her voice rose. "Something happened to my husband?"

"No, no, not exactly." He spoke in heavily accented English. "But I need to come in."

"Okay. Excuse the way I look, but I thought you were a friend I was expecting."

"No problem."

"Please, take a seat while I change my clothes."

"No, I'm sorry."

"What? You're sorry that you don't want to sit," Danielle stared at him, confused and afraid. What was going on? Why was this guy in her house?

"No, I can't let you get changed."

"Why not? What's going on?" Her voice rose even higher.

"Please, *geveret*, I must check to see if your husband is here."

Danielle didn't understand what he was saying. "Why would he be here? He's with his unit, up there in the north." Then she finally noticed the word *meshtera* on his uniform. Police

"*Geveret,* this will just take a couple of minutes. Sit, *bevakasha.* I must go check in the bedrooms and bathroom."

Danielle sat on the couch and pulled a cigarette from the pack in her pocket. Her hand was shaking so much as she lit the match, the flame went out and she had to strike another match to light her cigarette.

As he came out of the bedroom, the solider tried to make her more comfortable. "I told you this would be quick. Lucky for me our houses are like concrete boxes."

"What are you looking for?" she asked as calmly as she could, even though she had a sinking feeling she already knew.

"Your husband," he answered succinctly.

"I don't know where he is, I thought he was with his unit," she answered truthfully.

"I believe you, but I must check in the back too. I must do my job."

With his long, purposeful stride, the young man walked to the back room where the washing machine was located. Since the laundry room was only a breath wider than the washing machine and there were no closets, he returned to the living room before Danielle could start thinking clearly.

"Nu, geveret, I must ask. When was the last time you saw him?"

"Please, sit. You're making me more nervous by standing."

He continued to stand.

Danielle spoke in what she hoped was a calm tone of voice. "I saw him last week when he came home before he went to his assigned job."

"Did he tell you where his assigned job was going to be?"

"No, but I didn't think that was strange."

"He was supposed to report to his new base yesterday and never did. Of course we have made inquiries and believe that nothing happened to him, but from what some members of his group said, he was very unhappy with his assigned post."

Danielle answered spontaneously, "He isn't happy with anything, so that doesn't mean anything."

"I am afraid that this time it does mean something. We will contact you when we find him."

"Thanks," Danielle replied automatically. "By the way, where was he supposed to go?"

"All I can say is *chutz la'aretz*."

"Out of the country? Lebanon?"

"It is too bad. The army needs your husband. Did you know he is an excellent marksman?" he asked conversationally.

Still in shock, Danielle tried to make a joke. "I guess that's because he lived in the Bronx."

"I don't understand."

"Sorry. It was just a bad joke."

"Okay, I'm leaving now. This is the phone number to call if you hear from him or if he shows up," the soldier said politely. Then he added, "Now you can change your clothes, although you look very good the way."

"Out," she said. "Thank you, good-bye, and shalom," Insulted that he could make a suggestive remark at a time like this, she slammed the door behind him.

After chain smoking two or three cigarettes, she felt calm enough to throw on some clothes and run over to Rachel's house.

She banged on the door repeatedly, too upset to care that she was interrupting her friend's study time.

Rachel finally opened the door. "Hey, is that a new fashion you're trying to start?"

"What? What are you talking about?"

"Look at your shirt. "

Danielle looked down and sure enough, she had thrown on her favorite T-shirt inside out.

"Well, at least you know I'm upset enough to have to disturb you."

"Not really. We both know that's something you'd do anyway," Rachel teased. "Come sit down, and I'll make us some coffee."

Danielle headed for the bathroom to reassemble herself. "Rach, he's missing," she called as she pulled her shirt off.

"Who, Danielle?" Rachel asked as her friend came out of the bathroom. "You need to calm down and tell me the whole story."

Danielle sat down at the small dining room table and felt better simply recounting to Rachel everything that had just happened.

"God, Dani. I don't think you can do anything. When Natan comes home I'll ask him. I hate to say this, but I think when they find him they'll put him in jail. It sounds like he went AWOL. It'll be on his record."

"I don't think he cares. He told me to make plans to leave the country."

"When? When did he say that?"

Danielle thought for a second and then answered, "The first time was on the way to his parents' house when he had to report to basic. Since then we haven't talked about it much. Remember, he's only come home twice and called a couple of times. It hurts so much to think about. You know how it is. This is like being in the middle of a nightmare."

Rachel nodded in agreement.

"Just as I'm getting adjusted to one image, the whole picture suddenly changes and the landscape melds into something different. Now, in the blink of an eye, the landscape just changed again and it's even darker."

"I know what you mean. Natan and I are counting on enough pitzuim to start over again, but if we have to pay off those government loans with that money, then I don't know what we'll be able to do or where we'll be able to afford to live."

"The government is using us. No doubt about it. But now I really don't know what to do since I don't have a clue where Marv is."

"I hate to ask this," Rachel said, "but do you think he snuck out of the country?"

Danielle didn't respond.

"Dani? Danielle? Did you hear me? What do you think? Do you think he left?"

"I heard you, Rach. I didn't even think of that." She pulled a cigarette out of her pack and lit it.

"It's weird," she went on, "but I'm almost certain he's okay. I know he hated the idea of being in the army after the government royally fucked us, but I don't think he would just leave the country and abandon the kids and me. I think he's hiding somewhere. Maybe that's why I'm more angry than worried."

"What are you going to do?"

"I don't know, but I don't think there's much I can do. So, I'm going to continue to take care of the business, the kids, and the house and just wait. I have to believe he didn't just abandon us."

"Dani," her friend replied, "I sure hope you're right."

Chapter 37

The next few days went by in slow motion, with each day seeming longer than the one before. Danielle felt like she was living on automatic pilot, her body going through the motions as she tried to keep focused on everything she normally had to do. As usual, she took Ari and Lani to the gan, went down to the workshop to greet a tourist group, and tried to sell off as much merchandise as possible to their various customers in Tel Aviv and Jerusalem.

After congratulating herself for cajoling the buyer for an upscale gift shop in Jerusalem to take a few more of their silver mezuzahs, she returned the phone to its cradle. Hearing the tinkle of a little bell, she realized someone had entered the retail store.

"I'll be right there," she called. Taking a deep breath, she willed herself to smile as she opened the door.

A woman was looking at the displays at the front of the store. With a faded scarf covering her head and dressed in a long, drab skirt, she was carrying a baby in a sling across her chest.

Danielle greeted her customer with a cheerful, "Shalom, how can I help you?"

The woman answered her in perfect English. "You're Danielle?"

"Yes," Danielle answered automatically, although she was surprised at the query. "I'm the Danielle's the business is named after. Are you looking for something in particular?"

"Yes, you." The woman pulled something a piece of paper out of her pocket and gave it to Danielle.

"What the ..."

"I'll see you again soon," the stranger whispered. "But if you happen to see me around town, pretend you never met me. Lahitraot and shalom."

She quickly exited, leaving Danielle standing in the middle of the shop with a folded piece of lined paper. She knew who had sent it. Her stomach roiling and her windpipe tightening, she hoped she could make it to her chair without retching. As she walked blindly back to the office, she prayed aloud, "Please, God, let him be okay."

She sat down and nervously unfolded the paper, reading it in one glance: Go to apartment 202 in the last block of apartments this erev Shabbat at 6:30. Don't tell ANYONE. Love, Marv.

It was his handwriting. He was okay.

When Friday evening finally came, she asked Minna to stay with the children. She said she was going to a meeting at the cultural center to discuss the offer for a new community in the Gaza Strip. She'd stop in on the way back so that way people could vouch for her if there were any questions.

"Okay, Minna, don't let Ari wrap you around his finger just so that he can stay up a little later."

"But it's such a cute little finger, Dani," Mina replied with her hearty laugh. Ari had already coaxed her into helping him complete his Lego city while Ilana watched the two from her playpen.

"I'll be back in a couple of hours. Lahit."

She left before waiting for a reply and walked quickly to the designated apartment. As she approached the building, she saw a few men leaving the first floor apartment, which was being used as a synagogue. Overwhelmed with everything that was happening, she stopped to sit on a bench. She took a deep breath to calm herself as she looked around at the simple beauty that surrounded her. In one direction, the timeless desert hills stood against the horizon. To her right and down the delicate rise of sand dunes, a graceful line of palm trees decorated the pure white beach. Choking back tears for what she and her children were going to lose, she stood and forced herself to continue. She warily knocked on the door.

The door was opened by the woman who had come to the store. "Shabbat shalom, Danielle," she said. She introduced herself as Shoshana and invited Danielle to sit.

"Oh, you're American?" Danielle asked politely, recognizing the unmistakable Brooklyn accent .

"Yes, Midwood, to be exact, but maybe we'll have time to talk later. You came to see someone and you can't stay long." Shoshana disappeared into the kitchen.

"Danielle," a sheepish Marvin said as he came out of the bedroom.

"Oh, Marv." Danielle threw herself into his arms. "Thank God you're all right." Her tears started flowing uncontrollably after being pent up for so many anguished days and nights. "Marv, Marv, what are you doing? I've been so worried. Last week an MP came to the house …"

"Fuck the IDF. Fuck Begin, Sharon, and a double shtup to that one-eyed weasel Dayan."

"Fine, Marvin, but now you're the one that's hurting us, your family."

"Look, I'm sorry, but you have to understand. Right now, this is more important. The government's wrong. Very wrong. I refuse to be a soldier for a country that's screwing me. It makes no sense."

"Okay, I get it," Danielle said resignedly "So just explain to me what you're doing."

"I was just eating a falafel at some stand in Jerusalem, and this guy sat down next to me. We both decided it was great falafel, so we started talking . Turns out he was a rabbi from Brooklyn. Meir Kahane. Do you remember the name?"

"Yeah, I do. Wasn't he the head of the Jewish Defense League or something?"

"Bingo! But now he travels back and forth from the States to Israel and is involved with a group called Gush Emunim. They're starting to come here to Yamit."

"Didn't you mention them before? Aren't they religious?" Danielle asked.

"Yeah, but they don't care that I'm not. They agree with me. The government is wrong. Not only wrong for us, the Yamitniks, but wrong for the whole country. Big deal, so we get compensation. That isn't what this is about."

"What's it about, then, Marv?"

"Very simple. This is our land—Jewish land."

"Isn't that what we said to all those stupid journalists?"

"Right. But these guys are religious and believe every word in the Torah is sacred. They believe that this is part of the Israel that God gave the Jews according to what is written in the Torah."

"Like the world gives a shit about what was given to the Jews in the Torah," Danielle said. Still, she asked out of curiosity, "So what are the borders supposed to be?"

"The southern boundary goes up to El Arish, which of course includes Yamit and all of the Northwestern Sinai." Then he added, more excitedly than she had ever seen him, "They have a plan, Danielle. They're going to take a stand."

"And what are you going to do, Marv?" she asked, but she already knew the answer.

"I'm taking a stand with them." he replied, looking straight in her eyes.

She shook her head and looked away. "I can't, Marv. I have to think about the kids. If it were just us … And what's going to happen with the army?"

"Nothing. This group is going to provide a lawyer and we're going to fight the fact that I was drafted. In the meantime, I'm sticking close to them."

"You're going to stay here? In this apartment? Marv, Marvin, you're not thinking of us, me and the kids, at all."

"Of course I am. Remember, you are my wife, my life. I can only do this because of you and the kids. I'll stay in touch just like I did now, but I can't tell you where I'll be."

"But why, Marv? Why? Fuck Israel. We'll go back to the States just like you said. I already told my parents …"

She could feel her whole body tightening as her voice got louder, and she knew whoever was in the apartment heard every word she and Marv exchanged. She didn't care.

"Look, Danielle. My whole life my mother's been telling me that I'm the soul of my dead grandfather who was killed in cold blood before I was born. The only thing I knew about him was that the Nazis shot him point blank when he opened his front door. I don't know if he was strong or weak, good or bad. Of course, according to my mother he was a tzadik, but that doesn't matter to me. My parents never saw me, Marvin, and I'm their only son. I need to do something that I can be proud of, something that has meaning, and I'm willing to face the consequences, whatever they are."

"But Marv … Please, Marv, listen to me. You did plenty. You helped build this city. How many people can claim that? Remember those days when you had the key to turn on the water for the city? You built a business, you designed the logo for the city …" Her voice was rising hysterically.

"And in the end it will disappear, just like the shtetls of Europe—but this time just one clean sweep for the cause of 'peace.' Now we'll just disappear with a couple of signatures on a piece of paper with the whole world applauding. And I'm supposed to support the government that is willing to sell us out for a piece of paper that I could wipe my ass on?"

Hearing how serious he was, Danielle knew this battle was lost. There was nothing to convince him to turn himself in to the army, to admit he made a mistake, and to change her life back to normal.

"I guess there's nothing I can say to change your mind, Marv. I agree with you in principle. The government used us as pawns in a game we didn't even know we were playing. No doubt about it. You know that and I know that, but now is not the time. You're the father of two beautiful children. You're just being damn selfish and self-absorbed. Now is not the time to take a stand. We have to make an important decision like this together. Especially now. This will affect the rest of our lives. What the hell am I supposed to do? We have two children that depend on us."

"I can't, Danielle."

"I have to go. But let me just ask you a simple question, Marv. Do you think this group will stand by you when they realize you're nothing but a drunk?"

"My wife, my life, please, I love you," Marvin pleaded to her back as she walked out the door.

Chapter 38

Danielle felt as shocked and battered as if she'd been hit head-on in a collision. The only thing she wanted to do now was go home, crawl in bed, and wrap herself in the cocoon of her blanket, but she knew she had to stop in at the town meeting so that she had a cover story. On the return trip back through town, she relived the whole miserable rendezvous, trying to extract a specific moment that could have changed his mind.

As she trudged up the broad walkway to the Bauhaus-style cultural center, with its clean, simple lines, she glanced at the huge abstract sculpture of the Yamit logo intertwined with a star of David. A Russian artist and one of the original settlers in town, Tanya Sankov, had welded it from pipe and metal left over from the laying of the gas and water lines.

Before Danielle even opened the heavy wooden front door, she could hear the raucous voices of her friends and neighbors. She nodded to people she knew as she slipped into an empty seat at the back of the room beside her friend Sarah, who sat knitting madly like Madame Defarge. The last speaker, Bob Goldblatt, had just returned to his seat next to Laura Iscoff, who wasn't one of the settlers of the community but had done her anthropology PhD dissertation on the organization of the nascent city. Seeing them with their heads so close together, Danielle guessed she had come back to visit her friend Bob. *Or*, she thought cynically, *maybe Laura planned on writing another dissertation on the dismantling of a city.*

She scanned the crowded, smoky room. Sarah had welcomed

Danielle with a lifeless smile, although she appeared to be listening attentively to Rhoda, who had just taken the floor. Rhoda had returned recently from a trip to Tel Aviv and was explaining one of the government's options, which was still under discussion. Settlers from Yamit and the surrounding moshavim might be moved to a couple of new towns that the government was planning north of Rafiah in the Gaza Strip.

"There's an old kibbutz called Kfar Darom that they'd like to see reestablished," she announced.

"Sure," shouted Shimon Golani, the owner of a clothing store in the commercial center. "Why not? They'd save money and get the same group of suckers to build a town and start commercial ventures, so they have something viable to use in negotiations again. Not me, once is enough."

He nodded at his beautiful wife Shira, who always managed to look as fashionable, here in the middle of the desert, as if she were still shopping at Bloomingdales at the Short Hills Mall in New Jersey. Even through her morass of pain, Danielle noted their silent agreement and knew they had already made their decision to return to the States. Probably the rumor was true that Shimon had accepted an offer from some big Israeli import-export company in New York.

Dror agreed with Shimon's assessment. "It took so long for the supermarket to be a viable business. Look, it was just a little while ago that we still had to travel into Beer Sheva to buy necessities. We finally have a thriving commercial center with your store, Golani, the Frankels' hardware store, our supermarket, the jewelry store, and the fresh produce stand. Remember when we had no place to buy a cup of coffee or get an ice cream? No, once is enough for me. I'm not a boychik anymore. I've had enough excitement and Hannah agrees. As long as we get enough pitzuim, we'll find a nice neighborhood in Tel Aviv and then we don't have to worry."

Then the Gingy, who had told Danielle that he was there to make as much money as possible, said, "Look, if they won't let me make money the way I wanted, then they're going to have to pay me. Not only for every penny I spent, but the emotional wear and tear, and the future profits they're robbing from me." He clenched his fist like he was ready to punch someone. "I finally laid the foundation of the hotel that I've been dreaming about since the moment I set eyes on this place."

The murmurs got louder, and Danielle could hear Rhoda quite clearly say, "That *mamzer* Avi Pazner is a real son of a bitch. I had to screw him every time I went up to Tel Aviv. Then three months ago when I finally got the liquor permit for the restaurant, and paid plenty for it, I might add, that bastard didn't say anything. Why the hell would he even let me get started? He and all his political buddies are a bunch of scumbags!"

She brought up the idea of sticking together and rebelling against the government. "I got fucked by a husband who would rather screw *korvas* than his own wife. Then I get screwed by these bastards who will say anything as long as they can get into my pants. So this is what I learned from dealing with these no goodniks: standing alone, we're all fucked. Individually, all we can do is follow their insane plans. Alone we definitely lose because we're powerless, but if we stand up to the government as a group, then we have some strength and bargaining power. Maybe they'll forget this *fukahta* Peace Agreement and let us keep what's ours."

A few people on the other side of the room started applauding. Rhoda's words caused a buzz in the room, and Danielle could see people looking more hopeful. She looked around at all the faces that were as familiar and dear as her own family. What was going to happen to them all? Everyone in that room had come to this barren desert spot for nothing more than a dream. They had all left lives behind them to build a city that sparkled and gleamed with their hope for the future and pride of their accomplishments. Although it had been planned by the government, it had been built with the sweat and pain of everyone sitting in that room. She remembered the lonely weeks of sitting in the closet-sized room at the absorption center, waiting for the trucks to return for Shabbat, the men dirty and exhausted from their labor and their hands calloused and rough. How proud Marvin had been that they could live in a home he had built with his own hands!

Then there had been all the days spent waiting for permits, dealing with delays and disappointments. And then to finally reach a point where the city became exactly what the residents and government had planned and envisioned, and then suddenly, without warning, to have it torn out from under our feet. Every step of the way they'd had assurances from the government that they wanted and needed the settlers in Yamit. Moshe Dayan had even made a speech right at the front of this room!

Then Frankel, the former leader of the American *garin*, stood up. Everyone was suddenly quiet. Danielle hadn't seen him in a couple of weeks and was shocked by his appearance. Although he had not been a young man when he started this journey, now he looked gaunt and spent. The thatch of hair that was bobby pinned to his knitted *kippah* had turned gray. His eyes, however, were the most disturbing. They had always sparkled brilliantly, as if he had just heard a good joke. Now they looked dull and lifeless.

"My dear friends and neighbors. I have sat here and listened to the speeches and discussions about our fate and the future of our beautiful city. Now I feel I must speak. Many of you must have noticed I wasn't here for a few weeks. There is a reason. The last few weeks I've been in Tel Aviv trying to rally support for us and the future of Israel."

Whispers immediately filled the room in a buzz of excitement and hope.

Frankel continued somberly, "I spoke to as many members of Knesset that I could, and some were definitely sympathetic. More importantly, though, I spoke to Dayan, who many of you know is my cousin. Through his intervention I had a private audience with our prime minister, Menachem Begin. I am sorry to have to say this, but what he told me was not good. Up until the news of this peace accord with Egypt, I believed just like you did, that we would be here forever. If I thought otherwise, I would not have uprooted my family from our very fine life in Cincinnati where, as many of you know, I was the rabbi of a large conservative shul.

"But I wholeheartedly believed that the government's strategic vision was correct, and that our beautiful Yamit and the surrounding settlements provided a much needed buffer zone from Egypt. I also believed that holding onto the Sinai and the two oil fields in the Mitla Pass was imperative for the well-being of our country. So did Begin. Apparently the American president Jimmy Carter doesn't. Or more succinctly, according to Begin, he doesn't care."

Danielle looked around and noted that the hope that had momentarily illuminated the faces around her had disappeared. Suddenly everyone appeared tense and drawn, though they were focused on every word their former leader was saying. Rabbi Frankel was in his element as an orator, and although his message was contrary to what his audience wanted to hear, they were transfixed by his melodious voice. Their rapt expressions showed him they were listening to this disheartening news.

"My friends and colleagues, I am afraid we now stand alone in the belief of this region's necessity to Ha'aretz, our religious homeland. Our beloved Israel is tired of war and the death and destruction of young lives. There is also a strong peace faction, Shalom Achshav aligned with an American sister organization called Peace Now, that advocates giving back whatever land our enemies demand in the name of peace. Many of the politicians who clamored for this Sinai area to be developed are now calling for its dissolution, stating that by handing over the land, the developed moshavim, and of course the city we built, Yamit, it will show that we want stabilization and normal relations with our neighbors."

"When did we ever show that we didn't want normal relations?" shouted the Gingy from the back of the room. "Every war, going all the way back to 1948, was started by other countries. Egypt just started and lost the Yom Kippur War, and suddenly, *pitom*, Sadat wants to live in peace. I'm a third generation Jerusalimite. I'm no stranger to Arab deception and lies. I have no doubt that this will be a big mistake. What will Israel gain for this peace initiative? I will tell you." He spat on the floor. "Nothing." He stormed out as Frankel took a deep breath and continued.

"Our prime minister, God willing, will be making a trip down here next week. He plans on addressing our concerns and explaining the rationale, though of course peace requires no rationale. I assured him that although we are brokenhearted about the loss of our homes and the shattering of our dreams, we will do whatever it takes to comply with the terms arranged at Camp David. He professed his gratitude and assured me that in return we will receive the best terms possible in compensation."

Chapter 39

Danielle and Rachel sat at their favorite corner table at the beachfront restaurant watching Prime Minister Begin's security personnel check out the area.

"Life changes so fast, Rachel. If this were even just a few months ago, we'd be so excited that the prime minister was visiting our city. The kids would be out waving flags, people would leave work early, and we'd have a big party at the commercial center tonight. Instead, this visit is like he's walking on our graves."

"That's because he is," Rachel said.

"I wish this were over already. All anyone talks about is the damn pitzuim, or what we should be calling blood money."

Rachel nodded. "You're absolutely right. Natan and Rhoda got two big loans from Bank Hapoalim on the basis that tourism to Yamit would grow over the next ten years. That's how we were able to build that little patio and add the extra sink and appliances, so we could host orthodox tourist groups. We're in so much debt that I don't know if we'll end up with anything in our pockets. Every day I thank God I finally got that degree, because at least I'll be able to get a decent job somewhere."

"Shit, you're lucky. I don't have a clue about what I want to do. I was so thankful that we found Yamit. I can't imagine a better place in the world to raise children. It was like a dream come true."

"And now it's more like a nightmare. I guess now is a good time to tell you, Danielle," Rachel said sheepishly. "I already applied for something through some American government agency."

"You're kidding! Is it here in Israel?" Danielle was not surprised that Rachel already had a plan.

"No. Believe it or not, if I get this we would be based in Germany."

"Hmm. Herr Hitler would not be happy that the Fatherland will no longer be Judenriden," Danielle joked as she tried to maintain her composure and not cry. Her life just continued to crumble in front of her eyes. "What about Natan? He's willing to leave Israel?"

"Well, he's been talking to someone he was with in the army, and apparently there's an Israeli community in Frankfurt, so he wouldn't be totally isolated there." Rachel hesitated and then asked, "Have you heard from Marv, Danielle?"

Just as she was going to answer her friend with a lie, Danielle noticed one of the government security guards open the door of a white Saab that had just pulled into the dirt-packed parking lot.

"Rachel, I know this sounds stupid, but I think Begin just got out of that car."

"Oh, my God, you're right. Here they come."

The two women tried to act nonchalant as a cluster of men—the security team in front followed by several other men accompanying Begin—headed for the restaurant. Two men stayed back, standing on either side of the white Saab. As they entered the restaurant, the women could see that the prime minister's daughter Leah was with him. The friends looked at each other and raised their eyebrows, not saying a word as the prime minister passed their table. They watched as the procession continued to the back steps of the open air restaurant. Heads turned in each direction as they all scanned the deserted beach. Begin said something to his daughter and she nodded. Then, just as quickly as they arrived, the group departed. Danielle and Rachel looked at each other in amazement and then laughed.

"His daughter looks exactly like him!" Rachel said.

"You're right. That poor woman. But, Rachel, did you see how bad he looks?"

"What's new? I don't think he looked good even when he was young."

"No, no, that's not what I was talking about. He looked ill. His pallor was almost green. My gut has always been that this peace accord is being settled against his better judgment. I think it's making him sick."

"If you're right, that would explain his daughter being with him."

"Come on. Let's go get the kids. We'll have to eat dinner early so we can get good seats tonight when he speaks."

"Don't forget your camera, Danielle. This will be an historic occasion."

Chapter 40

Danielle looked around between snapping a few photos. This was new to her because she had always relied on Marvin to be the photographer. She hoped the pictures would be good to send to her family, so they could see what was going on. To her surprise, it didn't look like there were too many reporters. Now that the peace accord was decided, the journalists had all disappeared. There didn't seem to be much interest from the rest of the world that Begin was making a special trip to the town that was in the middle of the controversial territory.

It seemed like all of Yamit, as well as the surrounding moshavim, had come out to see and hear their prime minister. The cultural center was so packed, people were standing two rows deep along the side and back walls. Some of the older children were playing outside, though they kept running back into the building, afraid that they were going to miss something.

More than a few mothers were holding sleeping babies, while others rocked carriages to soothe their little ones. Of course every once in a while a baby started crying, and the mother quickly took him or her outside, but everyone was feeling restive. The noise was intense and getting louder. Danielle was grateful that Minna and her boyfriend Avi had been willing to stay home with her kids.

Izzy Frankel stepped onto the stage and asked for their attention. Slowly people stopped talking, and quiet and order fell on the agitated crowd. When the rabbi felt the room was orderly enough, he pulled his well-worn pitch pipe out of his pocket. Some people laughed.

He hit a note in the middle range and started singing "Hinei Ma Tov." The crowd joined in: "Henei ma tov umanaim." Camaraderie replaced the raucous noise as people held hands or wrapped their arms around each other as they swayed to the familiar melody. When she was younger, Danielle would have labeled this cornball and saccharine, but as she looked at the faces around her, she realized that—just like the song said—it was good and sweet to sit together as brothers and sing. By the end of the song, the room was filled with the melody. Frankel immediately led the crowd into "Hallelujah." The tune was so catchy and the words once again so simple, pleading for world peace, that Danielle had to wipe a few tears away.

After the last refrain, one of Begin's men joined Frankel on the stage and asked for the crowd's attention. The whole crowd hushed. Frankel introduced the speaker as Avi Schneider and then quickly left the stage.

Danielle was at first surprised that he looked so young, but on closer inspection she noticed the gray in his hair and tiny wrinkles at the sides of his eyes. Those just added to his dignified presence. He said he was one of Menachem Begin's diplomatic advisors and had been present at the Camp David Accords. He further explained that he had come to Israel as a young boy, when his father, who was an American pilot in WW II, had volunteered his services during the War of Attrition in 1956. He was honored that Mr. Begin had asked him to accompany him to Camp David, which had given him the unique opportunity of observing the negotiations first hand.

"It has been my great honor," he said, "to witness these historical proceedings. I have no doubt that these negotiations, mediated by President Carter and signed by both President Sadat and Prime Minister Begin, will leave its mark on generations to come. History will regard this peace accord as one of the deciding factors in Middle Eastern history. That being said, our distinguished prime minister has determined that he is obligated to speak to you, the pioneers and architects of this beautiful city and, of course, the thriving moshavim surrounding it. Our fervent hope is that once you hear him out, you will understand that the return of the Sinai was pivotal to the peace agreement between the two countries. Without further introduction, I give you the distinguished prime minister of Israel."

Before anyone could applaud, there he was, the prime minister of Israel, Menachem Begin, standing at the podium. Danielle quickly snapped a photo. At first glance, he appeared almost ugly, with his unstylish black-framed glasses, bald head, and unremarkable looks. But there was something familiar about him that she couldn't put her finger on it. Then she realized that his dapper, old-world European elegance reminded her of her father-in- law. Unlike most Israeli politicians who looked like they had just jumped off the kibbutz tractor, with their open neck shirts and wrinkled khaki pants, he was dressed impeccably. Just like her father-in law, who had grown up in the formal world of Old Europe before the Nazi horrors, it would be anathema for this man to be seen in public without his jacket and tie.

During World War II, he was arrested in Poland. Instead of being sent to a concentration camp, he, like Fredreich, was interned in Siberia. After surviving those hellish years, Begin made it to the dangerous shores of what was then known as Palestine, and became the head of a militant group called the Stern Gang. Again, he had to fight. This time not only the British, who were cozy with the Arabs, but the faction led by Ben-Gurion, who believed it was better to use diplomacy and make deals than to fight.

Although the prime minister of Israel was in his midsixties and short, he stood ramrod straight and exuded an air of dignity. Dignity that he had apparently earned from a life too familiar with sorrow and loss, while standing up for his beliefs, no matter the personal cost. Although Danielle was still confused about Israeli politics because of the numerous parties involved , she knew that Begin was the first prime minister that the Sephardic Jews had embraced. After so many years of a Labor government, which had looked down on the Jews from Tunis, Morocco, Yemen, and other Arab countries, this population felt Begin's government granted them respect and dignity.

An eloquent and experienced orator, the prime minister ignored the microphone and stepped in front of the podium to address his rapt audience. He began by saying that he knew most of them were *olim hadashim*—new immigrants—from America and Russia.

He went on, "I applaud those of you coming from America who

sacrificed lives of ease and comfort to live here and become part of our history as modern-day pioneers. You chose to leave the country of your birth, to live without many basic amenities, and to volunteer to become our first line of defense against our former enemies to the south. Those of you coming from Russia, after years of being persecuted for being Jewish or after years of having to deny your Judaism in order to survive, have resettled here in Israel to be free to live your lives as Jews. You knew it wouldn't be easy, but you were comforted that at last in a Jewish state you would be free to pursue your ambitions and to finally worship in freedom. And as for the native-born Israelis, all of us here know that you are just plain"—he paused for effect—"meshugga."

The crowd guffawed, people nudging one another. As Begin waited for the room to calm down, his aide took the microphone and asked silence. Everyone hushed and Begin continued somberly.

"My obligations as a prime minister force me to do something that I can only pray to HaShem is the right thing to do. That is why I stand before you this evening, and that is why the future of the Sinai settlements was brought to a vote in the Knesset.

"But allow me to digress. I am sure most of you here know my history, a history that reflects the eternal struggle of the Jewish people."

Danielle squeezed Rachel's hand as she silently beseeched their prime minister to retract the evacuation order.

"Just like many of you or your relatives, I have lost loved ones in the fires of the Nazi concentration camps. As a young yeshiva *bucher*, I cried to HaShem to save my blessed mother and father and my dear brother. But it was not to be written. So I continued my journey alone in anguish and pain, only to inhale the stench of the ovens from my prison cell in Siberia. Of course, before the camps and deportations, before the defining evil of the twentieth century, I watched incredulously as Christian friends and neighbors turned a blind eye to Jewish stores being wrecked and vandalized, Jewish students and professors being sent home from universities, and Jewish homes confiscated for our enemies. Unfortunately, I learned early in my life that the world is blind and deaf to the suffering of the Jew."

He paused, looking around his audience. "But miraculously, I escaped the far-reaching Nazi net. Instead, according to God's plan, I was interned in the frozen wasteland of Siberia and survived to escape to the shores of Ha'aretz. Upon reaching our sacred land, I was once again greeted by an enemy, and once again I fought for my survival, and for the memory of my family and all those who were killed for no other reason than that they were Jews.

"We, as a people, have fought unceasingly, since Israel was partitioned by the UN in 1948, for our right to live in peace in our own country. But as a leader in our interminable struggle, I am forced to make harsh and distressing decisions that affect us all. Many will disagree with the framework of the peace accord. It is understandable. To this day, many still disagree with my decision aboard the *Altalena*, demanding that my men lay down their arms as a direct refusal to fight our brothers in the IDF. But according to Torah law, a Jew must not raise a hand against another Jew. As it is written, we are one.

"As a people we have brought the world many gifts, and one of them is the concept of world peace. 'They shall beat their swords into plowshares … and neither shall they learn war any more.' That is a profound and momentous idea; one that has always been beyond the grasp of man. So it was with hope and trepidation that I entered the negotiations at Camp David."

After taking a sip of water Begin continued, "I believe the Jewish people have the unalienable right to our land, which includes Judea, Samaria, and the Sinai. But the leader of the free world believes differently. He is convinced that in order to have peace with Egypt, Israel must return every centimeter of land gained in 1967, no matter how important it is to our defense and religious beliefs. Since there was no possibility of our returning Judea and Samaria, which would usher in negotiations for Jerusalem, the only bargaining chip we had was Sinai, My partner in peace, President Sadat, was adamant on the return of the Sinai, including the evacuation of all our settlements. President Carter was in absolute agreement. Since I entered negotiations knowing that President Carter had made the statement that the Palestinian refugees needed a homeland, I was not shocked at the intransigence of the American president.

"After we had spent thousands of years living as strangers in others' lands. God finally returned us to his land, the land of Abraham, Isaac, and Jacob. We have fought for our right to keep our sacred country, and although I am loath to say it, I am afraid that we, as a nation, once again face another enemy. Although I cannot prove it, at the time of negotiations I had the distinct impression that there was collusion between the Americans and Egypt. If not collusion, then a bias toward the Egyptian demands. For although, I bared my soul to the American president, Mr. Carter he was intractable. When I looked him in the eye and told him that I made a promise to God that I would not hand over our Sinai settlements, he remained intractable. Instead of compassion, he looked at me and coldly replied, 'Then, Mr. Prime Minister, I suggest you bring it to a vote in your Knesset." This is a man who clearly had his mind made up before he went into negotiations. This is a man who clearly cares nothing about the survival of our state."

Danielle quickly snapped a photo as Begin took his handkerchief out of his breast pocket and wiped his brow. When he continued, his voice cracked slightly.

"In every generation it seems that the Jewish people are faced with a Haman. Unfortunately, this time he has the face of an American. We must be vigilant, but we must honor the vote of our Knesset that agreed to the evacuation. Remember, a Jew must not harm another Jew."

With these last words, his daughter Leah, who was sitting in the first row, ran up to her father to usher him off the stage. Stunned, the audience sat immobile until a voice at the back of the room shouted, "No, we will fight. You will see. *Am yisrael chai.*"

Danielle turned to the back of the room, and saw a man with a knitted kippah and a gray beard whom she didn't recognize. Standing near him was the woman who had set up her meeting with Marvin. The woman started singing "Am Yisrael Chai," but this time no one joined in. Everyone simply sat in stunned silence staring at one another. The dream was over and the end was near.

Chapter 41

Danielle was relieved, although a bit anxious, that she hadn't heard from Marvin in a while. The military police had contacted her once more, sending a letter that stated that if she had any news about the location of her husband, she was to report it to Commander Zev Oren. They had also sent someone to check out her in laws' house, sending both Tosha and Fredreich into hysterics, because they had thought he was at his assigned post. Now her mother-in-law called every day to see if she had news from him.

"No, Tosha," Danielle replied one day, weeks after the visit from Prime Minister Begin. "But trust me, he's okay."

"Do you talk to him?"

"Every once in a while, but I never know where he is."

"This is your fault," her mother-in-law yelled. "My son was a good boy and always did what he was told. He was an excellent student and never did anything to make us ashamed."

"Believe me, I didn't tell him to go AWOL."

"So who? Maybe I did?"

Danielle cringed, but figured it was better just to ignore that comment. "Tosha, listen I have to get off the phone now." Although she tried to stay patient and keep her equilibrium, when she looked at the mess around her she knew she had too much work to do and she had to get off the phone as fast as possible.

"A curse," Tosha said. "There's a curse on this family. Otherwise how would a boy that never gave us a problem turn into such a *farshtinkener oysvorf*?"

Danielle held the phone away from her ear as her mother-in-law's voice grew louder and shriller. She could hear her father-in-law in the background trying to calm his wife down.

"Okay, Tosha," Danielle said, interrupting her. "I'll call you if I get any news. 'Bye."

She quickly hung up the phone, but instead of going back to sorting clothes that the children had outgrown , she sat down and cried. The emotional turmoil was becoming worse now that Rachel was already gone, and other Americans were packing up their things to return to America or move to another part of Israel. Some were accepting the government's offer to relocate farther north in the Gaza Strip into an area called Gush Katif.

She knew that Rhoda was staying in Beer Sheva with her latest boyfriend, who, according to Rhoda, had a huge dick, slept with his Uzi, and came from some other primitive country called Uzbekistan. Rhoda was trying to convert loans that had been stipulated for the restaurant to cover a sheep ranch that was located deep in the Negev. She had told Danielle that it made more sense to be near the government offices, so that she could stop there daily to nudge them. Danielle could see her point, but knowing Rhoda, she assumed her boyfriend's big dick probably played a part in her decision. Maybe if she had the time next time she drove into the city, she would stop in to see Rhoda. Now that everyone was so involved with lawyers and the confusion of their shattered lives, the easy camaraderie among them was no longer so easy.

When people got together, the only topics of conversation were where they planned on moving after the compensation was distributed and how much they were getting. Any political ramifications were overshadowed by the anxiety of relocating, and the nauseating thought of dismantling the town they loved.

To each and every person, it seemed like the government had suddenly developed amnesia, but they, the original settlers of Yamit, certainly hadn't. How could they? They had built this magnificent coastal town in the barren desert from nothing. Their tenacity and their belief that they were doing something worthwhile for their country had kept them going. So Danielle agreed wholeheartedly with her circle of friends. The best thing was to get out before the government came in with soldiers to evacuate them. The hurt and disillusionment was so deep, staying until the very end would only increase the emotional turmoil and heartbreak.

Inside the green line, however, the country was jubilant. Journalists declared that this was the coming of a new era. Newspapers exclaimed that for once during its modern history, Israel could be assured of peace with a former enemy. The consensus was that even if it was only one border, one border was better than no border. Others believed that this augured a tentative beginning of more peace negotiations with other Arab countries. There was finally a chance that no more husbands or wives, brothers or sisters, daughters or sons would be buried in the prime of their lives. They could finally sleep well at night, knowing there wouldn't be another surprise attack from Egypt. No more hospitals filled with mutilated and broken people who would suffer for the rest of their lives. Maybe Syria and Lebanon would see that they could all live in peace and those countries would be good neighbors as well!

Danielle wanted to feel that way too, but all she felt was her own pain. The terrible disruption of the settlers' lives was minimalized or negated by the jubilation of the press. While Peace Now celebrated and trumpeted the coming evacuation, that diminished any hope that people would stand up for what belonged to them. So the settlers sadly accepted that once again they would be doing something for the good of their country. Of course, they would take the compensation the government offered. They had to restart their lives again.

As people made arrangements to leave, new faces started to appear. Since Marvin had become involved with that rabbi from Brooklyn, Danielle was acutely aware of strangers she saw walking around the commercial center. New families dribbled in to live in the apartments that were already abandoned. Unlike the original population, this new group was religious. The women wore long skirts and covered their heads. The men wore kippahs, and Danielle could see their tzitzits sticking out of their shirts as they ran back and forth to synagogue. She felt like she was spying on her own people, because she was so cognizant of this underground movement called Gush Emunim. She didn't know if other people were oblivious or they just didn't want to talk about it, but for Marvin's sake she would feign ignorance and keep her mouth shut.

During her last call from Marvin, she asked him what she should do with their collection of record albums, because it broke her heart to sell them. When they got married they had excitedly combined their collections, so between the two of them they had every original Beatles, Dylan, Cream, Rolling Stones, Doors, Grateful Dead, and then less popular artists that they loved ,like Kris Kristofferson, Maria Muldaur, Papa John Creach and his electric violin, and Taj Mahal. It was like a musical history of the times. As she had looked at all those albums, trying to decide what to do with them, she had cried uncontrollably. She recalled those Friday evenings before the kids were born when she and Marv would buy wine or beer to listen to some good American rock n' roll and dance around the living room. They always ended up in the bedroom. Those days had been over a long time ago.

Marvin said he didn't care know what to do with the albums, but then he suddenly asked, "Hey, remember how you used to dance to that song 'Midnight at the Oasis'?"

"Yes," Danielle answered, watching the smoke rise from her cigarette as she thought of more she had to do.

"You were so sexy. I even came in my pants once while I was watching you."

"That's great, Marv, but right now I'm not thinking of coming. In case you forgot, we're going. So what do you want me to do with all the albums?"

"Do whatever the hell you want. That's what you always do anyway."

"Marvin, I can't stay here and watch this all destroyed. Why can't you understand that?"

"'Cause you're on the side of the tigers, baby. That's what you don't understand."

She heard the slight slur in his speech, so she knew he was still drinking. "Does your great rabbi Kahane know that his sycophant is a drunk? Or doesn't he care as long as you follow his party line?"

"Listen, we each have one life and I'm doing what I believe is right. But I need my wife, my life, to make a stand with me."

"I'm sorry Marv, but I have to think about me and the kids. One of us has to act like a responsible parent."

"You still don't get it, Danielle."

"Maybe I don't, Marv. And I really don't give a shit. We have two kids that look up to us and expect us to be responsible adults. You certainly didn't think about them or me when you decided to stand with this meshuggeneh and go AWOL. Did you ever think that without your signature, I can't get the compensation money? I need to restart our lives as soon as possible. Like you just said, we each have one life, and I am not waiting until the army comes in to throw us out."

"Fuck you," he replied, and slammed down the phone.

As Danielle returned to her packing, she played that conversation over and over and came to some important decisions. Now she finally knew what she was going to do. She'd sell everything that she possibly could, and then she and the kids would live with her parents. She'd come back to Israel a couple of weeks before they handed Yamit over, and when Marvin resurfaced, he could sign the papers, they'd get the compensation money, and then she'd divorce him. That also solved the Isaac dilemma. It looked like his wife wasn't happy about getting a divorce and his father had had a stroke. If Isaac made it to America as a divorced man, she'd marry him when her divorce was finalized. Until then there was nothing to say or do. Communication between South Africa and Israel was frustrating. Letters took more than two weeks to travel between the two countries. Phone calls were too expensive, and she certainly wouldn't call from her end. She was just tired of waiting for these men to make her life right. Apparently it was up to her. That night she slept well for the first time in months.

Chapter 42

Months later, Danielle weaved her way through the crowded customs area at Ben Gurion Airport in Tel Aviv. She was certainly not looking forward to staying with her in-laws, but she waved and smiled when she spotted them through the glass partition. They, on the other hand appeared to be excited to see her, though Tosha was plainly disappointed that Danielle hadn't brought the children. She proceeded to let Danielle know just how much by making nasty little barbs in Yiddish about her to her husband during the long taxi ride back to their apartment in Jerusalem. Danielle could hear her whisper things like, "A *shayna punim* but a *calta neshama,*" and he would look out the window but whisper back, "Sha, Tosha." Danielle had to force herself to ignore it. On the other hand, Fredreich was genuinely happy to see her, and as soon as they reached the apartment he suggested a stroll through the neighborhood after she'd showered and changed her clothes.

"You shouldn't be late for dinner," Tosha said. "I made a delicious brisket and the tzimmes with the cherries that you like."

"Thanks, Tosha," Danielle said. "We'll be back in a couple of hours. I'm sure the exercise will give me a good appetite."

"Tosha, don't worry," Fredreich added. "I will bring my beautiful daughter-in-law home in time for dinner."

They walked down the street together, Fredreich taking her arm. As they strolled along Tchernichovosky Street, Danielle once again reflected on the beauty of the golden Jerusalem stone and the magnificent architecture, even here in the newer sections of the city.

Fredreich broke into her reverie. "So, my beautiful daughter-in-law, how long will we have the privilege of your company?"

"I think just tonight, Fredreich. Tomorrow I'll rent a car and drive down to Yamit."

"Will you be seeing my son?"

His simple, direct question caught her unaware. Even though she knew she might regret it, she told him yes, but she couldn't look him in the eye.

"Do not worry, Danielle. I will not tell Tosha. I think that is for the best."

"Thanks, Fredreich. It's been very difficult. We've been corresponding through a third person, and our letters cross sometimes, but it seems he's okay. This rabbi he met hooked him up with a good lawyer who believes he can have any charges against him go away."

"That is good, my beautiful Danielle. My son is very lucky to have you as his wife and the mother of his children. You have made a lovely home and worked hard in the business. That is what I tell Tosha all the time."

"I tried," Danielle said softly as they reached a busy intersection and had to wait for the light to turn.

"You will live near your parents when this is all over?"

"I think so. They're thrilled to have their grandchildren with them, and the kids are having a ball. You know my dad is the president of the temple, so he was able to register Ari for nursery school even in the middle of the term. Right now I stay home with Ilana while my mother works, and then when she comes home I go teach at the Hebrew school. It's okay temporarily."

"And Marvin will stay in the jewelry business?"

"I don't know, Fredreich. To be perfectly honest, right now we're just taking it one day at a time. This has put a lot of stress on our marriage." Danielle sighed and thought of the last letter that she had gotten from Isaac. Even though he said he missed her he had no idea when he would be leaving because his father had a relapse. Plus it was getting harder to move money out of South Africa. That was stress Fredreich didn't have to know about.

Always gallant, Fredreich pulled out Danielle's chair when they reached his favorite café. "My dear, I know that this whole time has been stressful for you, but this is one of the paradoxes of life. Problems are part of life and therefore part of any marriage. Accepting them and learning how to deal with them is a sign of maturity."

"Are you implying that I'm not mature?" she asked coquettishly.

"Not at all, my dear. As you know, Tosha and I went through our own difficulties and tribulations separately when we were young, but together we have worked to solve problems and to raise our children and provide them with a good home and education."

As he lit a cigarette, he scanned the faces of the other patrons at the outdoor cafe. Danielle thought maybe this would be a good time to tell him about Marvin's drinking problem and how it affected their marriage.

"Look, Fredreich, I need to tell you something."

He squeezed her hand. "Anything, my dear."

She took a deep breath and blurted out, "Did you know that your son had a drinking problem?"

Instead of responding, Fredreich turned away from her to get the waitress's attention. Danielle waited impatiently, though she assumed he would acknowledge what she had said after the girl took their order.

"My dear," Fredreich said to the waitress, "it is a pleasure to have a waitress with such beautiful eyes. Almost like Elizabeth Taylor's."

The young woman blushed. Danielle was sure she didn't even know who Elizabeth Taylor was, but she knew Fredreich was complimenting her.

"I will have a coffee with cream on the side," he ordered, "and a cheese Danish. My daughter-in-law will have an espresso. Yes, Danielle?"

"Perfect, Fredreich," Danielle answered politely.

When the waitress left to get their order, he turned to Danielle and asked about her friends Rachel and Natan.

She answered that they were fine and then returned to the distressing subject of his son's behavior. "Maybe you didn't hear me, Fredreich, but Marvin's drinking habits are hurting our family."

He shook his head and answered seriously, "In my family, all the men were good providers and took their responsibilities seriously. I am sure that once this terrible crisis is over, everything will be back to normal." He patted her hand and continued, "I think you would look beautiful in a Persian lamb coat. The next time I work in Frankfurt, I will make a coat especially for you. You know I am the best in the fur matching trade. I made coats for all the glamorous stars, even Marilyn Monroe. Actually, my dear you are built very similarly ..."

Normally Danielle would be entranced by Fredreich's story and flattered by his comparison, but now she only felt her body stiffen and a knot tighten in her stomach. Marvin's family was going to be no help in stopping Marvin's self-destructive behavior. Fredreich was presenting a classic case of denial.

For the rest of the time that they sat there, Danielle felt like she was watching herself from the outside. She nodded, laughed, and made humorous quips, but it was just her body. She had no help. Her father-in-law was not the man she had hoped he was. Now she just had to rent the car, make it through this evening, and get on the road early tomorrow morning.

When they had finished their coffee and Fredreich had paid the waitress, Danielle told her father-in-law that she was going to rent the car now so that she could get on the road as early as possible. Fredreich appeared surprised, but asked her if she knew where a rental place was. Danielle replied that she would walk toward the Old City.

"I would be glad to accompany you, my dear Danielle."

"No, thanks," she said emphatically, though with a smile. "I have a big emotional trauma ahead of me and I need to be alone. I'm sure you understand."

"Absolutely, my dear. Many nights I sit up alone, pondering my fate and this puzzle that we call life."

"Tell Tosha not to worry. I'll try to be back by 6:30."

She air kissed his cheek and he doffed his cap to her, and they both went their own ways in opposite directions.

Still upset that her father-in-law had ignored her concerns about his own son, and still unsure and insecure about her future, walked down the hill on Palmach Street. As she passed the Islamic Art Museum, still undecided which direction to go, it became clear. She would go to the Kotel, to the Wailing Wall. With that decision, she felt better and her stride became sure as she passed the beautiful and mysterious consulates from places like Panama and the Dominican Republic.

The walk was longer than she had remembered, so as she approached Liberty Park, she decided to sit for a few minutes to rest. Because she was so anxious about the coming days and seeing her husband again, a few minutes was all the longer she could sit still. She continued on her way, blind to the joy of the children playing or the colorful beauty of the gardens and giant shade trees. She was starting to regret her decision, but when she finally saw the Montefiore Windmill, she knew she was almost there. It was one of those quirky landmarks that she loved. Just like so many buildings in this city, it told a story. This one was about Moses Montefiore and his wife Judith, who became the greatest benefactors of the Jewish neighborhood outside the Old City walls. Their generosity and support had made the Yemin Moshe neighborhood self-sufficient.

She ran across the street quickly, before she got hit by one of the crazy drivers, passed through the Jaffa Gate, and turned into the Jewish Quarter. She loved the paradox of how the broad sweeping plaza was kept so clean it looked brand new, yet most of the buildings dated to somewhere in the fifteenth century. As she continued to walk, she recalled some guide telling her WOJS class why the oldest synagogues were below street level. When they were built, Muslims prohibited any Christian or Jewish structure to be as tall as their own buildings. As she passed the great arch of the Hurva Synagogue that had been destroyed twice, first by the Ottomans and then during the 1948 Arab-Israeli War, she thought, *Yamit will be in good company. All of Jewish history is filled with destruction.*

By the time Danielle saw the Dome of the Rock sparkling in the sun like the crown jewel of the city, her feet were killing her and her shoulder bag felt like a lead weight on her shoulder, but she knew she was almost there. She headed down the steps to the huge plaza, which was separated by a *mechitza*, to the women's side. She took the paper head covering offered to her by a little dark-skinned woman who sat by the entrance. Scrounging through the bottom of her bag, she gave the woman all the change she found buried there.

After she pinned the makeshift head covering to her hair, she gazed at the awesome sight surrounding her.

Since it was too early for evening prayers, the vast plaza was almost empty. She tore the bottom off one of Ari's drawings that she also found in her bag and swiftly wrote her request. Looking up at the ancient structure, she saw a few old women, shoulders bent shoulders and heads covered, totally absorbed in their prayers, and walked toward them. The closer she got to the gigantic wall, the smaller she felt. When she finally reached the spot that she marked as her own and touched the wall, she felt as if the Almighty breathed new strength into her. The immense burden she had been carrying was suddenly lifted from her shoulders. She crumpled the piece of paper into a crevice and softly chanted, *"Shema Yisrael Adonai eloheinu Adonai ehad."* She asked Him to give her the strength to get through the coming days. Tears filling her eyes, she kissed the tips of her fingers and placed them on the ancient Wall, and then she left.

Chapter 43

On her way back to her in-laws', Danielle stopped at a travel agency to rent a car. The rental agent was about her age and was glad to show off her English. She asked where Danielle was going, and when Danielle told her she appeared sincerely shocked.

"I thought everyone there was religious."

"Why?" Danielle asked, surprised.

Shira, the agent, shrugged and said that the newspapers had pointedly stated that there were mostly religious people from some group called Gush Emunim down there, ready to fight the government. For the last few days, though, the newspapers hadn't mentioned Yamit at all.

Danielle thought that was strange, but finished with the car rental. As she was signing her name, the girl unabashedly asked how much compensation she'd get from the government. Danielle looked her straight in the eyes and firmly said, "Not enough."

Danielle drove carefully through the Jerusalem traffic and miraculously found a parking spot across the street from her in-laws' building. She stood outside their apartment door and took a deep breath before she knocked. As Fredreich opened the door, she was surprised to hear a woman making small talk with Tosha. Tosha introduced Danielle to her upstairs neighbor Devorah, who worked as an assistant to one of the government ministers. Devorah stubbed out her cigarette and nodded to Danielle. Tosha went on to say that Devorah was the daughter of her camp sister. She would stop by every once in a while on her way home from work.

"I can't stay much longer," Devorah said in English. "I just wanted to say shalom and see if you needed anything."

"Danielle just came back from the United States to return to Yamit before they hand it over to Egypt," Tosha said.

"Interesting," Devorah said almost under her breath. She lit another cigarette and added, sounding perplexed, "I thought everyone in Yamit was religious."

"You're the second person who's said that today," replied Danielle. "It's the absolute reverse. We had very few religious people down there."

Devorah studied Danielle, blowing cigarette smoke in her direction. "I want to tell you something. The government is expecting a big *balagan*, chaos. Be careful. It may be dangerous."

"What?" Danielle exclaimed.

"Everyone knows the army is being sent down there," Devorah said. "But my boss told me to send a directive to all the newspapers, radio stations, and of course the television station not to send any reporters down there."

"What? But why?" Danielle was totally shocked at this information.

"Yes, this is *emet*, the truth. I can't say anything else, but when you watch the news tonight, you'll see the coming evacuation won't even be mentioned." She stood up. "And now, Tosha, Fredreich, I must go. My husband must be hungry. It was a pleasure to meet you, Danielle. I wish you and your family well."

"Thank you for that information, Devorah. We will be careful."

At dinner Tosha smugly told Danielle that she had heard from Marvin the previous week, and that he had said his lawyer had reached equitable terms with the IDF. Danielle answered that she had got the same news, and that she was looking forward to putting this behind them and staring fresh. Her father-in-law, trying to divert any arguments between the two women, said that they should make a toast to the future.

"The last time I took this out," he said, taking a bottle of cognac from a kitchen cabinet, "was when our Ilana was born. It has been too long."

After he poured a shot for each of them, he declared, "L'chaim."

As they touched their glasses, Danielle commented on how beautiful the glasses, and then instantly regretted it, because it started Tosha telling them a story.

"Yes, they are beautiful. Cut crystal from Czechoslovakia Do you remember, Fredreich, who gave to us these glasses at our engagement party in Sweden?"

"Yes, yes, Tosha, of course I remember. It was your brother Joseph and his lovely wife Magda."

"Ach, but this Magda was not as beautiful as his first love, his fiancée Miriam, the one that he—"

Fredreich interrupted his wife. "Tosha, Tosha, not now. Let us have a pleasant evening with Danielle."

She continued as if she hadn't heard him. "—never saw again after Auschwitz. Mengele had taken her for experiments."

Fredreich excused himself and get a bit of fresh air on the balcony while he read the *Jerusalem Post* and enjoyed a cigarette.

Danielle sat at the kitchen table while Tosha continued, tears welling up in her eyes.

"She was a twin and that, as you know, was Mengele's maniacal obsession." She sighed deeply. "When she and her twin sister, Francie, were transported to Auschwitz, they were seventeen years old, two years younger than I was. Their parents owned the farm next to ours, and my brother Joseph and Miriam were betrothed the year Hitler rolled into Poland. Oy! Was he crazy over her! Since they were children they ran around the orchard together and played Tarzan and Jane in the trees. He was only counting the days until their wedding. And could I blame him? No, she and her sister were like two beautiful porcelain dolls."

Danielle handed Tosha a tissue. Her mother-in-law continued after wiping her eyes.

"Miriam played the piano and had a beautiful soprano voice, like Kurt Weill's shiksa wife, Lotte Lenya. Oy, this was a girl who only had a good word for everyone. Her sister Francie played the violin and was a little more serious. I remember when Miriam would play American jazz, her father would shout that it was not fitting for a nice Jewish girl …" Her voice cracked. "Excuse me, Danielle." She left the table to find another tissue.

"Okay, Tosha. You don't have to continue ..."

But her mother-in law didn't hear her. She was lost in the midst of her nightmare. "At Auschwitz Mengele first drained their blood and infused them with the other twin's blood. Then he amputated parts of their body and stitched it to the other—"

"Please, I don't want to hear any more."

"Nu, you may wonder, how do we know? Joseph's Magda was a twin too. Her sister also didn't make it through the experiments, and Magda only lived because they thought she was already dead from typhus. They left her there to die right before the Allies came in."

As always, Danielle cried as Tosha finished her story. That was the only thing she could give her mother-in-law.

Chapter 44

Danielle was annoyed that her rental car didn't have a tape player. Now she was stuck listening to her own thoughts. Devorah had been right about the media coverage of the evacuations. Hoping Devorah was wrong, Danielle had watched the news the night before and turned the radio on as soon as she got in the car. There was absolutely no news about the evacuation. Since there was only one television station, she knew it wasn't an oversight. She had read the *Jerusalem Post* the previous day and scanned it that morning while she drank her coffee. Nothing. It was like Yamit had never existed.

On top of that aggravation, she would be seeing Marvin for the first time in months. This was it-the last stand. Either he would choose to stop drinking and live a responsible life, or she would have to divorce him and hope that Isaac would divorce his wife even though she detected a different tone in his last letter. He wrote that his wife promised to be faithful and begged him to keep their family together. Since he didn't want his children growing up in a broken home he promised to think about it. Danielle forced herself not to think about Isaac and the end of that fantasy. She had to keep her mind on the road and get to Yamit.

Since she didn't want to risk driving through the Gaza Strip alone, and also had to avoid Hebron, she had to go out of her way by taking the Tel Aviv-Jerusalem road, east toward Tel Aviv. Then she headed roundabout through Beer Sheva. The drive was colorless and boring, besides taking much longer than if she'd driven straight through the Gaza Strip. It also gave her too much time to think.

She did congratulate herself on finally coming to terms with her marriage, although she still had to deal with the loss of her beloved town. The media blackout added another complexity to puzzle over.

For some perverse reason, Danielle's mind kept returning to the news she had got from her friend Eileen when she returned to the States. Eileen told her that the month before she had been raped, there had been three other rapes close to the campus of her alma mater. However, none of the newspapers reported them. There had finally been an outcry on campus after another girl, the niece of a councilman, was found in her car, stripped of her clothes and brutally beaten. The other girls who had reported the crimes had just quietly disappeared from campus. The town council pushed for a thorough investigation, and the truth became apparent. Since the college administration didn't want any bad publicity, it had quietly "influenced" the newspapers to keep it buried.

According to Eileen, the Dean of Communications justified his actions by saying that they had just built four new dorms and were expecting an increased enrollment the coming fall semester. Furthermore, at the time of the attacks, the school had just been recognized as one of the top ten progressive universities in the country by *Time* magazine. To mark that honor, the administration had a huge party to celebrate the completion of the dormitories, once of which was the first dormitory in the country to provide amenities and special living conditions for handicapped and disabled students. Local and state politicians were invited, and a grand time was had by all. Connecting violent crime to the university could be disastrous for its reputation.

The story had taken Danielle's breath away when she realized how lucky she had been. Those other girls had been mutilated. It turned out that the perpetrator had been a campus security guard.

Danielle forced herself to forget about the past when she reached the Rafiah crossing. She had almost reached Yamit. To her chagrin, she had to wait as a contingent of small dirt-encrusted white and gray trucks rolled down the highway, heading south toward Egypt. As she tapped her fingers on the steering wheel and started counting the number of trucks, she suddenly realized that all the trucks were overflowing with appliances, tied onto their roofs and stacked in their cabs. Most of them also carried two or three young men, some wearing keffiyehs wrapped around their heads, smoking cigarettes, chatting, laughing. She wished she had a camera because no one would believe this odd procession of trucks weighted down with their precious booty.

She checked her watch, hoping she wouldn't be late for her meeting with that woman, Shoshana, from Gush Emunim. When she had spoken to her last night, Shoshana had warned her that no one was being let in to the city, including ex-residents. They decided to meet secretly at the yeshiva which was located outside the city limits, so as not take any chances. The few times she had spoken to Shoshana from the States, Danielle hadn't known whether to believe everything she said or not. After experiencing the strange media blackout and hearing what Devorah had said about the government expecting a showdown, she took what Shoshana said seriously.

After almost ten minutes, the last truck came into view. A couple of teenage boys, standing in a small space between the refrigerators and stoves that were tied precariously together on the bed of the last truck, shouted and waved to the boys in the truck ahead. Danielle pulled out behind them, tagging onto the end of the crawling procession and praying Shoshana had waited for her.

Chapter 45

"Thank God you're still here," Danielle called to Shoshana. The young woman was standing under an eave at the entrance to the yeshiva, exactly where she had said she would be. "I was so afraid you would leave."

"Nu, why should I? I have something else more important to do?" She smiled as she stuck a small prayer book into her skirt pocket.

"Thank you so much," Danielle said sincerely, and then told her about the strange holdup at the Rafiah Junction.

"Why do you think this is strange? They know that once they are living under Egyptian rule, they will again have nothing and have no means to get anything. This way they can either keep what they need or sell some appliances and make a little money."

"What a dummy I am. I never thought of that."

"The terrible thing is that many fedayeen are afraid of retaliation from the Egyptian government. If the government thinks anyone was helping Israel or sympathetic to Israel, believe me they will use any excuse to torture them or their families."

"You're kidding!"

Shoshana shrugged. "No, this is the way it is in the Middle East. And now our government is learning bad habits. You know now that I was not exaggerating about what is going on here."

"No, Shoshana. There was definitely a news blackout."

"Okay, so this is what we do. You are going to hide under this blanket in the trunk of the car and I am going to drive."

"What the hell?"

"Remember I told you that no one can go in that doesn't live there? You no longer live there but I do. So, I will drive in, say shalom to the guards, and deliver you to your husband."

"Like a Hanukkah present," Danielle said sarcastically.

Shoshana raised her eyebrow and gave Danielle a half grin that intimated she knew something Danielle didn't. "Exactly."

"But won't the guard recognize that this isn't your car?"

"No. I didn't go to work today and walked over here before the guards changed. So get in."

"Okay." Since Danielle figured she had no other choice, she opened the trunk but still hesitated.

"You're not claustrophobic are you?" Shoshana asked.

"If I was, I won't be now." She climbed into the trunk and Shoshana arranged the blanket over her. "Okay, shut it," Danielle said once she was situated as comfortably as possible.

She heard the slam of the trunk, waited while her eyes got adjusted to the stark darkness, and silently cursed her husband for this whole mess. An unexpected wave of nausea assaulted her as Shoshana backed the car out of the space and turned the steering wheel to head out the gravel driveway.

Please, she prayed, *let me not throw up.*

But she could feel every bump, and even though she instinctively started breathing in through her nose and out through her mouth, and although she willed herself not to, she needed to retch. Rolling onto her stomach, she vomited into the back corner of the trunk. She was wiping her mouth off on the blanket when she realized the car had stopped. From her dark, air-deprived prison, she could hear a muffled male voice greeting Shoshana, asking how she was. Danielle was so dizzy, she prayed she wouldn't pass out.

"Just living," Shoshana answered easily.

"This is a new car?" he asked in Hebrew.

"No, I missed the bus, so I borrowed this from the moshav."

"Beseder," he answered.

Danielle heard a sound, as if the guard had hit the side of the car with his hand, and then the car was moving. She was thankful she was still conscious. But they couldn't have gone more than ten feet when she heard, *"Rega, geveret."* Sweat formed on her upper lip and she thought she would throw up again.

Shoshana put the car in reverse and backed up. "Nu?"

And with a more respectful tone of voice he asked, "What can I do, rebbetzin? I have to question everyone going in. These are my orders."

Instead of accepting his apology, she answered him briskly without a trace of doubt in her voice. "On whose orders? From your general? From Begin the traitor? As for me, I take my orders from Ha Shem and Him only. Don't you know that it is written that it is a sin for a Jew to expel another Jew from his home?"

Then Danielle heard that disdainful tongue click, the sound written as *tsk* that she had never heard from anyone's mouth other than an Israeli. She could imagine the guard shaking his head and then after a slight pause, she heard that sound again, as if he'd hit the side of the car as a signal that she could go. Immediately Shoshana hit the gas pedal, and Danielle was back inside her beloved Yamit.

Shoshana opened the trunk to let Danielle out. It had just turned dark, but Danielle could see that Shoshana had parked in the almost empty lot of her apartment complex.

"See," Shoshana said. "Everything for a reason. You were held up at the crossing so that we could arrive here at nightfall."

"Oh, God, I must smell awful."

"Don't talk. Just come quick. I don't want anyone to see you."

Shoshana led her up the flight of stairs to the same apartment where she'd had seen Marv after he had gone AWOL. Shoshana unlocked the door, and there was Marv sitting at the kitchen table eating a salami sandwich, just like time had stopped.

"Oh, Marv," Danielle murmured as he embraced her. It felt so familiar and right and like he would never let her go, but the only thing she could think of was how bad she smelled. "Please, Marv." She pushed him away. "I threw up. My mouth and hair must be rancid."

"My wife, my life, what do I care? This is like old times. It reminds me of that time after that party when you threw up and I held your head."

"That's when I knew you really liked me," she said sheepishly, "tut then I was too drunk to be embarrassed. Now it was from lack of air. Just let me take a shower."

"Go brush your teeth. I don't care if you smell. I've been waiting for you too long."

Chapter 46

The next morning they joined Marvin's mentor, Rabbi Kahane, in the bomb shelter that he had claimed for himself and the young kippah-wearing rebels of Gush Emunim.

"So this is your wife, boychik!" the rabbi said. "You're just as beautiful as your husband says. It's nice to finally meet you. I'm glad you returned to be with your husband in this bogus showdown with the government." He nodded to Danielle and turned to Marvin. "See, I told you she would come."

Danielle scanned the bomb shelter, seeing that it had a toilet, a small fridge, and a two burner stove.

"So what do you think?" Kahane asked Danielle.

"I'm glad to be here, back in Yamit where we belong." She looked at her husband. "But I'm totally devastated that it will be destroyed."

"This whole 'land for peace' strategy," Kahane said, "and evacuating Jews from their homes is a gigantic sin."

"Believe me, rabbi, we know," she said. "It's more disappointing for us. The people who lived here."

"But none of you stayed. You should be ashamed. You took the terms of the government and ran with the compensation."

"Most of us have small children and thought the best course of action was just do what the government said, take compensation in order to jump start our new lives so that our children wouldn't be traumatized."

"Not one of you original settlers said boo, except your husband here." The rabbi patted Marvin on the back. "And he's not even religious."

"You blame us?" Danielle asked. "The newspapers shouted what a great and wonderful thing the peace agreement was, Sadat was a hero to the world for making his historical visit to Jerusalem, and who would believe that Begin's Likud government, the so-called hawks, would agree to peace with Egypt, our enemy in three wars?"

"And now," Kahane said, "they're not even allowing journalists to cover the end. Right, Belsky?"

Danielle was surprised as a new figure entered the bunker carrying some fresh bread and pita.

"You were right, rabbi," the newcomer said. "It worked coming in on that bread truck."

"I told you," Kahane said. "The guards know it comes in every day. What does it look like out there?"

"It looks like a deserted town slowly being covered with sand," Belsky answered.

"Covered with sand?" Danielle repeated.

"Of course," Kahane said. "Once the town council disbanded, nature took its course and does what nature does. It took over. Entropy now reigns."

After Danielle collected her composure from the shock of the description, she said, "Before I forget, rabbi, I have to thank you for helping us out. I don't know what we would have done without you. From the moment Marv met you, you've been a pillar of strength for him. And that you got him off on the charges the IDF had against him is just amazing. It's nothing short of a miracle."

"Everything is a *beshert a zach*."

"That's what my grandmother always said."

"Then your grandmother was a smart woman. Think about it," he said, leaning back on his chair. "From the thousands of falafel stands in this country, Marv and I happen to choose the same one at that moment in time."

Marvin added, "Not to mention we both liked the falafel. What are the odds of two Jews agreeing on something?"

"Well, once again, thank you," Danielle repeated. "Just let me know what I can do to help."

"Right now, nothing. Come, let's eat some breakfast."

Danielle put the fresh pita in the center of the table. As she cut up some cucumbers and tomatoes, she thanked God for the close call she had had the previous day. Marv had told her she could have died from carbon monoxide poisoning. Neither she nor Shoshana had thought of that. She took hard boiled eggs and yogurt out of the small refrigerator and joined the three men at the small table.

"I have to tell you, *kinderlach*," Kahane said, looking around the table. "This is very disappointing."

Marvin touched her leg under the table, and Danielle smiled at him as Belsky started to talk. Belsky had a squat, muscular body and the sad eyes of a basset hound. His knitted kippah was bobby pinned to his head. He spoke slowly and softly, seeming to visualize some distant memory as he answered his leader.

"My assessment is this was a terrible organization. I think Levenger and his followers did a lot of praying and though they probably wouldn't admit it, they believed that God would intervene at the last minute."

"Belsky, that's why I keep you around. You're a tzadik," Kahane announced as he smacked the tabletop.

"But as Jews we should already know better. Without organization and the will to fight, we're dead. We've been steamrolled and killed throughout history and never made a whimper. Look, look how long the resistance was able to hold the Warsaw ghetto against the Nazis."

"Danielle," Marv said, "doesn't my uncle Tszvi know that guy, that poet, the one that made it to Israel with his friends after he and his friends fought in the Warsaw uprising?"

Danielle nodded. "We took a ride to his kibbutz that time with your uncle and met him. His name, I think, is … Abba Kovner. He grew up in the same town as your mother's family. He and his wife fought together against the Nazis and made it safely all the way to Israel. What a story. They were so brave."

"Did he tell you," Kahane asked, "that the percentage of Jews that lived through the Holocaust was higher in the resistance than those that just followed the so-called Jewish leaders."

"See?" Marv said. "I knew it was better to do something than go along with the program." He chuckled and patted his own shoulder.

"You never heard the Yiddish expression, *'der oliem iz a goilem'?*" Kahane asked with a smile.

"No," Danielle and Marvin said at the same time. While she suppressed a giggle, Danielle noted how happy Marv seemed. Maybe this was what he had needed to stop drinking.

"You've heard the expression 'the masses are asses'?" Kahane asked. "Nu, kinderlach, that's what it means."

"Oy, Meir," Belsky said. "Before I forget, I brought the newspapers."

Belsky went over to the counter where he had placed the bread, and pulled out yesterday's *Haaretz*. He placed it in the center of the table as Danielle started clearing it.

"First the hamotzi and then we eat," Kahane said. " After we sing grace we'll take a look at this travesty."

As the men's voices joined in unison to thank God for his blessings, Danielle was surprised to hear Marvin participating. As she cleared his place, he winked at her. One thing was sure nothing her husband did would surprise her.

"So you see," Belsky continued, "this was the big protest the papers made about not being able to cover the Yamit evacuation."

"An empty white frame?" Danielle exclaimed, looking over Marvin's shoulder. "This is a protest?" She was starting to feel like Alice in Wonderland. Everything kept getting weirder and weirder.

Kahane leaned back in his chair and tugged on his gray beard. "Remember, this is a socialist country. All the papers are controlled by the Editors' Committee. *Davar, Hamishmar, Maariv.* Every one of them is. We pretend that this is a Jewish country, but in reality it's a socialist one. What we are seeing is a travesty. They are treating us, their own people like the enemy."

"Listen," Marvin said. "I think I hear a helicopter."

"Sure, what do you think? First Sharon has to scout out the enemy territory. Then tomorrow you'll see him shouting orders with a bullhorn—against his own people."

"We have ammunition, though," Marvin said.

At his words, a chill ran up Danielle's spine. She thought she was coming back to make a decision about her marriage, not a stand off between the government and its citizens, but she was as angry as any of the men, or even more so. The government had ripped her life into shreds.

"Yes, of course. But this whole protest makes no sense unless Rabbi Levenger is willing to get together with me and make plans quickly." Kahane added quietly, "I don't know what he was busy doing."

Chapter 47

That evening they started to walk over to the apartment where Shoshana lived with her husband, Rabbi Shlomi. In the dusky light Danielle could see soldiers walking around in groups of two or three. There was one group of them, laughing and smoking cigarettes, on the park bench where mothers used to share the latest gossip while they watched their children playing. Danielle glanced at Marv, who had a small backpack in one hand and was holding her hand with the other. She was glad he looked healthier and thought maybe he really had stopped drinking.

"So, did you talk to your Dad about his friend's jewelry business?" he asked.

"Yes. It's in a great location right in the center of town, and it looks like he would be willing to stay on for a while until you feel comfortable. Dad thought it would probably be a good idea to get certified as a gemologist."

Danielle thought how ironic this was. Here she was starting to feel more optimistic about her marriage, while she watched the demise of her idyllic town. She sadly noted that Belsky was right about the sand. The desert was reclaiming what belonged to it. Sadly, she saw that the beautiful gardens were neglected and the bursts of joyful color were gone forever. How different it had been when she'd first seen it. Then it had been just a colorless, drab landscape of sand and more sand, textured with small rocks and dirt, broken up by scrub and other hardy plants. But back then it was different. She'd had hope and a vision of how beautiful it would be. Now all she saw was the abandoned remnants of a synergetic dream. *If people knew the future,* she thought, *we would all probably do nothing.*

"Hey," Marv said, breaking into her melancholy reverie. "Let's go down to the workshop."

"You still have the keys?" Danielle asked.

"Of course. Who the hell was I giving them to?"

"Have you been down there?"

"Once my case was taken care of, I did. I didn't want to go back while they were looking for me."

"Good thinking, Marv."

"See, your problem is that you never watched enough television. I watched enough to understand the way these guys think. And by the way, my wife, my life, I made a present for you."

"Really? I love presents!"

"Of course. You're a woman." He squeezed her hand. "My woman."

They continued their walk through the deserted commercial center that less than a year ago had been bustling with commerce. Danielle looked around sadly, remembering the simple pleasure of strolling around the promenade, looking in the shop windows, while Ari and Battia ran up and down the steps, happy just to be alive.

Marv unlocked the heavy doors, and Danielle wanted to cry when she saw the empty desolation of the business that they had built with nothing but hard work and dreams. The retail store was just a memory. All of the beautiful displays of silver jewelry that had enticed the tourists were gone. Only two empty glass cases stood there, bereft and abandoned. Gray dust had settled everywhere.

"Come on." Marv pulled her through the deserted work space and into the small office. "Okay, now close your eyes."

"Marvin …"

"And give me your hand."

Danielle shook her head but did what her husband asked. She felt something metallic in her hand.

"Open."

She exhaled. "Oh, Marv, it's magnificent!"

It was an unusual silver arm band designed with the Yamit logo, with perfectly formed blue malachite stones embedded as palm leaves.

"The stones stand for us," he said sheepishly. "You, me, Ari, and Ilana."

"And the fifth one?"

"Hope. To our future"

"Oh, Marv." Danielle was stunned by this show of affection and threw herself into his open arms. "Thank you."

"You were right. I should have used you as a walking advertisement for the business," he said in a choked-up voice as he fastened the bracelet around her upper arm and then brushed her lips with his.

"Shh. It doesn't matter now. We'll start over. All dreams disappear in the morning. So this one disappeared too. But together we'll make another one, Marv. Just stay sober and I know we can."

"We never finished our walk," he said, his mischievous smile lightening the mood.

"That's true," she agreed playfully.

Marv grabbed her around the waist. "Let's go," he said. "We'll have the apartment to ourselves. Shlomi and Shoshana are staying with a group from Gush Emunim tonight."

She stood next to Marvin as he locked the door. As they carefully made their way up the darkened steps, she remembered the story of Lot's wife and tried not to look back.

Chapter 48

Danielle didn't know what woke her up first: the drone of the helicopter hovering over the town or the emptiness of the bed. She drowsily called her husband's name, but to her consternation didn't hear another sound except the slow dripping of a bathroom faucet. She grabbed her nightgown from the floor and threw it over her head, and then frantically checked each room in the small two-bedroom apartment. Marv was not there. In the kitchen Danielle saw his backpack sitting on the chair, but no note explaining where he'd gone. Looking out the window, she could see that the light had just broken through the darkness and figured it was about five o'clock. When she returned to the bedroom to get a cigarette, she glanced at the clock. She had been off by only three minutes. Trying to think rationally before having a cup of coffee was futile, so she figured she would make a cup of the detested instant coffee to go with her morning cigarette before she went to look for her husband.

She put the water on to boil in an old battered Turkish pot and then ran back to the bedroom to dress. By the time she came back out the water was boiled, and she managed to choke down a couple of sips of the bitter coffee to get enough caffeine in her to feel awake. As she became more alert, she decided Marvin hadn't been able to sleep and had gone to the Kahane bomb shelter. Feeling better and less perturbed, she decided to finish her coffee. She didn't want to wait too long, though. She wanted to be in the bunker before the IDF started marching door to door.

Just as she stubbed out her cigarette she heard a distant noise, and her stomach rolled with nervous queasiness. She ran back to the bedroom and quickly packed her few things. Spotting her new bracelet, she slipped it on. It looked like Marvin was serious about staying sober and saving their marriage.

She left the apartment, absurdly locking the door behind her. In the gauzy first flush of daylight, she started walking toward the bomb shelter on the other side of the town. Despite her anxiety, she delighted in the cool breeze coming from the Mediterranean that lightly kissed her skin. As she walked quickly down the main sidewalk that she would never see again, she looked at each house she passed, naming who had lived there, like the repetition of a child's jump rope song.

"That one belonged to Sarah and her nebbish of a husband George, with that wild little daughter Ruti. Then came Uri the garbage man, who always seemed to be having an affair with a few women at once. No wonder he was always whistling and smiling. Hmm, I don't know who lived there, but that corner one was the one Marvin carried me into by mistake the night of the big Hanukkah party."

As she continued she thought about Harlan, who had been born with cerebral palsy and had a useless short arm. Where was he now? Did he go back to the United States with his Israeli wife, who had been shrewd enough to recognize that he was a financial wizard? Then she heard a loud clap that sounded like thunder and knew the army had arrived.

She started walking more quickly in the direction of the noise. Teenage boys wearing knitted kippahs stood on a few of the roofs, and she wondered what they planned to do. Those skinny little yeshiva students were going to fight the army? Did they have weapons with them? But hadn't Marvin said they had ammo in the bomb shelter? Maybe that's what he had gone to get.

Some Israeli soldiers were coming straight toward her, but luckily they were still far enough down the road that they didn't spot her. The kids on the roof saw them too and yelled for her to join them.

"The ladder's in the back!" one shouted in English.

She quickly ran around the back and climbed up before she could remember how afraid of heights she was. Out of breath and shaken, she made it to the top, where a young man took her hand and helped her onto the flat roof.

"Nu, now you're one of us," he said with a thin smile.

"Thanks, guys. So what are you going to do?" she asked.

"Well, we know we can't win. But at least we can go down with a fight! So we have some sand and maybe we'll burn some tires."

"Look," another boy said. "Here they come. They're breaking the doors down."

"Oy gevalt! Look! That's Shloime's door they're breaking down."

"Isn't his wife pregnant?" Danielle heard someone else say.

"*Gott in Himmel*, they're dragging them out of there," shouted the young man who had helped her.

Suddenly they heard the whir of a helicopter, and all of them looked up to see it hovering right over their heads. Someone with a bullhorn, maybe Sharon himself, instructed everyone in houses or bomb shelters to give themselves up. They were commanded, by order of the Israeli government, that they were to place any weapons on the ground and come out with their hands above their heads.

"We're the criminals?" one of the boys said. "A Jew does this to another Jew? Kahane's right. We didn't plan this out well enough!"

"Look," Danielle said. "I think there's a television crew up on that roof behind us. I thought they weren't allowed in!"

"I think that's Benny Katzover," the man who helped her said. "He's a friend of Belsky's and came down on the bread truck with him yesterday."

"I was in the bunker when he came in and he didn't say a word about it."

"I'm not surprised. He's the best. That's why he's Kahane's right hand man."

"No, no!" another man shouted. "The guys in the other building started dumping sand on the army, and it looks like the soldiers are getting ready to spray water into the buildings where people are barricaded."

A barrel of sand went flying off a nearby roof, and soldiers who were trying to force the resistors to capitulate had to deal with sand flying in their eyes, momentarily blinding them. Still one of the soldiers called, "Watch out, he's got a Molotov."

From her position on the roof, Danielle saw it in slow motion. Her husband ran around a corner, waving a liquor bottle over his head and screaming something unintelligible. Before the agonizing scream left her throat, the shot rang out and the bullet hit its mark. Paralyzed from shock, she watched as her husband collapsed, blood puddling beneath his head.

Danielle could never explain how she made it off the roof and down to her husband as fast as she did. She pushed through the soldiers and reached him before the ambulance arrived. As she cradled him in her arms, screaming and crying, "What did you do? You idiot, what were you thinking?" she ignored the blood that was quickly covering her. As she rocked back and forth, a paramedic pried him from her embrace, and he and a soldier placed Marvin's lifeless body on the gurney. Danielle followed. She kissed her husband one last time and whispered tearfully, "I loved you, Marv. I couldn't live with you anymore, but I loved you. You saved my life and I will always be grateful. I only wish I could have saved yours. "

Walking slowly away, she heard Kahane and Belsky start to chant the Kaddish, the ancient mourner's prayer: *"Yitgadal v'yitkadash sh'mei raba."* As the IDF soldiers joined in, tears rolled down her cheeks as she grieved for herself, her children, and for the loss of Yamit.